*to Chrissy —
with best wishes*

MAXIMUM PRESSURE

Copyright © 2024 by Sheila Lowe

All rights reserved. Without limiting the rights under copyright reserved above, no part of this publication may be reproduced, stored in or introduced into a retrieval system, or transmitted in any form, or by any means (electronic, mechanical, photocopying, recording, or otherwise) without the prior written permission of both the copyright owner and the publisher of this book.

ISBN - 978-1-970181-47-0 (Paperback)
ISBN - 978-1-970181-48-7 (Ingram Paperback)
ASIN - 978-1-970181-46-3 (EPUB)

This book is a work of fiction. Names, characters, businesses, organizations, places, events, incidents are the product of the author's imagination or are used fictitiously. Any resemblance to actual events, locals, or persons, living or dead, is coincidental.

Cover Design: Scott Montgomery

Printed in the United States of America

PUBLISHING HISTORY
Write Choice Ink, Ventura, California
www.sheilalowebooks.com

ALSO BY SHEILA LOWE

FORENSIC HANDWRITING SERIES

Poison Pen
Written in Blood
Dead Write
Last Writes
Inkslingers Ball
Outside the Lines
Written Off
Dead Letters

BEYOND THE VEIL SERIES

What She Saw
Proof of Life
The Last Door

NONFICTION

Growing from the Ashes (memoir)
Reading Between the Lines: Decoding Handwriting
Advanced Studies in Handwriting Psychology
Personality & Anxiety Disorders
Succeeding in the Business of Handwriting Analysis
Improve Your Life with Graphotherapy
The Complete Idiot's Guide to Handwriting Analysis
Handwriting of the Famous & Infamous

Praise for Sheila Lowe

"*Dead Letters* is an entertaining thriller set in Egypt, Gibraltar, Arizona and London, starring two heroines, an expert handwriting analyst and her intrepid niece. This novel will get your heart racing and also give you a fun education on ancient Egypt history at the same time." — Matt Witten, bestselling author of The Necklace

"Lowe expertly delivers a solid criminal investigation while guiding her readers into a unique culture where tattooing and the murder of a young girl come together on the autopsy table. Hit the lights and siren because this is one fast ride from beginning to end." — Lee Lofland, Author of "Police Procedure and Investigation" and founder and director of the Writers' Police Academy

"This is a good read that's hard to put down. If you have any interest in reading handwriting, there's a lot of good information about that included in the story. You may even have to watch how you write in the future. You don't want anyone to think you're a psychopath..." — Long and Short Reviews

Dead Letters starts at high speed, and it stays there...Lowe presents a clear and compelling story—and thusly a respect for the reader's experience. - Pen World

"Utterly compelling! *"Outside the Lines"* joins the ranks of those rare thrillers that expertly blend nonstop plotting with keen perceptions of the characters—good and bad—who populate this wonderful tale."
Jeffery Deaver, *New York Times* Bestselling Author

"Dynamite" - Starred review – PUBLISHERS WEEKLY
"Lowe wins readers over with her well-developed heroine and the wealth of fascinating detail on handwriting analysis." - BOOKLIST
"The well-paced plot develops from uneasy suspicions to tightly wound action." — FRONT STREET REVIEWS
"[A] fast-paced, crisp, and gritty novel that penetrates the world of celebrity and the dark appetites of those who live in that world. — ARMCHAIR INTERVIEWS
"A perfectly paced mystery with an easy fluidity that propels the reader through the story at breakneck speed." — BOOKPLEASURES.COM

"Sheila Lowe's writing is fast-paced and suspenseful and made believable by her own background as a forensic handwriting expert. Yet another page-turner for Claudia Rose fans." — Rick Reed, Author of the *Jack Murphy Crime* Series

MAXIMUM PRESSURE

SHEILA LOWE

Write Choice Ink
ESTABLISHED 2021

Dedication

To Ginny Bolle, Becky Edwards, Cathy Dutton, Cathi Hofstetter, Kathryn McCarty, Sharon Perlmuter, and Espie Rodriguez, my Anaheim High classmates who won a character name in charity auction at the 2023 Anaheim Library Mystery Author Luncheon

MAXIMUM PRESSURE

SHEILA LOWE

Write Choice Ink
ESTABLISHED 2021

SOMETIMES THE WOLF CRIES GIRL

sometimes the hero stumbles
and falls right off the page
sometimes the princess rolls her eyes
and says "i don't want to be saved."
sometimes the dragon needs rescuing
and the villain aches to be helped,
sometimes, in the darkness,
the lost boy finds himself.
sometimes the prince is cunning,
and not at all what he seemed.
sometimes the witch's kindness
shows it's she who deserves to be queen.
sometimes we shouldn't define people
by someone else's point of view—
just because it's what we've been told,
doesn't make it true.

by srwpoetry

Chapter one

Friday afternoon, October 6

Everything had changed in Edentown, and nothing had changed. Twenty-five years ago, when Washington Boulevard was the main drag, the high school crowd hung out at the Fox theater on Saturday nights, then walked in a pack to Carl's Jr. for burgers. There had been a shoe store, a drugstore, a barber shop and a hair salon, a couple of high-end dress boutiques. The no-tell hotel above Guido's Café that rented rooms by the hour.

Those businesses were gone now, replaced by boxy modern high-rise office buildings, an ultra-modern museum, and a refurbished warehouse that housed upscale fast-food vendors, cheese shops, and a yoga studio. Enterprises that meant nothing to Claudia Rose in the context of her hometown. Making a right turn at Olive Avenue, she felt like Alice in Wonderland—as disoriented as if she had stumbled into an alternate reality.

As she made another right, more than a little uneasy that she might not recognize the old neighborhood, the breath she had held too long whooshed out like a popped balloon. Her shoulder muscles let go. She needn't have worried. Aside from the odd paint job here and there, the residential streets were much the same as when she had graduated from Edentown High School in 1999.

The question was, how many of her classmates would she be able to identify at the reunion, her first in all those years? She had driven the seventy miles from Playa de la Reina to work the registration desk at the opening event, a cocktail party in the school gym, with her best friend, Kelly Brennan.

Despite running late due to the standard stop and go traffic that made the 405 famous, she refused to hurry. It was a long time since she had last visited Charter Street, and now that she was here, it felt weirdly like peeping in on someone else's life.

There was the home her parents had bought when she was in junior high. It had been brand new, part of the creeping gentrification that devoured neighborhoods whole—Godzilla chomping its way to tracts of larger dwellings.

Claudia had loved that house, not least because she no longer had to share a bedroom with her younger brother. With its three-car garage and faux-French Country kitchen, the two-story rambler had seemed like a mansion after their old two-bedroom apartment. Now, her eyes were seeing it for what it was: an ordinary house on an ordinary street, looking smaller than the picture she'd held in her mind.

She stopped the car and sat there, calling up flashbacks of summer parties in the backyard. Hiding behind the bushes with her friends and getting high on weed; drinking beer filched from their parents' coolers. What had happened to the families she had once known? Some of her classmates must have kids attending Edentown High.

Her first wedding reception had been held in that backyard. Within five years, the marriage had tanked. More years after that, her parents put the house on the market and moved to Seattle. Today, it would sell for close to a million.

Claudia loosed a long, nostalgic sigh. It felt as though she was sitting in the front row at a stage play that had ended long ago, the drama wrung out of it. The curtain had been raised; the scenery revealed as a plywood façade.

The sound of her phone startled the melancholy out of her. Kelly's ringtone. She touched the answer button. "Yes, ma'am?"

"Where the blipity blam are you?"

"Keep your panties on. I'm five minutes away."

"I need you here *now*, girlfriend. Here I am, womaning the desk all by my lonesome, and people are showing up early."

Claudia knew better than to take the gripe seriously. Parties lit Kelly up brighter than fireworks on the Fourth of July. In the background she could hear the tuning-up sounds of a rock band. "Who's there?"

"The committee members of course—the three Cathys—"

Three friends who shared a name, each with a different spelling. Cathi Soden, Cathy Brewer, Kathy McCarty. Kelly reeled off more names. "Sharon Bernstein, Espie Rodriguez, Ginny Vernon, Eleni Boukidis, Becky Condren. Lemme think ... Mark Lukeman, Don Baker—"

Claudia broke into the litany. "Got it. I'll see you in a few."

"No detours."

Too late.

"No detours."

She ended the call and entered the school's address into the GPS—something she had not needed to do twenty-five years ago. The mile-long walk straight up Charter Street had terminated at the rear entrance to the school's swimming pool. Not anymore. The snippy electronic voice directed her to an underpass constructed years after she had left home.

Chapter two

Claudia entered the gym through the back door, at once hit by the disembodied voice of a young Christina Aguilera singing about a genie in a bottle. She paused there to take in the frenetic preparations for the reunion: A custodian on a ladder, hanging a "Class of 1999" banner. Caterers hurrying to offload chafing dishes of hors d'oeuvres onto a long buffet. Early arrivals milling around the portable bars, waiting for them to open. Volunteers decorating the round tables with baskets of chrysanthemums dyed in the blue and gold of the school's colors.

Her eyes were drawn to the back wall, where "EDENTOWN HIGH SCHOOL" was freshly painted in six-foot-high letters. The bleachers that normally stood there had been folded away for the evening's event, but Claudia had not forgotten the countless times she and her friends had stood on them cheering on their basketball team, the Pioneers, to a long string of winning games.

The registration desk was set up on the other side of the gym from where she had entered. Crossing the highly polished polyurethane floor, she could see Kelly laughing and bantering with a handful of classmates lined up to receive their name tags. Whether the reunion committee was ready or not, the party was getting started.

Claudia gave her friend a quick appraisal and dropped into the vacant chair beside her. "The dress rocks," she said approvingly.

Kelly had dragged her along on a shopping trip, determined to dazzle the mean girls with her adult fashion sense, even if most of the mean girls had matured and forgotten her existence. She had found a sultry blue-grey A-line that brought out the cornflower blue of her eyes. Claudia's pick was a one-shoulder black number that her husband, Joel, had judged as "extremely sexy."

Her eyes were sparkling, her extra-white smile gleaming as Kelly pushed a box of name tags towards Claudia. "You look a-*mayz*ing, you auburn-headed hussy."

Cathi Soden, the reunion chair, had told them that almost half of the class was expected to attend one or more of the weekend events, which meant they had more than two hundred classmates to check in.

"What took you so long?" Kelly asked. "I thought you'd gotten lost."

"As much as this town has changed, it would be no big mystery if I had."

Now that there were two of them, several people at the back of Kelly's line moved to stand in front of Claudia. She looked up at the first woman in line and got a vague sense of familiarity, but no name. The woman wore a pink chiffon dress that billowed on a slender frame, making it look a size too large. And something about the glossy chestnut brown pageboy hairstyle jarred with her pasty complexion, and hazel eyes that burned brightly.

The woman gave her a knowing smile, challenging her with a winding "wrap it up" motion with her index finger. "C'mon, Claudia, I sat behind you in AP English our entire senior year. We passed a bazillion notes to each other—"

Before she could control her face, Claudia's brows shot up and she felt her eyes widen in surprise. How could this pale shadow be the pudgy, rosy-cheeked classmate of her memory? "Omigod, Andie Adams. I didn't—I'm sorry, I—"

Andie's expression relaxed into a good-natured grin. "It's okay, I'm not the only one here who doesn't look like they did in high school. Unlike you, I might add. You haven't changed much." She glanced around the gym. "Isn't it weird, seeing all these 'old' people and knowing you're one of them?"

Claudia, thumbing through the "A's" for her name tag, felt compelled to protest. "Hey, forty-two is *not* old."

Andie laughed. "Depends on your attitude, I guess." She pointed to the box of names. "Could I get Nat's, too? You remember my cousin, Natalie Parker?"

A clear image of two teenage girls popped into Claudia's head—Andrea, sweet and shy—the ever-ready gopher to her bossy cousin, the bubbly captain of the cheer squad. "It would be hard to forget her," she said "Are you two still 'Nat'nAndie?'" The two had borne the nickname throughout their school years, as though one name covered both of them.

Andie shook her head. "I work for Nat, but these days we have separate identities."

Wondering whether there was a silent "finally" behind the remark, Claudia handed the badges over with a warm smile. "It's great to see you, Andie. Have fun."

"Why don't you come find us when you're done here. I'll save you a seat. We can catch up."

"Thanks, I will." The invitation pleased Claudia. After all these years, it felt good to reconnect with old friends.

As Andie started to walk away, Kelly chimed in, "Save a seat for me too."

She turned back. "Of course! See you both later."

Waiting until Andie was out of earshot, Kelly cupped a hand to Claudia's ear and whispered, "When was the last time that girl got some sun? She's as white as tofu."

"Her hands were like ice. Maybe she's been sick."

"Yeah, sick of following Nat around like a slave, doing her bidding."

"Let's hope they've both outgrown that by now."

Kelly gave a small snort of derision. "I doubt it. She just picked up Nat's badge for her, didn't she?"

Over the next half-hour there was little time to comment on whose hair was going grey or going bald, or to dish on who looked their age, how many divorces, or who had died in the Persian Gulf, or ended up on drugs or in prison. Activity around the registration desk finally lulled as friends found friends and drifted into the same social groups as in the past. Breathing sighs of relief, Claudia and Kelly finally had a moment to look around the gym. At the center of a knot of men was the football team's winning quarterback, surrounded by backslapping teammates and admirers.

"All the jocks, back together again," Kelly observed.

Claudia followed her eyes. "Is Brandon Bailey wearing his letterman jacket?"

"I can't believe it fits. He must have needed a can opener to get into that thing."

"Aw, we shouldn't begrudge him the remembrance of his glory days."

"And, not to put too fine a point on it, he may not have as much hair as he used to, but he won us a shitload of trophies."

"They're all in the display case in the main building." Claudia lowered her voice. "I haven't forgotten how hot you thought he was when you bagged him after that last playoff game."

"Oh, Claudia, you don't get enough credit for being smarter than everyone else." Kelly tilted her chin with pride. "One of those trophies should be mine. And by the way, weren't you in the locker room that night, too, mackin' on Matt Macedo?"

"'Mackin' on?'" Claudia echoed. "How old *are* you?"

For a few silly moments they were transported back to their senior year, giggling about their conquests after the big game. The reminiscing was cut short by a late arrival.

If his extraordinary height had not identified him, his mass of orangey-red hair would. There was no mistaking this classmate. Kelly craned her neck to look up at him. "Have mercy and pass the defibrillator. Can it be Vince Ramsey?"

"Hello, Kelly Brennan," he said, unsmiling.

In 1999, Ramsey had been a skinny six foot five, lacking the bulk required for football, and with no interest in basketball. He had a superior intellect, though, a dearth of social skills that had made him an easy target for mockery. The jocks dubbed him "Sideshow Bob" after a character on *The Simpsons* TV show—a murderous psychopath with frizzy red dreadlocks.

At the time, Claudia's nascent interest in psychology had led her to deduce that it was not, as their fellow students taunted, antisocial behavior that drove Vincent, but shyness. More than two decades of education and professional experience told her that he was probably on the autism spectrum—Asperger's, perhaps. It made her glad that she had gone out of her way to be nice to him.

This Vincent Ramsey, garbed in a well-tailored, fashionable suit, with a busty blonde beauty clinging to his arm, was in a vastly different league than the gawky nerd they had known. Somewhere along the way, his confidence had received a major boost. She was pleased to see that he had grown into his looks, and teetered on the brink of handsome.

"You're not someone I expected to see here," Claudia said with a welcoming smile. Vincent's return gaze was as impassive as she expected it to be.

"Of course you didn't expect to see me," he said. "Nobody here knows who I am."

"Trust me, Vince, they know who you are," Kelly said, silently measuring his height with her eyes.

He brushed aside her comment with a shrug. "They don't know me personally, but they've certainly heard of my company."

"What's the name of it?"

"NumbersBox. It's been publicly traded since 2012."

The Fortune 1000 tech company was a household name. Kelly gave him an approving thumbs up. "That's a big wow, Vince. EHS was the first school in the district to have a computer lab, and you *owned* it. But who knew we had our own Bill Gates?"

Claudia extended her hand, and got a disappointing limp shake in return. "Congratulations. I had no idea you were the brains behind NumbersBox."

"Pfft. Don't you mean you can't believe I'm so successful?"

"No, I don't. There was never any question you were the smartest guy in the room."

Successful or not, he was projecting the same attitude of superiority that had gotten him humiliated over and over in school. He took the name tag Kelly handed him and clipped it to his lapel. "That may be true, but

I know one thing. I have no one from Edentown High School to thank for my success. I built my company from the ground up."

Ignoring the hubris in his self-important statement, Kelly cast him a wry grin. "You've come a long way, baby. Now you can treat them all like shit, the way they did you."

Drawing himself up straighter, Ramsey flattened his lips in the semblance of a smile. Someone must have told him it was the thing to do in a social situation, but the result was more alarming than charming. "I have no need to stoop to that kind of behavior. Money and success are their own revenge. And if you don't mind, it's 'Vincent.' 'Vince' makes me sound like a vagrant."

And with that, Vincent Ramsey turned on his heel and strode away with his unacknowledged companion in tow.

Kelly's face screwed up as if she had sucked on a lemon. "Can you say *schadenfreude?* I don't care what he says, he came to gloat. He's a bazillionaire and we're all just peons."

"After what he went through in high school, he deserves to gloat," Claudia said.

Kelly's retort was cut short by their former prom queen, stopping by to greet them. "Look at you," Kelly said admiringly. "Perfect skin, perfect figure. It's impossible to look that young twenty-five years later, Rayanne. Did you make a deal with the devil, or what?"

She beamed at the flattery. "That's so sweet of you. My twins will be freshmen here next—?"

The rest of her sentence was lost on Claudia. For a breathless moment she stared at the man who had stepped in front of her. His hair was the same—thick, black, and curly—with the addition of a few silver threads and a neat beard. In a tan corduroy sport coat and black turtleneck sweater, forty-two looked very good on him.

"I bet you don't remember me," he taunted with an impish grin.

"Are you serious?" Startled by the quiver of sense memory that hit her, Claudia got up and went around the table. Feeling a little faint, she pushed aside the camera that hung around his neck and threw her arms around him. The embrace felt at once strange after all the years, and yet, not strange at all. He even smelled the way she remembered. All at once embarrassed, she let go and stepped away. "How are you, Matt?"

"Happy to see you." Matt Macedo reached out and hugged her again. "You look—well, the same as ever. You look great."

The hint of sorrow in the lines around his eyes stirred her curiosity, but with a couple of people waiting in line behind him, she let it go for now. "You look the same too," Claudia said, returning to her post and starting to look in the box for his name. "What are you up to these days? Or does that fancy Nikon around your neck tell the tale?"

Matt huffed a chuckle that turned lines at the corners of his eyes into crinkly smile lines. "Cathi asked me to grab some candid shots. Just like when we worked on the *Edentown Echo*, right? In real life, I'm a documentary filmmaker."

"Filmmaker? I'd love to hear more about that later." She found the tag that read "Matt Macedo" and handed it over, the brush of his fingers against hers creating a tiny hum of electricity on her skin. Maybe the remnants of first love lingered forever.

"I want to catch up on old times, but there's also something I want to talk to you about," he said.

Her curiosity meter jumped higher, but the next man in line was getting impatient. "Hey Macedo, can you pick up the pace? There's drinks to drink, people to see."

"Hold your horses, Wilson," Matt said with a grin. "I'm talking to a very important lady." He turned back to Claudia. "Let's get together later," he said, walking away with a pleased smile that tickled the edges of his mouth.

Kelly leaned over and whispered. "He still likes you."

"Don't be stupid. That was high school, and I'm happily married. He probably is, too."

"There's no ring on that finger."

"Why am I not surprised you noticed that?" Claudia said, feigning annoyance as she handed Chris Wilson his name tag. "Feel free to pursue him to your horny little heart's delight." She was half-kidding, but Kelly's gaze held a speculative glint that followed Matt across the room. "Maybe I will," said her friend. "Maybe I will."

At last, the box was virtually empty, and they decided that anyone who was left was not coming. Claudia started gathering their supplies. "Let's go see if there's any food left on the buffet."

"We stop at the bar first," Kelly said, dumping the trash in a heap on the table.

Before they could walk away, a male voice spoke from behind them. "Hey, don't I know you two?"

Claudia swung around with a little burst of pleasure. "Mr. Dickson."

He was not a lot older than they were, and still had the boyish Tom Cruise grin she remembered, and the humor that lit his deep-set grey eyes. His hair, brown and tousled, was longer than it had been when he was their driver's education teacher. Taking a swig from the half-empty rocks glass in his left hand, he pointed at each of them in turn. "Kelly Brennan. Claudia Bennett. Tell me I'm wrong."

"Good recall," Claudia said. "Are you still teaching here?"

Joshua Dickson made a face of mock dread. "God, no. I escaped this bunch of hellraisers right after your class graduated. My wife wanted to be near her mom, so we moved back east. I'm a New Yawka now." He exaggerated the East Coast accent to a ridiculous degree.

"Are you just here for the reunion?"

He shook his head. "I've got some family business to wrap up here. Visiting my uncle. And Sue Goldman said it was reunion time for the class of '99, so I figured I'd show up and surprise everyone. Can't let Sue be the only old teacher." He paused for another swallow. "It's cool to see some of you folks again."

"It's great to see you too, Mr. D," Claudia said. "You were one of my favorite teachers."

"Call me Josh; we're all grownups now." He turned to Kelly, who was being uncharacteristically silent. "Tell me the truth, Ms. Brennan, How many speeding tickets have you had? If anyone was gonna get caught speeding, it'd be you."

Instead of the flirty attitude Claudia expected from her friend, the look Kelly threw him was nothing less than withering. "Don't worry, *Josh*. Your *awesome* teaching skills made us all *perfect* drivers."

An amused grin spread across his face. "Good to know I had such a good influence."

Kelly kept a straight face. "Sarcasm is just one of the many services I offer."

Sensing that her friend was winding up to launch a rocket, Claudia dove in to head it off. "You went to school here too, didn't you, Josh?"

"Proud graduate of the Class of '92 and captain of the baseball team," he said with a sloppy salute. "We're classes adjacent. Hey, I've got a question for you. Why did the graduate bring a ladder to the ceremony?" He paused for a beat, then delivered the absurd punchline. "Because she wanted to get high honors."

Claudia groaned. Kelly's reaction was an exaggerated eyeroll. "To hell with maturity. Your jokes haven't improved over time."

Dickson chuckled good-naturedly. "The music I listened to in high school is on Oldies radio now. So, what have you girls been up to for the past twenty-five years? Married? Babies?"

"I'm a forensic handwriting examiner," Claudia said when Kelly said nothing. She shot her friend a side glance, startled to see a scowl.

"You were into that handwriting stuff back in high school, weren't you?." Dickson said. "Good for you, sticking with it."

"I'm amazed you remember."

"I sure do. You analyzed my handwriting."

"Wow, that's right, I did," Claudia said. "That was back when I didn't know what I was doing. I'll have to dig into some old boxes and see what I said about you."

"Just don't blackmail me with it," Josh Dickson said with a friendly wink. "What about you, Kelly-girl? What field did you go into?"

"Family law," she said curtly.

"You don't say? I never would have guessed that in a half-million years. I'll know who to call next time I get arrested."

"*Family* law," Kelly repeated. "I don't defend criminals."

He chuckled. "Same lovable wiseass I remember."

She opened her mouth, but Dickson beat her to the punch. "I gotta go harass Bailey—Good ole Number Twelve—see you gals around." Without waiting for them to say goodbye, he ambled away towards the bar.

Kelly watched him go. "What an asshole."

Chapter three

Claudia turned to her, astonished. "I thought you liked Mr. Dickson."

Kelly shrugged, but her lips pinched together in a way that said the shrug was not the casual gesture she'd meant it to be. "Everyone loved Mr. Dickson," she said dismissively. "It's cool that teachers show up at these things."

"Remember how he and Ms. Goldman used to hang out together at lunch? They were the youngest teachers in the school; just babies if you think about it."

"They weren't prepared for a bunch of miscreants like us."

Claudia grinned. "It was fun speculating about whether they were hooking up."

"I still think they were. You know, he was never hot in the 'hottie' sense of the word, but that 'cute' little boy look—there was something about him—" Kelly searched for the word she wanted.

"Appealing? Sweet? Charming?" Claudia supplied.

"Exactly that. It hasn't aged well. By the way, thanks for not ratting me out to him about the tickets. Did I tell you I got a date with that cop who pulled me over last week?"

Claudia was not surprised. It would not be the first time her friend had sweet-talked herself out of a sticky situation.

True to her word, Andrea had saved them a seat at the table she shared with her cousin Natalie, and Natalie's husband, Tom. There was another woman who Claudia recognized as Rachel Thomas, and a couple she did not know. Kelly did, though, and she wasted no time taking charge of the conversation.

"What has everyone been doing since graduation? Or since the last reunion." She pointed a finger at the man Claudia didn't know, who was in the act of popping a Swedish meatball into his mouth. "I believe in picking on the one who just stuffed their face. Gary Mills. Go for it."

A stocky man with a round, friendly face, Gary was mostly bald with a few strands of light brown hair arranged in a combover. Unlike most of the other men in the room, who wore suits or sport coats, he had opted for a more casual look—salmon-colored polo shirt and jeans. As all eyes at the table turned to him, beads of nervous sweat broke out on his brow. Blushing, he grabbed a glass of water, drank too fast, and choked on it. "Sorry, folks, this is harder than you'd think."

His wife, a pleasant-looking woman, handed him a napkin with an encouraging smile. Gary made a quick dab at his damp forehead and sucked in a deep breath. Punching a fist into the air, he yelled, "Edentown football rules!" drawing laughter, and the same shout back from nearby tables. He settled back in his chair with a sheepish grin. "God, I loved high school. Didn't we have a great time?"

"Well, I guess some of us did," Kelly said. "But you're not getting off that easily. What about since graduation, huh?"

"I worked in my dad's hardware store until nine-eleven came. Then I joined the Air Force, did a couple tours in Afghanistan. That was the friggin worst, man—not like winning the state championships with Bailey and the team, that's for sure." Gary reached a possessive arm around his wife. "Dar and I were married by then—this is Darlene, everyone—she went to that *'other'* school across town, which we won't mention." Everyone acknowledged Darlene, and Gary went on. "When I got out of the service we moved to Spirit Lake, Idaho, bought a farm and raised our four kids. That's about it." Now that he was done, Gary gusted a sigh of relief and passed the verbal baton. "Your turn, Nat."

Natalie Parker had been a stunning blonde in high school, and still was. Over the years, her mouth had acquired a severe set that hardened her looks, but not so hard that it detracted from them. She wore a short, tight dress that showed off a shape as youthful as when she had led the cheer squad. Her makeup and outfit were so perfect that Claudia wondered whether she had used a professional stylist to dress her for the occasion.

"She's sitting sidesaddle so we can't miss the Louboutins," Kelly whispered behind her hand. Claudia suppressed the giggle that bubbled up. It was true; Natalie had pushed her chair back from the table and arranged the sexy ankle strap sandals to ensure that the unmistakable and expensive red soles could be seen.

Eyeing her and her conventionally handsome husband—every inch the successful criminal defense attorney in a four thousand dollar suit—Claudia thought their sharp veneer of success had a brittle quality. *Barbie and Ken,* she thought, and not in a nice way.

Natalie glanced around the table, waiting to speak until all eyes were on her. "I graduated UCLA poly-sci with honors. My original plan was to go to work on a political campaign right after college. But I'm sure you've heard that old saying, 'Man plans, God laughs?' Well, God was laughing at *us*. I got pregnant. Tom and I were so totally in love that we decided to put my career on hold so I could support him until he got his law license. We ended up with two gorgeous little girls."

"Lucky for them, they're both mirror images of their mom," Tom said, to an outbreak of subdued groans.

His wife threw him an adoring smile. "The minute they were in school, it was time for me to step out into the public eye. I don't think anyone was surprised when I got elected to the city council. It was a 'local girl makes good' kind of thing. I've been serving ever since. In all modesty, I'd like to say, we've been getting some massively great things accomplished for Edentown."

What modesty?

"Nat's going to be our next mayor," Tom announced. Natalie trotted out the ingenue she had once been. "Let's not get ahead of ourselves, Tommy. There's a whole lot of fundraising to be done before we can make that happen."

He grinned at them all shamelessly. "And if any of you would like to contribute to the campaign—"

"Now, Tommy, you have to stop that." The look Natalie threw him was as coy as a teenager with a crush. "But you can all send your friends to my website—NatalieforMayor.com."

The Mills couple murmured congratulations. The rest of them made agreeing noises. Resisting the urge to puke at Natalie's fake humility, Claudia picked up a mini quiche from her plate and bit into it so she wouldn't have to say anything. Kelly nudged her foot under the table in solidarity.

"Did you all know that Claudia is our most famous classmate?" Andie said, redirecting the spotlight away from her cousin. "She's a handwriting expert."

Claudia looked at her in surprise. Had Andie grown a spine of her own over the last twenty-five years? Her cheeks were flushed an attractive pink, and she looked decidedly pleased with herself.

"I saw you on TV a while ago," she said. "You were on one of those forensics shows, talking about the Unabomber's handwriting. I couldn't believe how much you could tell about him. And you carried yourself so well too."

Annoyance, rapidly extinguished, flitted across Natalie's face and she pasted on a fake smile. "You should have told me, Andie. You know I like to keep a list of famous alumni. Claudia, I'll have to make sure you're on it."

"You're thinking of a documentary about several bombers," Claudia said, addressing Andie and ignoring her cousin. "The bombers had all sent letters to the media or left them at crime scenes. The producers wanted to know if there was such a thing as a 'criminal' handwriting that could be identified.'"

"And, is there?" Natalie's insistent voice grated. The gaze Claudia turned on her was cool. "No, there isn't. Certain red flags for pathology can be read as danger signs, but it's all a matter of potential. I don't make predictions about criminal behavior."

"What about you, Andie?" Kelly interjected. "What have you been doing with your life?"

With the spotlight turned on her, Andrea blushed brighter, and in that space of a few seconds, her skin glowed, making her almost pretty. Cinderella, invited to the ball. Claudia was struck afresh by the contrast between the girl she remembered—the drudge perpetually in the shadow of her glam, confident cousin—and the adult she had grown into, with her sharp cheekbones and pallid complexion.

"I never got married or had kids of my own," Andie said, a little breathy. "Any maternal instincts I have get satisfied through my nieces—and they truly are beautiful. After we graduated I took a gap year, travelled the world some—yes, I did, all by myself, and proud of it! Then Nat ran for office, and I worked for her campaign as administrator."

"Make that 'irreplaceable chief of staff,'" Tom said. The broad wink that followed his remark made Claudia dislike him more. It gave her the suspicion that he was being sarcastic.

"Still 'Nat'nAndie,'" Gary Mills said fondly. "Just like the old days."

Andrea gave him a sweet smile. "Why don't we hear from Rachel next. Her job is far more interesting than mine."

Natalie's full, red lips formed a pout. "Oh, you don't think working for me is interesting?"

Speaking across her, Rachel said, "I'm an embalmer—a mortician." Her chin jutted, defying anyone to criticize her choice of career.

Defiance was Rachel's default mode, Claudia recalled. She had been one of the so-called "bad" kids, flouncing around school in a perpetual sulk, smoking in the bathroom, using drugs, and not caring who knew about it. She was one of a small handful of girls who had dressed in all black and painted her nails black, too.

Tonight, Rachel had honed her Morticia Addams style with a silky black tunic and flowy harem pants. Raven-hued, razor cut bangs hid her eyebrows. Large dark eyes, heavily outlined in black, were magnified under lush fake lashes that fluttered against her pale skin.

"Mortician, eh?" Gary gave an exaggerated shudder. "That's not a job you hear about every day. How'd you come to—"

"Death fascinates me." Rachel's diamond-hard stare could have turned him to stone. "I find it comforting to restore people's loved ones—to make them look as close to the way they did in life as I can. Sometimes there's not a lot to work with, and that's a challenge I enjoy. I'm damn good at it, too."

Natalie interrupted the question Gary's wife started to ask. "What about you, Kelly?" she asked, pointedly ignoring the daggers Rachel's eyes were hurling at her, and deftly shifted the attention off her. "Are you still raising hell like you always did?"

Kelly considered her over the rim of her wine glass. "Raising hell whenever I can, Nat. Rachel's good at death. I'm good at divorces, having practiced on several of my own. I'm a family law attorney."

Natalie patted her husband's hand. "I am happy to say Tom and I will never be in need of your services. We're more in love than we were when we met. Aren't we, honey?"

Tom smiled dutifully. "Of course we are, dear."

Gary Mills spit out a loud laugh. "Good boy, Tommy. He knows the right answer."

For a split second it felt like everyone at the table was waiting for Natalie to bark at him. Claudia jumped into the breach and returned the attention to Rachel. "I think being a mortician would be a difficult job."

"I like to believe I provide a valuable service," Rachel said primly. "It's an important one."

"*Six Feet Under* was my favorite show," Gary said, and for a time, the conversation turned to TV shows. When that ran down, he said, "Hey, did you guys see Mr. Dickson? I can't believe he's here."

"*What?* Mr. Dickson is here?" Andie's wide-eyed gaze swept the gym, looking for their former teacher.

Rachel sat up straight in her chair and looked around too. "He's here? Didn't he move out of state years ago?"

"He told Claudia and me that he piggybacked the reunion on some family matters," Kelly said.

Spotting him several tables away, Gary raised his glass in the direction of their erstwhile teacher. "Here's to Mr. Dickson, one cool dude. He used to make driver's ed a blast; let us get away with all kinds of shit."

"I guess he didn't bring his wife. He's hangin' with Ms. Goldman, as usual."

"Reunions are boring if you didn't go to the school," Claudia said. Joel had managed to excuse himself at the last minute. As a homicide detective there were no excuses when he was called out to a crime scene. And she couldn't blame him for being relieved that he could beg off attending the event.

Rachel scraped her chair back. "Excuse me, folks. I need to go see if the little girls' room is still where it used to be."

Natalie rose too. "I'll come with you."

Andrea followed suit. "Me too."

Kelly, examining her wine glass, decided she needed a refill and headed for the bar. The band started playing songs from the nineties and the Mills' excused themselves and went out to the dance floor, leaving Claudia on her own. She gathered her purse and stood, intending to search out Matt, when she saw him approaching her table.

"Did you forget about me?" he asked.

Claudia smiled back at the twinkly eyes she had found so attractive back in her senior year. "I was just about to come looking for you."

"Glad to hear it. It's too loud to talk in here. Let's find a someplace quieter."

She thought for a moment. "How about the bleachers out by the pool?"

"The bleachers it is. First, though, may I buy you a drink?"

"Yes, you may. Chardonnay, please."

They made a stop at one of the bars, and strolled across the gym with Claudia's wine and a beer for Matt, pausing along the way for brief chats with old acquaintances.

Exiting through the rear door to the pool area, Claudia shivered. Heavy coats were not required on Southern California October evenings, but she had misjudged the temperature, and the cool air penetrated her thin dress. Matt handed her his beer bottle to hold and shrugged out of his jacket.

"You don't have to do that," she protested as he draped it around her shoulders. "Now *you'll* be cold."

He grinned. "Are you kidding? I'm a tough guy."

"Chivalry lives on." She handed back his bottle with a rumbling of disquiet. Had his gesture meant something she didn't want it to, or was she imagining an intimacy that did not exist? He wouldn't have put his jacket around her if Joel had been there. But then, she would not have been out here alone with Matt if Joel had been there.

Following the low lights that prevented them from missing the edge of the pool and inadvertently stepping into the gleaming water in the dark, they walked around the Olympic size swimming pool and climbed to the top row of bleachers.

"Don't sit down yet," Matt cautioned. "Lucky for you, I was a Boy Scout."

He reached into his jacket pocket and produced a handkerchief, his hand pressing against her hip. Claudia suppressed a small gasp. Seeming not to notice her discomfort, Matt wiped off the dewy metal bench and made a mock bow. "Madame, your dress is now safe from the elements."

Testing the bench before perching on it, she chided herself for being absurd. "What's the Boy Scout motto?" she said. "'Be prepared?' Matthew, you deserve a merit badge. Now, tell me what happened after you dumped me and went away to school. I bet you got married and had nineteen kids."

"I did get married, but we didn't have any kids." Matt's eyes glittered with sudden tears. He turned his face away. "My wife died about a year ago. I've been trying to dig my way out of it ever since."

That would explain the aura of sadness she felt around him. She felt like a jerk. "Oh, Matt, I'm so sorry. What happened?"

"Heart attack. She did everything right, took care of herself. I guess she had a heart defect she never knew about" He covered the emotion with a cough and a slug of beer. "How about you?"

"No kids for me, either. Got married, got divorced. Got married again, to a homicide detective. Which is why he's not here tonight. He got a called out." Claudia grinned. "I'm reasonably sure he was happy about that. I accused him of having someone bumped off so he could get out of attending the reunion."

Matt laughed. "That would be a little extreme. I guess he's not a party animal?"

"Oh, he is so *not*. But then, I wasn't going to come either. Kelly talked me into it."

He nudged her with his elbow. "I'm glad she did."

"You said you wanted to talk to me about something. What's up?"

"Yes. But first, I need to—and this is *not* the main reason why I brought you out here, but—"

"Go on, Matt, what is it?"

"I know it's way past time, but I have to say it. When things—when you and I—ended—I had a tough time getting over you. I wished—?"

Where is this going?

Claudia, sipping her wine, kicked herself for suggesting they come out here. Joel was not the jealous type, but she had a feeling he would be less than thrilled at her sitting in the moonlight with her first serious boyfriend, talking about their past. She said, "It wasn't easy for me, either Matt. But you were going to school on the other side of the country, and it would have been nice if you'd given me a heads-up."

"I know, I know. I'm sorry. It all happened fast, and, well, I guess it worked out for the best—like I said, I was happy with Caren. But—" he hesitated again. "You can't help wondering how things might have been, 'if.'"

Now that he's single again? Is that what he's thinking?

"That was a long time ago. We're different people now. Tell me about your films. Anything I should have heard of?"

He gave her a crooked smile and allowed her to lead him down a safer path. "As a filmmaker, I've been interested in crime and forensics for a long time." He reeled off several well-known true crime shows to his credit that included episodes of *Forensic Files* and *Dateline NBC*.

Claudia found herself feeling pleased on his behalf. "Wow, look at you in the big leagues. I'm so proud of you."

He returned her smile. "If I'm in the big leagues, so are you. I've seen you on national TV. And there was that article in the *L.A. Times*. You've made a name for yourself. I'm proud of you, too."

"Thank you." In the brief silence that followed, Claudia realized how still and quiet the night was. No birds chirping, no planes flying overhead. Just a big, bright full moon gazing down at them, waiting to see what he would say. "Can I take a wild stab that my work is the reason why we're out here?"

"You're right," Matt admitted. "I'm working on a new project—something I believe your handwriting expertise could add to in a significant way."

She felt a stirring of interest. "You've got me curious. What's it about?"

"It's a documentary about a teenage girl who went missing and was never found."

A sudden presentiment whispered in her ear: *be careful.* She knew at once where this was heading, and she was not at all certain it was a ride she wanted to take. "You're talking about Lucy Valentine," Claudia said.

Matt leveled a long, enigmatic look at her. "Yes, of course."

Chapter four

May 9, 1998

Authorities are on the lookout for a missing girl who was last seen a week ago at Edentown High School, where she is a junior. Lucy Louise Valentine, 16, told friends that she wasn't feeling well and was leaving her PE class early to go home.

Police said Valentine did not return home and has not been seen since. She is Caucasian, five feet two inches and 94 pounds, with black shoulder-length hair and brown eyes. When last seen she was wearing a black short-sleeve shirt, black and green plaid shorts, torn black stockings, and ankle boots. She wore a silver necklace with a gargoyle pendant.

"This is a parent's worst nightmare," the girl's mother, Stephanie Valentine said, in tears. "We have our problems—what teenage girl gets along with her mom? But there's no way my Lucy would just up and leave like this. Someone has taken her. Please, please bring my baby girl home."

Police are concerned for the teen's safety. Any sightings should be reported to—

Sylvia Bennett pointed the remote at the TV and switched it off.

"Hey, I was watching that," sixteen-year-old Claudia protested.

"I don't want you watching that garbage." Her mother crossed her arms over her ample chest to emphasize the point. "It's too depressing."

"That's so not fair. I need to know what's happening. I need to know if they find her."

"No, you don't. And starting tomorrow, I'll be picking you up after school every day until they catch the pedophile who did this."

Claudia gaped at her. *"What?* No way. That's insane."

"Get used to it."

"But none of my friends' moms—"

Sylvia gave her 'the look.' "If your friends' moms told you to jump off a cliff, I guess you'd listen to them. You sure as heck don't listen to me."

"Omigod, this is *so* embarrassing! I'm not a child."

"Obviously, there's a crazy person out there, preying on girls your age. You should be scared to walk home alone."

"It's not like you care what happens to me. I bet you'd be happy if someone grabbed me off the street."

Sylvia made a sharp tsk of annoyance, but she didn't put up the argument Claudia secretly yearned for. She headed back to the kitchen, leaving her daughter to brood on her long-held belief that the stork had delivered her to the wrong family. She had never fit into this one.

She stared at the blank TV screen, pondering the unfairness of life. How could she know someone who was there one day, then vanished like a puff of smoke as if she had never existed. Things like that happened to other people in other places, not to a student at Edentown High, where it was comfortably boring. She and her friends liked to complain, but they had felt safe and secure in their ennui.

Unlike Lucy Valentine.

Wherever Lucy was, whatever had happened to her, Claudia had a jittery feeling in her stomach that told her she was anything but safe.

She would not describe the missing girl as a friend. They knew each other from some of the same classes—PE and driver's ed and English Lit. Kelly hung out with her sometimes, and Rachel Thomas—the three of them were in a Goth phase. Lucy kept her distance from most of the other kids, who considered her weird, and were not particularly nice to her. Kelly said Lucy was like a cactus with big, prickly thorns that nobody could get close enough to touch.

Claudia shivered. *Not prickly enough.*

The day after Lucy was reported missing, school was in an uproar. Girls who, at any other time, would not have given her the time of day pretended to weep for her to come back safe and sound. Uniformed police stood in front of the whiteboards in each of her classes, asking who had seen her and whether anyone knew of her possible whereabouts. No one did. Or if they did, they were not telling.

The next step for the cops was to glom onto the few students who *others* identified as knowing her best. That included Kelly, who was treated to private questioning.

How did Lucy seem in the days prior to her disappearance? (shrug; normal). Was she the type of girl who would run away? (shrug; maybe) Did she have any enemies? (shrug; like, who?). Did she have a boyfriend? That question produced the longest, most promising answer: she liked someone, but she never said who.

When Kelly was released and found Claudia hovering in the hallway, waiting for her, she told her that Rachel had been in the principal's office first, and had left with a tearstained face. She'd sworn she knew nothing—she was scared for Lucy.

No formal classes were held that day. How could anyone be expected to concentrate on English Lit or Algebra with cops on campus, plowing through the student body, searching for anyone who might—just might—have some teeny-weeny tidbit of information that would lead to Lucy's whereabouts. Students crowded the quad, huddling together at the lunch tables, speaking in hushed voices.

"What do you think happened to her?"

"Maybe she got kidnapped on her way home."

"I think she ran away."

"I bet she joined a satanic cult."

"Yeah, she was a kinda weird chick—all that Goth shit."

"Don't say 'was.' That makes it sound like she's dead."

"Maybe she is."

And on it went, the endless speculation and innuendo. There was no other topic of conversation that day or the next or the next. Claudia had sat at one of those tables and absorbed it all, wondering. Sharon Bernstein, a popular girl who wore a cute bun on top of her head, claimed that Lucy had left behind a note.

"Did you actually see it?" Cathi Soden asked, impressed that her friend might be in the know.

"No, but I heard about it from Cathy Brewer."

"Did *she* see it? What did it say?"

Sharon shrugged helplessly. "All I know is, Cathy's older sister babysits Lucy's kid brother while their mom is at work—which is *all the time*. She's the one who said about the note—Cathy's sister. I bet the cops took it."

"I bet they did, too," Cathi agreed.

The idea of a note piqued Claudia's interest. She had recently read a book about handwriting analysis and was learning what the written word revealed about the writer's personality. Her Granny Arlene had given her a copy of *Navigating Personality Secrets in Handwriting* for her birthday. How could handwriting reveal so much about a person—their social skills and the way they think; their fears? Claudia devoured those pages and wanted more.

She bought a notebook and made a list of what to look for in handwriting that matched specific personality traits, and practiced on her friends. Word got around fast about her new skill. Most days during lunch period classmates sought her out, wanting to know what their handwriting revealed about them, or their boyfriend, or girlfriend.

Not everything she read in the book was reasonable to her. She hobbled through the definitions of each stroke of handwriting as she had learned them, vowing that when she got to college she would study psychology, so she could accurately understand what it all meant.

"I've seen Lucy's handwriting," Kelly declared after being freed from her interrogation—the cops called it an interview, but she was smarter than that. On TV shows when the police questioned you it was an interrogation, and that was good enough for her. Besides, saying she was interrogated gave her a certain prestige with the other kids, who were burning with curiosity about what had gone on in the principal's office.

Claudia hid her suspicion that Kelly was grandstanding. Her friend had a way of saying or doing things to draw attention to herself, whether or not they were entirely accurate. "Seriously? Where did you see it?"

"Yes, seriously, you doubter. It was on that essay Miss Goldman made us do in grammar class. She had us diagram each other's work. Since I sit—*sat*—next to Lucy, we exchanged papers. I couldn't help noticing her handwriting because it was so not like anyone else's."

"What did it look like?"

"I've never seen writing like it. It's tiny. Really, really small. In fact, it's so small you can barely read it. And it was faint, which also made it hard to read." Kelly wrinkled her nose in a "thinking about it" expression. "That's all I remember. No, wait, the words also had gigantic gaps."

Claudia got out the book and went through the chapters to find the features Kelly had described. Tiny handwriting. The book said that meant someone who concentrated closely on what they were doing. That didn't fit what she knew of Lucy, who had been on the spacy side. Very wide gaps between words could mean someone who felt isolated—or it just might mean they needed elbow room. That could be true. Faint writing—according to the book, it was a sign of sensitivity. But when you put all of that together, what did it mean? Those definitions were pitifully inadequate to describe a teenage girl who had apparently disappeared from the earth, leaving no trace of what had happened to her. There had to be more to analyzing handwriting than that.

She wished she could put it all out of her mind. But no matter how hard she tried, Claudia could not stop thinking about it. If Lucy Valentine had indeed left a note as Cathy's sister claimed, and if she understood handwriting analysis better, what would the missing girl's handwriting say about her?

Hearing Matt utter Lucy's name made the memory of her disappearance as raw and as new as if Claudia had deliberately kept her feelings about that long-ago event seething under the surface, waiting to be recalled at this very moment. She pulled his coat closer around her, burrowing into its warmth. Not that it could insulate her from the sick fear that ate at her now—exactly as it had in 1998.

"You've been researching the case?" she asked, amazed that her voice was steady, as if she wasn't trembling inside.

Matt's expression was hidden in the shadows, but there was a barely suppressed intensity that Claudia remembered well. It bristled around him as it had in the past when he got excited about an idea. "Enough to know that I have to make this film. Maybe I can dig up some evidence the cops missed. They thought she was a runaway, and figured she would show up on her own. I suspect they did a half-assed job of looking for her."

"*Everyone* thought she ran away."

Or that's what we said to each other to comfort ourselves when we were afraid of what had really happened to her.

"But why would she run away? Nobody came up with a single good reason."

"Her mom said in that press conference that they didn't get along." Claudia's lips formed a wry smile. "Not that any teenage girl gets along with her mom. I sure didn't."

"I'm serious. Do you believe it stands to reason that she just up and left, and there was never any sign of her, ever again?"

Back when Lucy disappeared, she had spent a lot of time thinking about it, and she could not disagree with him. She considered his question.

"You're right. I can see her taking off and hiding out somewhere for a few days if she and her mom had a big enough fight. God knows, I wanted to do that more than a few times, but I could never get up the nerve. To do that willingly—to leave and never go back—you'd have to hate your mother, wouldn't you? And I didn't get that impression from her mom on TV."

"How would she take care of herself? Unless she had someone helping her." Matt took a long pull of his beer and stared at the dark surface of the swimming pool. "Every time there's an abduction in the news, it all comes back. When I read about Jaycee Dugard—she was rescued after *eighteen years* of being locked in a garden shed—"

"I remember. She was kidnapped on her way to school at twelve years old." Recalling the media coverage and how it had awakened her old fears, Claudia grew pensive. "The monster who took her got her pregnant twice. She was scarcely more than a child herself. His handwriting had red flags all over it."

"You saw his handwriting?"

"They published a letter he wrote to the judge. A machine could have written it, it was so precise and exact. That kind of writing—the writer is so tightly wound that when they let go, you can expect some kind of explosion."

"See, Claudia, that's why I need you on this project." Matt's voice cracked on an emotion that she was feeling, too. "When I hear those stories, it makes me wonder if Lucy might be out there somewhere, a captive in someone's basement or backyard."

"God, that's a horrifying thought. I'd rather believe she ran away and she's living happily with a different identity somewhere."

"I've put in a request for Lucy's police file, but I have my doubts that it's going to tell me anything the media hasn't already made public, which is basically nothing—a girl went missing and was never found. I can tell you one thing; the cops weren't thrilled to have me suggesting—even by inference—that their investigation wasn't 'all that.'"

Claudia imagined Joel's reaction if someone challenged one of his investigations. It would not be pretty. "I'm sure they don't like it, but do you think they'll actively obstruct you investigating a cold case?"

Matt finished off his beer and set the bottle on the bench beside him. "They made no bones about it. I won't get anything more than the initial missing persons report—the one Lucy's mom filed. I was told I won't get access to any follow-ups or investigation by the detectives."

"Why would they care if you saw the whole file?" Claudia questioned aloud. "It's been twenty-six years. I'd think they would welcome any help in clearing it."

"It's a cold case, but it's considered open-unsolved, which means it's active—even if the trail is ice cold and they haven't done diddly on it in more than two decades. And *that's* why I've got to resurrect the story."

She nodded approvingly. "What's your plan?"

"Once I get the file and find out who the lead investigator was, I'll try to contact him. Or her."

"Think they'll talk to you?"

Matt's grin showed white, even teeth. "With my charm and boyish good looks, what do you think?"

Claudia laughed. "I think if the detective is a middle-aged single woman, you'll be fine."

He made a silly face. "You're a real pal."

"I try. Now, let's get serious. Tell me how you think *I* can help. I didn't know Lucy all that well. Kelly knew her way better than I did." She asked the question, but before she heard his answer, she had a strong hunch that she knew what he was going to say.

And then he said it. "Lucy left a handwritten note. Were you aware of that?"

The conversation with Sharon Bernstein popped back as if it had just happened. "I had heard there was a note, but nobody seemed sure it was true. I never heard anything more about it. As far as I know, it was never confirmed. Have you seen it?"

"Not so far, but if it's true, the original ought to be in the police file—the one they won't let me have. Can you work with a copy? If I can get one and have you take a look at it, and you could do your thing—" he broke off with an expectant look at her.

"That depends on what 'thing' you mean. What do you want me to do?"

"First, I want you to tell me if you believe it's really Lucy's handwriting."

Her eyebrows rose. "You think somebody else might have written it?"

"We have to consider all possibilities, and if there is one, a note would be an important component."

Claudia took a pause before answering. "Sure. But to authenticate it, we would have to have exemplars—samples of her known handwriting that were written around the same time for comparison." She heard them both saying "we," and told herself it was a monumentally bad idea. A better idea would be to return to the cocktail party, where there were plenty of other people and no temptation. The trouble was, Matt had snagged her attention.

"I heard that Lucy's mom passed away," he said. "I know this is a longshot, but I'm going to try contacting her younger brother. He was a kid of eleven when it happened, so I don't know how much he would remember what went on at that age? I'm counting on their mom having held on to Lucy's schoolwork, or birthday cards, or, well, anything she wrote."

"Kelly once described her handwriting to me," Claudia said. "From what she told me, it sounded outside the norm, which could help identify whether the note is hers or not. It's a big 'if' you can get a copy, of course. All the same, even if you don't find anything to help authenticate it, I could use it to develop a personality profile from the handwriting. It would show her state of mind when it was written—assuming it *was*

Lucy who wrote it. And if she did not write it, the writing will reveal the personality of whoever who did."

"Perfect." Matt let the word hang in the air for a few seconds. "So, are you in?"

His enthusiasm was contagious. A chance to peek inside Lucy's mind through her handwriting might help settle the mystery of her disappearance. In spite of her misgivings, there was no way she could refuse.

Chapter five

Saturday Morning, October 7

The Class of Ninety-Nine reunion committee had chosen the perfect October weekend for its celebrations. Dry, crisp temperatures. By noon, the Southland would be painted with a warm glow hovering in the mid-seventies. The T-shirt weather was a major plus for the all class classic car show in the high school's main parking lot. It was scheduled to follow a pancake fundraiser breakfast in the gym. Festivities would conclude that evening at a banquet at the official reunion hotel, the Edentown Hilton.

Getting reacquainted with their classmates at the cocktail party had been 'interesting' in the sense of the Chinese curse, "may you live an *interesting* life." Andie, as sweet as ever, had acquired some much needed self-confidence. Rachel was still ghoulish and arrogant. Claudia had laughed out loud at Kelly's description of Natalie as "glambitchous." It fit.

And then, there was Matt.

Sleeping without Joel's warm body next to hers made for a restless night. Claudia rolled out of bed early, having agreed to help serve the pancakes. Still half-asleep and feeling the effects of last night's wine, she showered as quietly as water pounding against a wall could be quiet, and got dressed. Her hand was on the doorknob when Kelly's sleep-slurred voice stopped her.

"Where are you sneaking off to?"

"I'm not sneaking. I'm being quiet so I don't wake you up."

"Too late." Her friend sat up with a groan, rubbing the sleep from her eyes. She had staggered into bed late the night before, too wasted even to think about washing her face. Black mascara had smudged, resulting in raccoon eyes.

"Sorry. Go back to sleep. I'll see you there."

Kelly flopped back on the pillow and pulled the blanket over her head, muffling her voice. "My car is at the gym—"

"Take an Uber, the same way you got here. Unless you can be ready in five minutes. I'm already running late."

"Forget it; I need another hour of beauty sleep. And a Bloody Mary. Or two. My head feels like the Incredible Hulk did the Stomp on it."

"Getting too old to paint the town red?" Claudia teased. She closed the door behind her before Kelly could lob a parting shot.

The one-hundred-year-old high school was a ten minute drive from the Hilton; twenty minutes in early morning rush hour traffic. When she got close, Claudia could see signs of the car show setting up. It wasn't supposed to start until nine, but people of all ages already swarmed the parking lot, comparing high-gloss paint jobs on the restored jalopies, immersing themselves in the nostalgia of lost youth. Judging from some of the vehicles she spotted, alumni from the 1940s and even earlier had joined classmates whose vintage Mustangs and Camaros and Corvettes were on display. Her '85 Jaguar would have fit right in.

She drove past as leisurely as she reasonably could without tempting the driver behind her to honk his horn—he was gawking too—and around to the small parking lot at the rear of the campus behind the swimming pool.

It was early enough that the lot was empty, and she had her pick of spaces. The shortcut around the pool deck would take her to the back door of the gym, which she and Matt had used the previous evening.

Rounding the bleachers, Claudia squinted in the sudden blinding glare of the sun glinting on the water. It took a few seconds for her vision to clear, and as it did, her eyes were drawn to a dark shape on the bottom of the pool. A sharp breeze rippled the surface, distorting it. The water stilled, and time stopped.

She blinked, then blinked again, trying to wrap her head around what she was seeing. He was floating face down, longish dark hair waving around his head like the arms of an octopus. Pale fingers splayed.

Then reality set in.

She yelled to him, clinging for just an instant to the ridiculous notion that he was simply taking an early morning swim before the events of the day. That would have made more sense if his attire had been a Speedo, rather than a sport coat and trousers. And if he had not been hovering, motionless, near the filter at the bottom of the pool.

In those first moments of incomprehension, Claudia could pretend to herself that she had not recognized the man, facedown as he was. That they had not engaged in friendly conversation little more than twelve hours ago. She sped along the deck to the gym door. No one was in sight when she began to yell for help.

She was still yelling when she got close enough for the feeble hope to be dashed that he might somehow be alive.

Chapter six

Saturday morning, October 7

The first responders were there seven minutes after Claudia's 911 call. They secured the area surrounding the swimming pool, allowing no one to enter or leave without permission. When she explained about the pancake breakfast about to be held in the gym, the officer in charge sent some of the uniforms to speak to kitchen staff, who would have been there since early morning getting set up.

It was decided that the breakfast could go on. An officer was assigned to stand guard at the back door of the gym, not allowing anyone through while the outdoor investigation continued. Others were deployed to the car show to canvass the attendees, asking whether anyone had seen anything suspicious.

After they had fished Joshua Dickson's body out of the pool and the coroner's van drove away with it, Claudia sat on the bottom bleachers, shivering as if it was she who had been in the cold water. She felt strangely hurtled back in time, to the day of Lucy Valentine's disappearance. This time, though, instead of Kelly, Claudia was the one being interviewed. Or interrogated—Kelly's word. It was foolish to feel guilty undergoing police questioning, when she was innocent of anything other than being in the wrong place at the wrong time.

The chief investigator introduced himself as Samuel Booker. A fiftyish African American man with a shiny shaved dome, wearing a neat brown suit and tie.

Claudia played the "my husband is a homicide detective at LAPD" card, which had helped her talk her way through more than one difficult situation over the past couple of years. Regretfully, she told the detective she had nothing to contribute that would be of any help. Yes, she had once known the victim. Joshua Dickson had been a popular driver's education teacher when she had been a student at Edentown High twenty-five years ago. He had attended last night's reunion event. Everyone liked him. She had learned how to drive under his tutelage.

"Have you been in contact with him?"

"No, he moved to the East Coast a long time ago. My friend and I spoke with him briefly last night. That's the first time since we graduated that either of us saw him."

"And that was it? No more conversation later in the evening?"

"None at all."

"Doesn't it seem unusual for a teacher to come to a reunion such a long time later?"

"No, there's nothing unusual about it. Mr. Dickson wasn't the only teacher attending the reunion. Ms. Goldman was here, too—Sue Goldman. As I said, he moved away, but she still teaches here. She might be in the habit of attending these things. She and Mr. Dickson were friends. You should consider talking to her; she might know something."

"I'll do that, thank you," said Booker scribbling in his notebook. He was old school, like Joel, who refused to use his phone for making notes like the younger detectives. "Would you happen to know whether Mr. Dickson knew how to swim?" he asked.

The spectral vision of her former teacher floating under hundreds of thousands of gallons of water flashed back. In his dark clothing, he had looked like an overgrown crow.

I'm not his keeper, she wanted to retort. *I just found his body.*

There was no reason to be rude. She searched her memories for one the detective might find pertinent. "My boyfriend in high school was on the swim team. I remember him telling me once that Mr. Dickson substitute coached the team. I assume he knew how to swim."

"Mhm," Booker said. "Do you happen to know whether Mr. Dickson was drinking alcohol at the party?"

"He was carrying a rocks glass when he spoke to my friend and me. That was just before the party got going. I think it might have been whisky, but I was not paying attention. Maybe the bartenders would remember how many refills he'd had, but there were a good two hundred people attending if you include spouses, so I wouldn't count on it. Unless maybe something made him stand out to them."

"Like what?" Booker asked.

"His demeanor? Something like that, I guess. When we talked to him, he was cheerful; jovial. That was typical of him when I knew him. And, it was that kind of occasion, right? I have no idea whether he got so drunk that he might stagger outside and fall in the pool."

Booker nodded, as if he had expected her answer. "Okay, Ms. Rose, thank you for your cooperation. Last question—do you know of anyone who had a reason to harm Mr. Dickson?"

So far Detective Booker had kept the discussion low key. His question turned it up a notch.

"Why? Do you think there was foul play?"

He looked back through heavy lidded eyes, dispassionate and cool. "I don't think anything yet. I'm just gathering information like we do at any unattended death."

She smiled. "They must teach that phraseology in detective school; it's the same response I've heard from my husband."

He continued to gaze at her in silence.

"Are we done, then?" she asked when she saw that he was not going to respond.

"You didn't answer my question, Ms. Rose."

"Which one?"

Booker repeated: "Do you know of anyone who had a reason to harm him?"

"Oh. No, I don't. Everyone I knew loved him."

Detective Booker got up, smoothed the creases in his trousers. *"Now* we're done. I have all your contact information in case anything else comes up."

"I've told you everything I know, Detective. But you're welcome to call me if you think of anything."

"Thank you, Ms. Rose. Now we are done. You are free to go."

By the time Detective Booker had released her from the interview, Kelly had arrived and wanted all the intel.

"You found *another* dead body? What the hell, Claud? If you keep it up, the cops are going to think you're a serial killer."

"Don't say it." She could read her friend's mind: *It's not that long since the last one...*

The truth was, it had been a few scarce months since Claudia stumbled upon a murder victim. She had been searching for her niece who was missing from an archaeological dig in Egypt. And that wasn't the first time, either. It was not that she looked for them—she didn't *want* to find them—it just seemed to have become a bad habit—one she would love to break.

The two of them walked around the outside perimeter of the high school to the main parking lot, where the car show was in high gear. "Okay, spill it," Kelly prompted. "Everyone's buzzing, and nobody knows anything. It's just like when—"

"I know," Claudia said glumly. "Cops at school. Lucy Valentine."

"What do they think? Some poor drunk kid who shouldn't have been back there?"

The victim's name had not been released, pending notification of next of kin, but Detective Booker had not instructed Claudia to keep it from her best friend. "It was Mr. Dickson."

Kelly stopped walking. Her mouth dropped open. "No way. Omigod; what the actual f—"

"You sound like you're sixteen."

"I *feel* like I'm sixteen." Her eyes opened wider. "You're not joking, are you? It really was Dickson?" Kelly started walking again, faster, so that Claudia had to lengthen her stride to keep up. "No. You wouldn't joke about something like that. What the *hell* happened?"

"I heard one of the cops say the likely story is, he was tanked and fell into the pool. They have lights out there—I was outside with Matt, chatting last night. It wasn't hard to avoid the edge. But if Dickson was that wasted, all bets are off. With his suit and shoes weighing him down, once he fell in, he couldn't get out."

"Crap, that's horrible. I wonder what he was doing at the pool."

"Needed some air, maybe?"

"When he talked to us he wasn't on his first drink. He was at the happy slappy stage. I saw him at the bar a couple of times later, and he was well on his way to oblivion." Kelly's grin was self-mocking. "It takes one to know one." Unexpectedly, she teared up. "I can't believe it. This is so sad."

"Er, weren't you the one calling him an asshole last night?"

"He *was* an asshole, but this is something I wouldn't wish on anyone."

Claudia shook her head, her mind still wanting to deny what she had seen. "I couldn't believe it when I saw him down there—"

"Wait—down where? Didn't he drown?"

"Yes. He was *down* on the bottom of the pool."

"Why would he be on the bottom? Drowned people float."

"They don't when they first drown. Joel had a case like this. He told me that once the body starts to putrefy, it starts to fill up with gas, like a balloon. It would take two or three days for that to happen, though. Eventually, it would rise—"

"Stop!" Kelly had gone green around the gills. She made the 'time out' sign. "TMI."

"Matt and I were out there on the bleachers, talking, until around nine. Mr. Dickson must have come out there after we left." For just a moment, Claudia closed her eyes. "When I first saw him in the water, I sort of knew it was him, but I didn't know for sure until they got him out and rolled him over."

She had witnessed them pull him out of the pool while she stared on, water pouring off him and out of him, drenching the deck. The image had stayed with her. She had a feeling it was going to be indelible.

"Just think. If he'd gone out there a little earlier, or you and Matt had stayed a few minutes later, it might never—" She broke down sobbing.

For Kelly, dealing with her emotions meant gallons of tears. A swimming pool full.

Claudia thought about calling Joel to tell him what happened before he heard it in the media. But he was working on his case, and she didn't want to hinder his investigation. Besides, she needed some time to process the experience of discovering her teacher dead.

If she told herself the full truth, she was putting it off because her husband would want to rush to the rescue. She didn't want to feel as though she needed rescuing.

Chapter seven

Kelly went off to sit with the football players and cheerleaders, while Claudia joined Matt and some of the people they had worked with on the staff of the school newspaper, the *Edentown High Echo*.

Everyone was seated and making their way through the salad course, when Cathi Soden, the reunion chair, stepped up to the podium to deliver her welcoming remarks. Then she made the announcement they were all whispering about—the death of their former teacher.

"As you all know, we have a very active grapevine," Cathi said. "So most of you have probably heard the horrible news about Mr. Dickson's shocking death." She paused for the expected buzz of reaction to go around the room. "We're told it happened last night, sometime after the cocktail party. The police have asked for a list of everyone who registered for the reunion, and they are going down the list, contacting everyone as a matter of procedure. If any of you saw something, or have any information, please contact them right away." She took a breath and looked somberly over the crowd. "And, in the unlikely event you *haven't* heard, Josh Dickson was found early this morning in the school pool by one of our classmates. Let's take a moment of silence to think about our beloved teacher and his family."

A prolonged hush fell over the banquet room, during which Claudia sent Cathi a silent *Thank You* for not mentioning her name. Then, someone coughed, and the moment was over. Cathi thanked the committee members for their contribution to the success of the event, and the brief program concluded with a prize for the classmate who had traveled the farthest.

Someone pointed out, and was shut down, that Mr. Dickson had flown out from New York, making him the actual winner. Someone else pointed out that he was not a classmate and would not have been eligible. Patti Lindstrom, who had come from Illinois, accepted the certificate for a free night at the Hilton with thanks.

As though someone had held a match to dry brush, the moment Cathi left the podium and returned to her table, the buzz started again, and swelled. Despite the fact that Claudia's name had been omitted, it was on the cascade of conversation all around them, and at their table.

Lupe Garcia, who was the student editor of the *Echo* in their senior year, had taken up a career in journalism, and had later gone on to become the managing editor of the *Edentown Gazette*. Lupe had a reputation as a pit bull when going after a story, and she wasted no time turning a laser focus on Claudia. "How did you happen to find him? Tell us what happened."

Josh Dickson's death was the very last thing Claudia wanted to talk about. "Not much to tell," she said. "I was taking a shortcut to the back door of the gym to help serve the breakfast—which I never got to do. How did the pancakes turn out, by the way?"

Her attempt to change the subject fell on deaf ears. Teri Bergman had also been a reporter on the school paper. "God, that must have been such a shock, to find him like that," she said, an indecent curiosity showing through her attempt to appear sympathetic.

Claudia halted the forkful of salad greens halfway to her mouth. "Yes, it was. But hey, you know what else was a shock? Finding out that Vincent

Ramsey is the CEO of NumbersBox. That's a huge company. Isn't *that* interesting?"

"What's so interesting about that?" Teri said at the same time Lupe drawled, "You didn't know about that? Oh, I forgot, you live in L.A. It was major news here in our hometown—how many years ago, Billy?"

"I dunno, hon. Maybe ten. He—" Billy, Lupe's husband, broke off as the main doors to the banquet room swung open and a line of black-uniformed waitstaff marched in, bearing a copper dome-covered dinner plate on each hand. For the next several minutes, any meaningful conversation was suspended during the ceremonial delivery of the entrée.

As soon as the plates were on the table and the waiters were making their way back to the kitchen, another *Echo* reporter, Joe Martin, leaned towards Claudia. "I didn't know that about Ramsey," he said, his knife rudely pointed at her. "Are you serious?"

"Dead serious," Claudia shot back, regretting her choice of words as soon as they left her mouth. "Vincent mentioned it last night when he checked in."

Joe twisted around in his chair, his eyes traveling the room until they fell on Vincent Ramsey and his date, the same blonde he had brought to the cocktail party. Her attention was currently on the male to her other side. Vincent, his mouth pressed into a thin line, sat straight as a ruler, gazing into the distance, as usual, giving the impression of inhabiting his own world, where others were not welcome. *"Sideshow Bob*, the CEO of a company that important?" Joe mocked. "Remember what we used to say? He's so skinny, he wipes his ass with dental floss."

Matt glanced up from his food. "You can sneer all you like, Joe, but he's made more money than God, 'Sideshow Bob' or not."

Billy Spencer, Lupe's husband, added a derisive chuckle. "You're just jealous of that babe he's with."

Joe threw him a sullen glare. "I bet he's paying her by the hour."

Lupe laughed. Billy coughed, conspicuously loud, but she brushed off the hint. "Don't be such a little bitch, Joe. I think Billy's right, you're jealous of our highly successful alumnus. Or is it carrot top himself that you have the hots for?"

Joe ignored her. He reached for the bottle of Cab on the table and poured himself a hefty glass. Contemplating the boeuf bourguignon and mashed potatoes on her plate, Claudia wished she had ordered the salmon. The company was starting to give her indigestion.

"Anyone notice Miss Goldman isn't here tonight?" Teri said into the hiatus.

Lupe reached for a dinner roll from the basket and broke it in half. "Too torn up over Dickson, I bet."

"Yeah, used to be hella close," Teri said. "Maybe they still were."

There was something suggestive in the way she said it. Billy flicked her a questioning glance. "You think they were getting it on again after all this time?"

"Did you see them last night? They were superglued together. Couldn't see daylight between them."

"Maybe for a while," Lupe said. "But I think they must have had a fight. *Something* happened."

"Like what?"

"I ran into Ms. G in the ladies' room. Her eyes were red and her face was puffy. It was so obvious she'd been crying. She was wiping mascara off her face and I asked if she was okay. She brushed me off, claimed she had something in her eye." Lupe frowned. "Come to think of it, I don't remember seeing her again after that."

"Because you had your eyes on her the whole evening?" Joe derided, probably still smarting from the last zinger Lupe had aimed at him.

She stopped buttering her roll to pull a face. "Hardly. But I do think she must have left early."

"I used to have a huge crush on Dickson in high school," Teri said, pointedly gesturing to the bottle of Chardonnay across the table. Billy gestured for her to give him her glass, and poured for her as she continued her confession. "He was so adorable and funny back then. That crush died a hard death last night. He was so sloppy drunk, he could hardly stand up. No wonder he fell in the pool."

Claudia pushed her plate away. Had these people been pathetic losers the entire time, or had they grown into it? Long ago, when she had wanted desperately to be accepted, to be part of their clique, she had thought they were the cool ones. Back when teen angst pushed her into doing stupid things, she would have done just about anything to get them to like her. A sharp spike of anger hammered her chest and threatened to explode. "Does anyone remember that a guy we knew and liked is dead?"

"And you're the one who found him, but you don't want to talk about it," Lupe said, unchastened. "What's up with that?"

"What's up with that is there's nothing to say, other than it's a tragedy that he's dead, and I wish I hadn't been the one to find him. Period. End of sentence. What else do you want me to say?"

Teri popped a forkful of rice into her mouth. "How can you be so sure that's what happened, Claudia?"

"What the hell are you talking about?"

"What if he had some help?" Billy added.

"Yeah, Lupe just told us he and Miss Goldman were arguing," Joe said. "Maybe she didn't go home after she went to the head. Maybe she waited and got him to go outside—"

"You know that's slander, right?"

Billy laughed, as if the whole thing was a huge joke. "Don't be such a priss, Claudia, we're just funning."

"Someone dying tragically isn't my idea of fun."

Matt dropped his fork with a clatter on his plate, drawing all eyes in his direction. "Why don't you guys knock it off and leave her alone. To find someone dead—someone she knew—has got to be a traumatic experience. And unless the coroner comes back with something different, the cause of death is gonna be accidental drowning."

Having Matt jump to her defense left Claudia with that twitchy feeling again. She put a restraining hand on his sleeve to let him know that she didn't need him to defend her. Reining in her temper, she glared at each of her tablemates in turn. "I get that you people are curious, but there's nothing more to say about it. Can you please let it go?"

"Yeah, Matt," Lupe said with a self-satisfied smirk, having gotten a rise out of her classmate. "I know you two were hot and heavy in high school, but you don't have to protect her now; she's married to a cop."

"How come your husband didn't come with you?" Teri asked.

"He's working. And I'm a big girl. I can go to my reunion by myself."

Lupe's speculative gaze went to Claudia, then Matt. "I saw you two slinking out the back door together last night."

Claudia gave her a tight smile. "I know you're forever nosing for news, Lupe, but you're sniffing in the wrong dirt pile—there's nothing to see here. I'm sure that out of a couple hundred classmates, there must be something genuinely salacious you can go after."

Lupe stared at her for a long moment, then said, "You're right, there is." An uncomfortable silence fell as she pushed back her chair and walked away, leaving a collective sigh of relief to ripple around the table.

"Just Lupe being Lupe," Billy said apologetically.

Without her provocative presence, the conversation became more relaxed and general. Claudia stuck it out through dessert, but when the band started playing and Matt asked her to dance, she refused with a smile. "I'm going up to my room for some peace and quiet. And don't ask if you can come with me; the answer is *no*. I have to make a call."

To my husband.

"When can we talk some more about the documentary project? I'm eager to get going on it, and I could use your help."

She could see the disappointment in his face. The fact was, she did want to hear more of what he had in mind. "How about first thing tomorrow, before we all go home?"

He gave her what she was sure was meant to be his winningest smile. "Are you sure that's the best I can get?"

She considered relenting, but knew it was an unwise move. "I'm sure," she said firmly. "Let's meet in the hotel café at eight-thirty."

He leaned in and gave her a quick hug. "Yes, ma'am. Eight-thirty it is. See you then."

Claudia made her exit soon after. Classmates were making the rounds, stopping at other tables to say goodbye to friends. She waved goodbye to Andrea, who was walking out with Natalie and Rachel, followed by Natalie's husband, Tom. They all still lived in Edentown, so had not needed rooms in the hotel. She was sure Kelly would want to hang at the bar with friends before following her up to their room. Fortunately, if she overindulged tonight, she wouldn't need a ride.

On the elevator ride up to the fourth floor, Claudia dug out her phone and found a text message from Joel that she had missed in the noisy affair.

> Having fun? Early bed. Love you.

He must have been exhausted to call it a night so early. The long hours, the driving to interview witnesses, and the report writing murder investigations required took its toll. She hoped his activities had led to an arrest.

The day had done a number on her too. If she admitted it, there was some relief that she didn't have to talk to anyone else tonight, even Joel. With a slight pang of guilt, she texted back a 'love you too' message and dropped the phone back into her purse.

Chapter eight

Sunday, October 8

On Sunday morning, Café Citrus was half-empty. A scattering of sleepy-eyed patrons drooped over their phones and coffee cups. Claudia slid into a booth opposite Matt Macedo.

In his black T-shirt and jeans, his hair wet, Matt looked as refreshed if he had just taken a five mile run and showered after a long, peaceful night's sleep. Claudia, after waking up every other hour, reliving her brief conversation with Josh Dickson and then finding his body, was less than bright-eyed and bushytailed. She studied the menu as if it could give her the answers to all the questions in the universe.

Matt ordered ham and eggs with pancakes. Yogurt and granola and black coffee was all Claudia could stomach at that time of morning. The thought of anything with grease made her queasy. While they waited for their order, Matt launched into his vision for the documentary.

"The working title is *Looking for Lucy*. I know it's not very imaginative, but it's good enough for now."

"It tells the tale," Claudia said absently. She meant to pay attention, but her mind was drifting back through time to 1998.

"Let's form our own search party," Kelly had suggested. *"She used to go into the woods. What if she got lost or hurt? Or fell into the canyon? We can get a bunch of our friends together and go through the park around the school, and Edentown Woods."*

"That's a ton of ground to cover," Claudia said doubtfully. "Didn't the police already search there?"

"Obviously we can't do it all, but if we do it like on TV—like where everyone links their arms and walks in a long row, searching for clues—we can be doing something."

The thought of taking action was definitely more appealing than sitting in her room, fretting. Claudia reached for the phone extension next to her bed. "I'll call the Cathi's first, I bet they'll want to go. And Lupe, too, and—"

"—I'll call some of the guys." Having come up with a plan, Kelly fairly glowed with fervor. "What if we find her—wouldn't that be amazing? Alive, I mean."

"Omigod, I hope we do."

They had gathered at the pink of dawn on Saturday morning, more than twenty of them, certain they would uncover some important clue to the missing girl's whereabouts. Setting off into the massive woods with an element of excitement, it was like they were on a scavenger hunt, which made Claudia wince. But they'd showed up, and that was worth a lot.

Edentown Woods was a regional park that abutted Edentown High School. There was no possible way they could begin to cover even a fraction of the 4,000 acres of canyon and woodlands, grassy meadows and ponds, the shrub-covered hillsides, but it made them feel as though they were contributing something to the search for Lucy Valentine.

For some, it didn't take long for boredom to set in. A couple of hours into the search, when they'd found nothing more than bits of trash and dog poop the owners had failed to pick up, the searchers began to drop out. One by one, they made excuses and quit. A handful of diehards stayed until dusk was crowding in, but in the end, they, too, were obliged to give up. Having found no answers, they all left and went home.

Claudia was one of the last to go. She was worried they had missed something; she kept going over and over it in her head. Had Lucy run away from home after all, like they said on the news? Or, as Kelly believed, had she gone into the woods and was lost or hurt? She tried unsuccessfully to push away the most horrendous possibility of all—that someone had taken her. And done what with her? The questions nagged like a toothache. The seed of fear that had been planted with the news of Lucy's disappearance sprouted and grew into blazing anxiety. Claudia began to invent excuses to stay home from school, not even telling Kelly that she was scared to death to go outside and—

"Hey, are you okay?" Matt's voice snapped her back. He was looking at her oddly and she realized that she must have been staring off into space. She produced a faint smile. "Sorry. Lost in the past. I was thinking about that search party we organized—were you there? I don't remember."

Matt looked startled. Before he could answer, the waitress came by and dropped off their order, which seemed to give him the space he needed. "No. I don't remember why, but I couldn't go that day."

"Her only real friends were Kelly and Rachel. The rest of us hardly knew her at all."

"I knew her since grade school," Matt said dejectedly. "She was a loner even then."

Claudia stirred granola into her yogurt, not wanting it. "What was it that made you want to tackle this now, after so long? Was it the reunion—thinking about school, that reminded you of Lucy?"

He pushed some eggs onto his fork, ate an unenthusiastic mouthful, and set the fork on his plate. As the silence continued Claudia began to wonder whether he had returned to the same dark place she had. She waited him out. When he turned his eyes up to meet her gaze, the range of emotions she saw there mystified her.

"I've thought about her so many times over the years—never knowing what happened," he said. "I felt responsible."

"How on Earth could you be responsible?" Claudia asked, unware that Matt had any feelings about Lucy at all. The pain in his voice came as a surprise.

"I know it doesn't seem reasonable, but when you're a kid, it doesn't have to, does it? I felt like I should have been able to save her."

There was something more, she could feel it. "Save her from what, Matt?"

"From whatever happened to her, whether she ran away, or—" He chewed the corner of his lip. Raising his eyes to meet hers again, he said, "Lucy and I dated when we were juniors," then hastened to add, "For a little while."

Their junior year was long before Claudia and Matt had begun seeing each other. Eons in teen years. Yet, the unexpected announcement deflated her. "As shy as she was, I'm surprised she would date at all," she said.

Matt smiled, but it was a weak effort. "She was—" he stopped to think about it. "Shy isn't the word. Maybe 'reclusive' is more accurate. It's not that she was afraid of people...more like she was choosy."

The waitress stopped by to refill their coffees. When she was gone, he huffed a sad laugh. "I'm not even sure how we connected. Maybe we both recognized horrible self-esteem in each other. It was like a magnet, bringing us together. It started in study hall. I was better in math; she was stronger in English. We started studying for tests together, comparing notes, helping each other out. Did you know she wanted to be a writer?"

She wanted to be a writer.

That simple sentence brought a sharp spasm of pain. She knew so little about Lucy, and those words brought her to life. Claudia shook her head. "No, I didn't know that."

"She was into Edgar Allan Poe—thought he was so cool. Thinking about it now, she probably saw herself as being like him—a tragic, romantic—a mysterious figure."

"And that's how she ended up. A mystery. I have a mental picture of her wearing black every day. She used to hunch her shoulders up like she was protecting herself; from what, I don't know."

Matt nodded in agreement. "I know what you mean. She was brittle like a piece of glass, so fragile, it might crack if you looked at it too hard."

"There was a guardedness about her, as if she expected to be attacked. My mother used to call it 'leading with your chin' when she was accusing me of being on the defensive." Claudia's sigh was full of memories. "Which was a lot."

"As I recall, your mother was a major pain in the ass," Matt said. "No offense intended."

"None taken. You have a good memory. And nothing has changed on that score. But back to you and Lucy. You went from study hall to dating?"

"I wanted to ask her out, but it took a while to get up the cojones. I was so stunned when she said yes that I hardly knew what to do about it. In the end, it wasn't a big deal. We got together a few times. Mostly, I'd go over to her house and watch TV with her when she had to babysit her little brother. We went to a couple of movies; hung out at the mall. Made out in my car." Matt puffed a long breath through pursed lips. "No matter how close I thought we were getting, it was like I never really got to know her. Even when we were making out it felt like there was a barrier there, you know?"

"Kelly said something similar about her—that they were friends up to a point."

"Kelly wasn't a horny teenage boy who expected more."

The yogurt Claudia had managed to get down churned in her gut with unwanted suspicion and questions that were forming. Before she could voice them, Matt had something else to add.

"When she disappeared, it was two or three months after we'd stopped dating. Someone must have told the cops I'd been seeing her. They came to our house and questioned me. My parents had to take me to the police station."

"That's a lot, Matt. I never heard anything about it."

"My dad made sure it was kept quiet." His eyes fixed on the middle distance, remembering the experience. "I'll never forget how it felt. They kept trying to trip me up, get me to admit I'd done something to her. They pushed me for a confession—said I'd killed her and hidden the body, and I'd feel better if I came clean."

Feeling suddenly chilled, Claudia wrapped her hands around her coffee mug. "Were your parents present when they questioned you?"

"My dad insisted on it. He threatened the police chief with a lawsuit if it ever came out that they were treating me as a person of interest when there was zero evidence against me."

"I don't understand why they would pursue you if you'd broken up months earlier."

"The only answer is, they didn't have anyone else to go after. I made a mistake in telling them Lucy broke up with me. She was seriously cold about it too. There was no 'sorry to do this, Matt.' Just, *'I like someone else, so I'm breaking up with you.'* She just kicked me to the curb like a pair of old shoes with holes in the soles."

Claudia rolled her eyes at the drama. "Who was the other guy that she liked? Did the cops go after him?"

"I *begged* her to tell me, but I never could get it out of her. I thought maybe it was someone older, or from another school. And no, I don't think the cops did much looking."

"So, they tried to make it sound like you were so angry that months later you went after her and hurt her?"

"That's about the size of it."

The elephant in the room sat on the table, waiting to be noticed. She had to ask the question that was uppermost. "How upset *were* you that she dumped you?"

"It didn't help my ego any, I don't mind admitting it; the rejection hurt. But I can honestly say I wasn't all cut up over it." Matt caught her gaze and held it. "What you really want to know is the same as the police—after all those months, was I hurt and angry enough to do something to her? The answer is, unequivocally, not even close."

He said it convincingly. But if he was lying, he'd had twenty-six years to perfect his story. "It drove me crazy," he added. "A couple of times I even followed her to see if she met him."

Claudia stared at him. "Jeez, Matt, like that doesn't sound some kind of stalkerish. Where did you follow her?"

"Mostly, to the woods behind the school. She'd go off by herself and she would have seen me if I got any closer. If she was meeting someone there, I never saw him."

"Let's back up a bit. How did the police know you were her ex-boyfriend?"

His mouth bunched in a sardonic twist. "Good question. I never saw Lucy hanging with anyone except that Rachel Thomas girl, and your buddy, Kelly Brennan. I'd bet my favorite socks it was one or both of them."

"Kelly would have told me about it," Claudia objected. "Especially when you and I started dating in our senior year."

Would she, though? There had been times when Kelly kept important things to herself and did not tell Claudia until long after the fact. Would she have told the police investigator about Matt and Lucy being together? In normal times, Kelly liked being in the spotlight, but after her "interrogation," about Lucy, she might not have wanted to draw attention to herself. It could have been to her benefit to point the finger at someone else. On the other hand, Kelly wasn't vicious, nor did she have any reason to throw Matt under the bus. Claudia didn't think so, anyway. But her mind was humming with this new information about Matt being Lucy's boyfriend. She wasn't sure about anything anymore.

"Lucy and I lost our virginity to each other." He pushed his half-eaten food away, flushing with embarrassment.

"I'm finding out all kinds of things about you," Claudia said stiffly. It took a supreme effort to hold her tongue when she wanted to yell at him, *why am I just learning this?* What else didn't she know about Matt that maybe she should before she got more involved with this venture of his? In light of what he had just told her—that he and Lucy had had sex—shouldn't he have been more affected when she broke up with him? On the flip side, as he had said, he'd been a horny teenage boy with expectations. Such creatures were not known for being sensitive to anything outside their own needs and desires.

Matt topped up their coffee mugs with the carafe the waitress had left on the table. "I'm trying to be as honest as I can with you so you'll understand why it's so damned important to me to get this project made. It doesn't matter that nobody outside my family knew about me being questioned." His shoulders slumped, and he looked as miserable as Claudia had ever seen him.

"Ever since Lucy's been gone, it's felt like a dark shadow was following me around—like one of the dementors out of *Harry Potter*. It colors everything I do, and I need to put it to rest. Not just for me, but for Lucy and what's left of her family. Now that I have the resources and the connections to produce this project, I'm going to get it made. And If she is dead, I want to find out why, and who—"

Claudia studied him through newly opened eyes. He was a good story weaver, convincing in his earnestness. Was that sufficient? She made a mental note to ask Joel to check him out before she dove in with both feet. "Where do you plan to start?" she asked.

"With Lucy's brother, Troy Valentine."

"If she left a note," she mused, "I suppose that's where it would be, assuming the cops gave her mother a copy."

"And assuming Troy hasn't thrown out her stuff," Matt said. "He lives in Studio City. You're in Playa de la Reina, right? That's a half-hour drive from there. If I can get him to agree to a meeting, would you go with me and see what he remembers?"

Claudia frowned. "I don't remember telling you where I live."

Matt snorted. "Do the words 'investigative reporter' mean anything to you?"

Chapter nine

Sunday, October 8

It was midmorning when Claudia got home from Edentown. Joel was in bed and snoring. He must have had another late night. Feeling as though she had been away for a week, rather than two nights, she inched her way under the covers and pressed herself against his bare back. Her arm snaked around his chest, and she nestled her cheek to his warm skin. He stirred and mumbled something. She shushed him back to sleep.

Over the two-hour drive home, she had found her thoughts shifting back and forth between the disappearance of Lucy Valentine and the death of Josh Dickson. It would require some serious mental scrubbing to rid herself of the image of his body on the pool deck. She considered asking her friend and sometime-therapist, Zebediah Gold, to hypnotize it out of her, but discarded the idea as a non-starter. Knowing Zebediah, he would remind her that she was powerless to change what had happened to Mr. Dickson, and thus would need to deal with his tragic end head-on.

As for Lucy, Claudia was less powerless. It was true that she couldn't change the ending to her story, or even bring it to completion, but she would do what she could to help Matt with his investigation. In the wisdom that came with hindsight, there was a chance they could get further with it than the police had. In addition to analyzing any relevant handwriting they came across, she could use her training in psychology to observe the people he interviewed.

Matt had offered to pay her for her professional services, but that didn't feel right, and she had told him so. This was not the first time she had been invited to participate in a film venture. She knew that until he sold the project, any expenses would come out of his own pockets, which were not deep. She didn't miss the gratitude in his eyes when she insisted on volunteering to work the case pro bono until he sold it to a network. They could talk about payment later.

Joel woke around noon, happy to welcome her home. They stayed in bed and made love until their stomachs growled and sent them downstairs to the kitchen.

Claudia foraged in the refrigerator for grilled cheese sandwich makings. He sat in the breakfast nook, nursing a beer, listening to her report on all that had happened during her stay in her hometown. She could have predicted his reaction to her finding her drowned teacher: a slow, incredulous shake of his head. "Why does it always have to be you?"

Focusing on her culinary efforts allowed her to avoid his eyes while she searched for a clever answer. Not finding one, she gave it up. "That's more or less the same thing Kelly said too." She could see that the news had disturbed him. He would not say so, but he didn't have to; she was intimately acquainted with his every expression, every shade of meaning.

"It's not something I do on purpose," she said, and heard the defensiveness in her voice. "Besides, this time it wasn't a murder victim. He was drunk, fell in the pool, and drowned."

Joel bit off a chunk of the sandwich she handed him and washed it down with beer. "They're sure of that?"

"What else would it be? Everyone at school thought he was a cool guy. He moved away right after we graduated, so no enemies in town." Claudia set her sandwich plate on the table and sat opposite him. "I wonder how high his blood alcohol was."

"The autopsy report will say. Probably another day or two before it comes out." His cool grey eyes grazed her, probing her, and reading her the way only he could. "Tell me more about this Matt guy."

"What do you want to know?" She gave him the side eye. "Are you jealous?"

"Should I be?"

She laughed and made a show of licking melted cheese from her fingers. "Typical detective; answers a question with a question. Kelly has her eye on him, so I don't think you need to worry."

Joel, who professed to be afraid of her lascivious best friend, chuckled. "Dude doesn't know what he's in for."

Claudia put up a not-so-fast hand. "Except, he thinks she might have narced on him to the cops about him having dated Lucy Valentine before she disappeared. So, how kindly is he going to feel towards her?"

He was unconvinced. "Twenty-six years later?"

"Have you ever been on the receiving end of an interrogation as a sixteen-year-old? Yeah, I didn't think so. That wouldn't be so easy to forgive and forget—if she was the one who ratted him out. I plan to ask her. More likely to have been Rachel, though."

"Rachel was one of the school paper reporters?"

"No, the mortician. She was in the same driver's ed and PE classes that Kelly and Lucy and I were in. They used to hang out sometimes."

"Not you?"

"We had different interests. I wasn't part of that whole goth cabal those three had going. Kelly and I were always close, but we had other friends too."

Joel finished his sandwich and pushed his plate away. "From what you said about some of those newspaper folks, I'd be inclined to keep my distance from them."

"Normally, I would too," she agreed. "But some of them are on Matt's list to interview for the documentary, so I'll be talking to them again."

"What does he think they can add?"

Claudia gave him a pert grin. "Just like you tell me, you don't know until you ask, right? Some of the newspaper kids wrote articles about Lucy going AWOL. I don't know whether any of them were interviewed by the police, but it was a big event in our lives—big enough that they're bound to remember some details. And who knows if one of them will remember something that another doesn't."

Joel's sigh might as well have been accompanied by an eye roll. "And there she goes again—Grapholady, unofficial private dick."

She reached across the table and flicked his chest with her finger. "There's only one dick in this story—Mr. *Dick*son."

"That's a name I'd have to change," he said.

"I couldn't believe Kelly called him an asshole."

Joel looked interested. "You didn't tell me that."

"I need to find out what made her say it. It was right after we talked to him on Friday night. She was being very unKelly-like—not at all friendly. *Everybody* liked him. He was the most popular teacher in school."

"Because of his age?"

Claudia nibbled the last corner of her sandwich and chewed it thoughtfully. The smiling young teacher had rarely ever yelled at them the way some of her other teachers did. In his daily uniform of neat black slacks and short-sleeved white shirt—he was nothing if not consistent—he had been close to—but was not quite—a peer. He had kept an appropriate distance for his students to know where the line was drawn between them and *Mr.* Dickson. During the time Claudia was his student, she could not recall anyone ever misbehaving badly enough for him to send them to the principal's office.

"His age, and because he was fun to be around, constantly cracking dumb dad jokes. We had to learn the rules of the road—literally—it *was* driver's ed—but he came up with ways to make it more interesting." A smile found its way to her mouth as she reminisced. "He used to joke about smoking pot, and other stuff that would have horrified our parents." The smile fell away. She pushed crumbs around on the plate with her fingertip. "I can't stand to think of him dying that way—and all alone. And his poor wife and kids."

"Didn't you say he was screwing around with that other teacher?"

"That's just a guess. It's what Lupe said, but she could easily have made it up just to be provocative—she likes to do things like that." Claudia paused to consider the question. "Was it true that Dickson and Goldman could have picked it up again—assuming we were right about them getting it on in the past? A one-night stand 'for old times?' Sure, they could. And if Lupe *was* telling the truth and they had a fight Friday night, and he was so drunk that he fell into the pool, that could be why he went outside—to get some air."

"You don't think maybe Sue was mad enough to have followed him out there and given him a shove?"

"That's what Joe Martin said last night, but he was joking. No, I certainly don't think so." The thought of it made her feel ill. "Can you imagine—you're plastered, not thinking straight, fighting to get out of the water, a soaking wet suit and shoes weighing you down, and nobody coming to help?"

Joel got up and pulled her up, too. He folded her into his arms. "I'm sorry you had to be the one to find him, babe."

If anyone knew about dead bodies, Joel did. As a homicide detective he had seen more than his share, and some in far worse condition than

Josh Dickson had been. She had seen some in far worse condition, too. "It never gets any easier, does it?" she said.

"No," he said. "It never does."

She left her husband clearing up the debris of their lunch and went upstairs to her office. If she was going to help Matt, she wanted to be armed with all the information she could glean, so she could hit the ground running when he was ready to get started in earnest. She woke up the computer and googled Lucy Valentine.

The articles that came up were published in the days and weeks following Lucy's disappearance. *The Edentown Gazette* reported on the candlelight vigil the students had held for her outside the school, hoping to spread the word. There was a photo of student body president, Joe Martin, who had led them all in prayer for her safe return.

The *Gazette* had published Lucy's junior yearbook photo. It made her look younger than sixteen years—eleven or twelve if someone were to guess. A sullen pout marred features that didn't even pretend to smile. There was also a photo of her mother, Stephanie Valentine, who stood at a bank of microphones, distraught, begging for her daughter to come home. Her eleven-year-old son, Troy, stood at her side looking lost. In the sheer madness of it all, and in her desperation to find her daughter, had Stephanie remembered that she had another child who also needed attention?

According to what she read, Lucy's father lived with his second family in the Chicago area. Both parents had been questioned, as were their neighbors, Lucy's schoolmates, and her "unnamed ex-boyfriend,"—that would be Matt. The implication that the boyfriend was somehow involved in her disappearance was only thinly veiled.

The house where Lucy lived with her mother and brother had been thoroughly searched. "Ransacked by the cops," according to one neighbor who was disgruntled by the media presence in the neighborhood. The search uncovered nothing of any consequence.

Claudia thought of the note Sharon Bernstein had told them about. None of the articles mentioned it. Was it just a rumor? Or had the police withheld that information in the event a suspect in the disappearance was found?

On the first anniversary the *Gazette* ran a short article—a single paragraph with a useless update: Lucy Valentine had disappeared a year ago. There were no new clues to the girl's whereabouts, Edentown Police were stymied. The case was at a standstill.

On the five-year anniversary, and then the ten-year, the *Gazette* published more or less the same article, noting that they had spoken to Lucy's mother again. Each time, Stephanie Valentine promised to keep her daughter's memory alive by hounding the police until they were able to tell her what happened to her.

Years later, when Stephanie died of cancer, friends said it was caused by the loss of her daughter. Her obituary stated that she had gone to her grave refusing to give up her belief that her girl was alive and would someday come home.

Nothing Claudia read was new. Feeling sad and slightly depressed, she printed out the articles and put them in a three-ring binder. She hoped it would not end up being a "murder book" like the police maintained.

There was nothing on her calendar for the week ahead that couldn't be changed if necessary. If Matt was able to reach Troy Valentine, and Troy agreed to a meeting, she would be ready to hit the road.

Chapter ten

Monday, October 9

"I don't want to talk about it," Kelly said the next day when Claudia called and quizzed her about her attitude towards Josh Dickson. "He's dead. Show some respect and leave him in peace."

Putting the phone on speaker, Claudia leaned back in her office chair and sipped coffee from the mug she had brought up from the kitchen. "That doesn't sound like you. Did something happen that I should know about?"

"What the hell, Claudia?" It was not often that Kelly got angry, but she sounded angry now. "I said I don't want to talk about it. Would you drop it?"

"Yes, ma'am. Forget I brought it up."

"What about Matt?"

The unexpected segue made Claudia's head spin. "What about him?"

"Is he fair game?"

"Jeez, Kelly, he's a grown man and I have no interest in what he does romantically. If you want to go there, give it a whirl. But..."

"But what?"

Up until now, she had given Kelly no more than the basics about the documentary—he wanted to reinvestigate the disappearance of Lucy Valentine and had asked for her help in talking to some of the people who had been peripherally involved. Having gotten on the wrong side of her friend already today, Claudia was not eager to do it again. But if she was genuinely interested in seeing Matt socially, Kelly needed to hear the rest of the truth.

"Remember when Lucy disappeared? Someone told the police that Matt had been dating her before she went missing. He asked me whether it might have been you who told them."

"*Me?*" Kelly sounded astonished. "What the hell? Like I'd do that. Jesus, Claudia, what kind of person do you think I am?"

"Don't shoot the messenger. His other choice was Rachel Thomas. Do you think she would have—"

"No! Why the hell would she?"

"I don't know. But speaking of that, why didn't you ever tell me Matt had been dating Lucy?"

"Why would I? You didn't start seeing him until the year after she took off, or whatever happened to her. Besides, what was I supposed to say? He was more into her than she was him, and she broke up with him. Period. End of Story. *Fini.* Nothing to tell."

"Apparently, there *was* something more. Lucy told him she liked somebody else. Did you know that?"

"No, but I wasn't all that close to her, so no harm, no foul."

"Did you ever see her with another guy?"

Kelly fell silent for several seconds, and Claudia could almost feel her digging in her memory for an answer. "I don't think so." She amended it to, "Not that I remember. The truth is, she pulled away from me, too, around that time. Like I said, we weren't that close to begin with. Maybe I did something to piss her off. I never asked. If someone doesn't want me around, screw 'em. I have better things to do."

"Matt is hoping the documentary might bring somebody out of the woodwork who knew something that they might have been afraid to tell back then. Over the years, perspectives change; things look different."

"Looking for Lucy, huh? I hope you two do find some answers. But if there was another boyfriend, she kept it on the downlow. You should ask Rachel, though. She was closer to Lucy than I was. She'd know if there was someone."

"She's on Matt's list to interview. He must have told the cops that Lucy dumped him for someone else. Either they didn't believe him and didn't bother to check, or they couldn't find out who it was."

A beep on her phone indicated that someone else was trying to get through. "Speak of the devil. Matt's calling."

"Tell him I didn't rat him out. In fact, tell him to call me. I have a few choice words—"

"Okay, bye." Claudia tapped the end button and hastily switched over to the new call. "Hey, there. What's up?"

Matt sounded pleased. "I got hold of Troy Valentine. I wouldn't say he's *willing* to talk, but he has agreed to meet with us. Well, me. I didn't tell him anyone else would be coming. Didn't want to dump everything on him and possibly spook him."

"Did you ask about the note Lucy supposedly left?"

"No, I just told him I'm making a documentary about his sister and would like to talk to him about his experiences at that time."

"But you said he's not willing...?"

"It's a time in his life he'd prefer not to relive. Can't say I blame him for that. But I used all my skills of persuasion."

"You can be very persuasive," Claudia said. "You got me to join the project."

"Yes, I did. Can you meet me at his place tomorrow morning at eleven?"

"Absolutely. Text me the address."

The low-slung house nestled in a leafy grove of trees. Its wide deck was the perfect size for outdoor parties, and boasted a long rattan sofa and glass-topped table and chairs shaded by a tall striped umbrella. Directly behind the house was a shrub-covered hillside and Coldwater Canyon. A highly desirable Los Angeles County neighborhood.

Troy Valentine was tall and slim and barefoot, dressed in a black T-shirt and linen drawstring pants. With honey-colored curls to die for and a long jaw peppered with a short beard, he was as fair as his sister had been dark.

"Half-sister," he corrected Matt. "Our shared DNA came through our mother. She married Lucy's father after mine bugged out, never to be heard from again." He made a face. "Then it happened again. Makes you wonder, doesn't it?"

This information was delivered with Matt and Claudia standing on the porch. Troy flicked a curious glance at her. He had cornflower blue eyes and a nice smile. "I don't mean to sound unwelcoming, but wasn't it supposed to be just you, Matt?"

Claudia smiled back. "Shame on you, Matt, that was rude. I hope you don't mind that I tagged along as a second pair of ears." She gave Troy her name, and her hand, which he gave a firm shake.

Matt apologized. "My bad; I totally forgot my manners. Is it okay for Claudia to be here?"

Looking a little put out, but too polite to protest, Troy stepped aside. "Yeah, I guess so. Come on in."

"She knew Lucy."

His eyes widened. "You knew her?"

"Yes, though not well. We had some classes together."

"Well, why didn't you say so?" Troy welcomed them inside with a much warmer bearing. "Careful you don't trip over some over some sneaky toy waiting to get you," their host warned as they followed him in. Seeing their surprise, he grinned. "Don't tell me—I look too cool to be a dad? The boys are in daycare this morning. Trust me, it would have been impossible to have a decent conversation with those two mini-demons running around, demanding attention—and they would. It's their superpower."

"How old are they?" Claudia asked, feeling bad that Lucy had missed out on being an aunt.

"Three-year-old twins. And, naturally, the most adorable children *in* the entire world." He led them into a sparsely furnished spacious living room, continuing over his shoulder, "Dennis, my husband, will text me when he's on the way home with them, so we'd best get this show on the road. Can I get you something to drink? Tea, coffee, soda, something stronger?"

"I'm good, thanks," Claudia said, giving Matt a side-eye when he asked for a beer. Was he a day drinker, or did he think it would make Troy more agreeable when they asked him for his help?

"Hang loose, I'll be right back." Troy headed for the kitchen area though a double-wide doorway. "Grab yourselves a seat."

They were wending their way around toddler-sized plastic airplanes and magnetic tiles in various stages of construction when Troy returned with two bottles of beer. "It's a pogo jumper stick," he said, talking about a toy whose purpose Claudia was unable to figure out.

"Good to know. I would not have guessed that." The short, pole-like device was anchored to a something that looked like her purple yoga block. She took a seat on the lived-in sectional sofa that took up all of one wall. Matt accepted one of the bottles and joined her there.

Pulling up a chair from the dining table across the room, Troy swept a hand at the array on the floor. "We want our kids to have more fun than either Dennis or I had." His lips twisted. "That wouldn't be hard to do."

"You mean because of your sister's disappearance?" Matt said. It was his interview, but Claudia wanted to muzzle him. If Troy was as reluctant to talk as he had indicated, it made sense to move into the reason for their visit by degrees, rather than dropping it on him all at once.

"That," Troy said. "And also, before. But that's not what you've come to hear about."

"You started to tell us about when your father left," Claudia said, hoping to get more background on the Valentine family.

"I was around eight when husband number two found someone younger and more housewifey to suit his taste. They moved to the Midwest to start a new batch of Valentine babies. He'd adopted me when I was too young to be asked. Thus, I am a Valentine, though I'm thinking of switching back to my original name, McFly. Yes, just like in *Back to the Future*."

"I remember hearing that your mom worked a lot," Claudia said.

He made a derisive sound. "A lot? How about *all* the time? Like, nonstop."

"What did she do?"

"Personal assistant to a bigshot Hollywood executive who *demanded* her absolute attention. Even when she was at home and we were doing something, he used to call her like every fifteen minutes. It could be nine at night, and she had to answer. Every single time. The fact that she had kids meant *nada*." Troy huffed a dispirited laugh. "All of her apologies to

Luce and me for putting us off, making us wait for her attention—none of it changed anything. Work had to come first. Every time."

"That must have been hard on you both." Claudia attempted to catch Matt's eye and subtly send him a message to give Troy space to continue.

"My sister and I reacted differently to the benign neglect," Troy said. "She got angry and acted out. I got depressed and ate. I was quite the little porker as a kid."

"How did Lucy act out?"

"Oh, you know, refused to do anything Mom told her to do; backtalk. Wouldn't do her chores. Anything that smelled like rebellion, Lucy was right on it. I can tell you, I tried to stay out of their way when they were on the warpath, which was a shit ton. They were constantly screaming at each other."

"I see what you mean about not having fun," Claudia said. It sounded like her and her mother when she was sixteen.

"I was so damn lonely. But if you think it was bad before Lucy left, it was nothing compared to what came after." Troy's expression darkened. "Once all hell broke loose, it was curtains for poor little me. Well, not in the sense of 'curtains' meaning dead, of course but..." He trailed off.

"Bad, huh?" Matt said.

"Bad?" Troy looked at him as though he had lost his mind. "Are you crazy? It was *hair-raising*. All those cops swarming through the house from top to bottom, ripping it apart—including *my* room—like I was hiding her in there or something. Everyone pushing me out of the way, not explaining what was going on. Basically, they told me to shut up, everything was gonna be peachy." His eyes glistened with a sudden sheen of tears. "It wasn't peachy. It never was again. *Never*. Goddammit, I *hate* digging up all this old crap. I told you I don't want to go back there."

The sorrow on his face made Claudia want to go over and hug him. Or walk away and leave him to his anguish.

"I know it's hard," Matt said sympathetically. "I'm sorry to ask you to do it. And I appreciate that you are doing it even though it's painful. But you want to know what happened to Lucy, don't you?"

Glaring at his tormentor, Troy dashed away the tears with a fierce movement of his hand. "Frankly, I'd be happy if I never heard her name again. There was nothing I could do about it then, and there's nothing I can do now, no matter what happened to her. It's not like we had a sweet, cuddly relationship. But I'm not going to stand in the way of you investigating what happened. I'm doing it for my mother. She never gave up believing Lucy was out there, somewhere, living her life. She had absolute faith that she would come home someday. This is for her sake."

"I read that in her obituary," Claudia said. "That she never stopped believing Lucy would come home. I'm truly sorry for your loss."

"Thanks for the thought," Troy said tartly. "But I lost my mother back in 1998 when Lucy left. I used to think it was my fault—that she was indifferent to me because I wasn't loveable enough. As a grownup I understand that she loved us both in her own way. But after Lucy, she lived in her own world, and there wasn't room in it for me." His sorrow leaked out and surrounded them like a thick fog. "What is it you want to know?"

Matt set his half-empty bottle on the coffee table and took out his phone. He held it up for Troy to see. "Do you mind if I record this?"

"What is it, a podcast?" Troy said, letting them see his misgivings. "Wasn't it supposed to be video?"

"It *is* video. Just like I said on the phone, I'm making a film documentary. Once I've got everything together, I'd like to come back with a camera."

"You mean I have to go through this all over again?"

"I promise to make it as painless as possible."

"Jesus on a skateboard." Troy let out a loud groan and gave in. "Yeah, fine. Whatever."

"Why don't we start with the day Lucy went missing," Matt said. "Tell me everything you can remember."

Claudia sat back and took note of Troy's body language. He must be thirty-seven now, but as he started to reminisce, and his memories returned to his twelfth year, his face seemed to appear younger, more vulnerable. He closed his eyes, and as if he were dreaming, his eyes moved slowly back and forth against the lids. He visibly steeled himself as he began to speak.

"It was a Wednesday. She didn't come home after school, Lucy didn't. Mom was late getting home from work that day. Nothing unusual about that. I remember whining to the babysitter that I was starving. She came flying in around seven or so with a sack of greasy food from McDonald's or some other junk food shithole. No time to fix dinner. I would never feed my kids that way."

Troy opened his eyes, but he didn't look at them. "I was kind of old to have a babysitter, but I guess it made her feel less guilty to know I wasn't home alone the whole time. Sometimes it was just Luce and me, but that day, the sitter was there. Mom got home and stuck a burger and fries in my face and started ranting about how Lucy was supposed to be home by now—kind of ironic, don't you think?"

"Your recall is terrific," Matt said when Troy paused in his narrative.

"Are you kidding me? The most dramatic day of my life? Don't you remember yours?"

"Now that you mention it, I do. It was when the police questioned me about your sister."

Troy frowned at him, clearly confused. "What? Why would they question you?"

"Could we come back to that?" Claudia interjected. "We're here for *your* story, Troy. Matt can tell you his later."

"Claudia's right," Matt said. "Please go on."

It took him a few seconds to get wound up again. "It got later and later, and Luce didn't show up. Mom was getting madder and madder. But when she hadn't got home by my bedtime—I know, you're going to ask me—nine-thirty—she started to get worried and quizzed me about her friends. She had no idea who they were. And what the hell did I know? She had a couple of girlfriends who would come over once in a while—Um, wait a minute, lemme think." He closed his eyes for a few seconds, then nodded when he got it. "Kelly, and—um, I think Rachel. Does that sound right? Good. But I didn't know their last names, and I sure as hell didn't know how to reach them. There was also a guy who showed up a few times, but I don't know his name."

"Just one guy?" Claudia asked. "Do you maybe remember a second guy?"

"Just the one." His answer was unequivocal. "She didn't have that many friends, and definitely no guy friends, other than the one I mentioned."

"Had you seen this guy close to the time she disappeared?" Claudia felt Matt tense beside her as they waited for Troy's answer.

"You ask the hard questions. Lemme think." Again, Troy's eyes closed. "No, he'd only been over to the house a few times. Maybe she started meeting up with him somewhere else. He was out of the picture for a while by the time she left."

Matt let go of a long sigh. "Yeah, that would be me."

Troy gawked at him, openmouthed. "*You?* Wow, I did not recognize you."

"It's been a long time, dude. I wouldn't expect you to."

Light dawned on his face. "Oh, *that's* why the cops talked to you. Man, I did not see that one coming. I need to hear more about this."

"Sure, I'll be glad to talk about it later. But right now—"

"Okay, fine, I get it. Stick to my story. So Luce didn't want her kid brother bothering her when she had friends over—which really didn't happen all that often. But when she had someone over, she would yell at me to stay away from her room, so I never knew *what* was going on in there. Anyway, that's beside the point. *That* night, it was close to ten when Mom finally called the cops. A couple of them came over in a black and white patrol car.

"I was looking at them through my window—those flashing blue lights on the roof; I couldn't stop looking. Scared the bejesus out of me. It made it seem real that we didn't know where my sister was. I mean, Lucy and I didn't much like each other, but she was my big sister."

"How were the police? Did they take it seriously?" Matt asked.

"They kept asking Mom the same question over and over: Had she run away before?"

"And, had she?"

"She'd stay out for a few hours longer than her curfew, but no, she never ran away. About the fifth time they asked her that, Mom got frustrated and started yelling at them—Lucy was a smartass and a rebel, but she wouldn't run away. Where would she go?" Troy took a long swallow of beer and gathered himself. "The cops eventually got hold of those girls—Kelly and Rachel. Maybe through the school the next day. I heard them tell Mom that both girls said they hadn't seen Lucy after she left her PE class."

"I was in that class too," Claudia told him. "I remember Lucy saying that she didn't feel good and wanted to go home. The gym teacher sent her to the nurse to get a pass."

Troy's gaze swung to her. "That's what the teacher said too, but I remember the cops telling mom that she never went to the nurse's office or got a pass. She must have just walked off campus—which sounds like something she'd do. There wasn't school security like there is now. No cops on duty." His eyes bored into Claudia as if he was trying to peer inside her brain and see what she had seen. "You must have been one of the last people to ever see her."

Like that's not creepy.

"Me, and the rest of the PE class," she said, trying not to feel defensive, as if there was an accusation in his statement.

Matt brought them back on track. "She never made it home."

Troy dragged his gaze away from Claudia. "That's actually not true."

"What do you mean?"

"That night, when the cops searched her bedroom, they found a note she'd written to Mom."

Chapter eleven

Claudia's heartbeat sped up. This was what she was here for.

Matt's eyebrow quirked upward, and she could feel his excitement too. "If she left a note before she went to school, she was planning to leave," he said.

A quick headshake from Troy. "No."

"No?"

"It wasn't there that morning. I was in her room after she left for school, and there was no note." His face reddened. "She kept a stash of pot hidden in her dresser. Sometimes, when she wasn't there, I'd sneak some—not enough that she would notice—a pinch at a time, just because I could. I kept it in a baggie, didn't smoke it. I mean, wasn't I the flea's eyebrows because I had it?"

"Typical little brother," Claudia said. "I had one too. Where did they find the note?"

"Right there on her dresser."

Matt's confusion was plain. "If it wasn't there in the morning, and you didn't see her come home, when did she put it there?"

"Here's the thing. Before we lived in that house, the last owners used to rent out the room that was Lucy's. They'd had an outer door installed to give the renter privacy—they could come and go through that door to the backyard without going through the house and leaving through the front door. Sometimes Lucy would sneak out that way at night."

In Claudia's private opinion it was absurd to give a young girl that much freedom. If Lucy had been her daughter, she would have walled up the opening. On the other hand, at Lucy's age, if she'd had a room with a door, she would have used it for nighttime forays too. "Did your mother know she sneaked out?"

Troy shook his head. "Nah. When Mom got home and she'd had a couple glasses of wine to help her unwind, she'd sleep like the dead. She never knew Luce was out cruising God only knows where. My room was next to hers, and sometimes I'd hear her come in after midnight." He shot them a crooked grin. "She never would say where she'd been. The one time I nagged her to tell me, she threatened me on pain of death not to blab she'd been gone." His smile turned sad. "She was totally convincing about the death part. Being her pesky little brother, you can bet I blackmailed her for candy and money, but I never told. Even when the cops were grilling me like *I* might have done something to her."

"So, she could have snuck in at any time that day and left the note," Matt said.

"Yep, and my mother was too upset to notice it until the cops showed it to her."

Claudia leaned forward eagerly. "What did the note say?"

"All I remember is thinking she must have been high when she wrote it."

"What made you think that?"

"All I know is, it didn't make sense. I've forgotten what it actually said."

"What happened to it?" Matt asked.

"The cops took it, until Mom begged for it back. It was the last physical link she had to my sister. They were convinced she'd run off and would come home when she ran out of couches to surf—which is stupid when she didn't have those kinds of friends. Not that we knew of, anyway."

"Any chance you held onto it?" Claudia held her breath.

"I don't know." Troy shrugged listlessly. "Probably."

His answer was underwhelming. "Probably? More yes than no?"

"Mom kept Lucy's room exactly the way it was. Amazing she let the cleaning lady go in there to dust and vacuum. Every birthday and Christmas there would be a new wrapped gift for her for when she 'came home.'" He put the phrase in mocking air quotes. "Talk about living in a creepy fantasy world. It was like being in a goddamned ghoulish museum. A few years in, the bed was covered with stuff that she would have been too old to care about if she had come back."

His lack of enthusiasm was discouraging, but Claudia kept her eyes on him as if she could penetrate his brain with her power of mental suggestion. She *willed* him to come up with something helpful. As though he felt her, he sat up straighter.

"You know, after Mom gave up on buying gifts, she gave them to a charity. But she packed up all of her favorite Lucy things into one big box—her stuffed animals, favorite clothes, her favorite grunge CDs and posters—she was over the top Looney Tunes for Nirvana and Pearl Jam, Alice in Chains. *If* she kept the note, that's where it would be."

Claudia wanted to weep for Stephanie Valentine, and for Troy. She said nothing, just let him keep talking. For all his lack of enthusiasm in the beginning, a fireplug of emotion had opened and sprayed them full force.

"My mother spent a lot of time in Lucy's room. After she got her cancer diagnosis she was in there most of the time. Even slept in her bed." He blew a soft puff of breath through his lips. "I gotta tell you, the biggest irony of all is when our workaholic Mom stopped going to work, stopped answering her boss's calls. She finally quit her job. I have no idea how she paid the bills. All that time, I desperately wanted her to be home with me and help me not to be scared all the time. But then she was home every day, and it was like she didn't even see me."

"How sad," Claudia said. "I'm so very sorry."

"I lived with her until she passed. I went to Cal State Northridge so I could be close while I was going to school. After she was gone, I cleaned everything out and sold the house, which was *not* fun, I can tell you. Everything went to me. With both her and my sister gone, there was nobody else. But her will specified that I could never get rid of that one 'Lucy box.' I had to 'keep it safe for her return.' I'm just lucky she didn't say I had to keep the house as a shrine."

"I guess that means you hung onto the box?" Claudia asked, mentally crossing her fingers that he would answer in the affirmative.

Troy looked at her as if she had grown an extra head. "Do you think I was going to defy my dead mother's wishes?"

"No, of course not."

"And you think Lucy's note is in it?" Matt persisted.

"That's what you want to know, isn't it? If you insist, I'll dig through the treasure trove that is our garage and look for it."

"I would love to have it for the film. It would add dramatic effect to show Lucy's actual handwriting."

Troy rose from his chair, but Claudia's optimistic hope that he was going to the garage to start looking for the box was dashed.

"It's about time for the fam to get home and I need to have their lunch ready." He held out a hand to Matt, who was rising too. "I'll look for the box, maybe later tonight after the boys are asleep. I'll text you the moment I find it."

"Thanks, Troy, I appreciate it."

Claudia stood and took his hand next. She couldn't stop herself from pressing the question. "I hope you find the note."

Troy's eyebrows rose. "What makes it so important to you? The cops didn't think it was significant. I'm telling you, it was gibberish."

"She's a handwriting expert," Matt said not giving her a chance to answer for herself.

"No way." Troy's eyes lit up with interest. "What would you be looking for?"

"It depends. The first thing I'd like to do, if you have some other samples of her handwriting—like homework, or letters to compare—I can verify that she wrote the note."

"Verify? Who else would have written it?"

"We don't know that, do we? If she didn't run away—Well, the first step is to authenticate it. The next thing, which is separate and apart from the authentication piece, is to develop a personality profile from the handwriting."

"That's so dope. Can I show you mine too?"

Claudia smiled at his interest. "Of course. If you like, I'll analyze it as a thank-you for your help on this."

"Omigod, I would totally love that. I guess the kids are too young to analyze?"

"Toddler's scribbles can be analyzed, but it's a specialized area. If I'm going to analyze kids' writing, it needs to be when they've learned to write and are comfortable with it. I have them draw some special pictures to go along with the writing."

Troy walked them to the door. "You just gave me some incentive to get my butt into the garage tonight."

Claudia followed Matt out onto the deck and turned back. "If you need more incentive, I'll do your husband's too. And that's not an offer I make very often."

He stuck out his hand with a grin. "My friend, you've got a deal."

Chapter twelve

They snagged a corner table at a funky local gastropub, and ordered lunch for their post-mortem on the visit with Troy Valentine. Getting the true story from the boy who lived through it had brought it home more vividly than any news article could have.

"I thought that went as well as it could," Claudia said. "Who's next on the list?"

From across the table, Matt contemplated her with amusement. "Are you always like this?"

"Like what?"

"All work, no play?"

"Alas, yes," she said, and proved it. "I hope Troy locates that 'Lucy box.' And, that the note is in it."

"He sure jumped at your offer to analyze his handwriting. Dollars to doughnuts he'll move heaven and Earth to find it."

Claudia groaned. "That's two clichés in one sentence, and you've hit your limit. He seems well-adjusted, but I'm curious to get a look at his handwriting. I want to see the effects of the trauma."

Matt was taken aback. "You can see trauma in handwriting?"

"It might show certain artifacts if the person hasn't been able to deal with it. In Troy's case, it wouldn't be at all surprising if he was holding on to some hidden anger. Or, it could be he's worked it through and let it go. That shows up in handwriting too."

"Seems like a nice guy." Matt said. "But then, people who knew Ted Bundy believed he was a nice guy because he was good-looking."

"Troy is no serial killer—" Claudia stopped herself. "But it does reminds me of Steven Stayner. His brother became a serial killer."

Just then, the waitress arrived with their food. Matt didn't speak until she had set it out on the table, and was walking away. He picked up his fork and attacked the mound of chicken salad on his plate. "Stayner? I don't remember that name."

"Steven, the younger brother, was kidnapped by a pedophile when he was seven. He disappeared like Lucy, without trace. When was fourteen, the pedophile took another little boy. Steven didn't want to see the same thing happen to him. He escaped and rescued the child."

"That's pretty damned heroic. I remember that story now. It had a good ending."

"Only for a while. When he was twenty-four Steven was killed in a hit-and-run motorcycle accident—no helmet."

Matt's forehead furrowed into a batch of wavy lines. "Omigod, Claudia. How could a family live through that?"

"There's more, and it gets even worse. Steven's older brother, Cary, sexually assaulted and murdered several women in Yosemite at a lodge where he worked. Right around the time we graduated."

"A year or so after Lucy disappeared?"

"Yeah, but I'm not making a connection."

"How do you know there's not?"

"That would be a truly horrible stretch." She knew he was not entirely serious. She sat back in her chair and considered him from under half-lowered eyelids. "Tell me the truth, Matt, do you think it's possible that Lucy is alive somewhere?" When he faltered, she had to wonder what he was thinking.

"I'm reserving judgment on that," he said. "We're just starting the investigation. There's no way to know yet where it will take us."

Accepting his answer for now, Claudia changed the subject and told him about Kelly's denial that she had talked to the police about him.

"And you believe her?" He looked doubtful.

"She was adamant about it. But you should ask her yourself. She's the same fun girl she was in high school." Claudia gave him a knowing grin. "Way more fun than me."

It was his turn to look at her sideways. "Oh, I remember Kelly. She had a reputation as a party girl. Sure, if you say so, I'll call her. And Rachel Thomas. She's on my list too."

They agreed to touch base once Matt had arranged a time to meet with Rachel, who had never moved away from Edentown and worked at a funeral home there. That would mean a ninety minute drive south back to Orange County if they were going to interview her in person. And that was if traffic was flowing well.

A forgery case was waiting for her in her mailbox that would require her to testify if it went to trial. Two brothers were fighting over their grandfather's estate. One of them had produced a will that named him sole heir. The other claimed the signature was forged. It didn't take long to conclude that Claudia would have to give her what was bad news for him—the signature was genuine. On the upside, knowing the truth would help his attorney strategize and perhaps get a settlement.

After giving her client her opinion, she stretched out on the sofa in her office and lost herself in a John Sandford novel until Joel got home. He brought dinner in a sack from El Pollo Loco, which made Claudia think of Troy's story about his mother bringing home a bag of food from McDonald's on the night Lucy vanished.

They sat in the kitchen, eating and talking about their respective days. Joel had been stuck at his desk, doing paperwork on the homicide he and his partner had just closed. Claudia told him about the visit to Troy. He was more interested in talking about her videographer former boyfriend.

"I checked out Matt Macedo like you asked me to."

That got her attention. "You didn't find anything, right?"

"As it happens, something did come up."

Claudia's stomach turned over. "Like what?"

Joel took a healthy bite out of a grilled chicken breast and pronounced it mouthwateringly good, then gave her a look that made her nervous. "Are you sure you want to hear what I found?" he asked.

"Why wouldn't I?"

"You aren't going to like it."

She hoped he was joking, but his tone was too serious. "What are you talking about? You're not going to tell me there's a problem, are you?"

"It happened a long time ago—twenty years. The charges got dismissed, so there was no trial, no conviction, just an incident report." He made his face the careful blank he adopted when he didn't want her to see what he was thinking. It felt like he was temporizing and that made her worry more.

"Twenty years ago? He would have been twenty-two, hardly more than a kid. What did he do, Joel? Stop keeping me in suspense."

"It was a domestic battery call. He and his girlfriend were drunk and arguing. A neighbor called 911. Patrol went and checked it out. The report said he had a scratch on his face. He says she hit him and he grabbed her arms to make her stop—that's how the scratch happened." Joel looked at her. "They didn't see any marks on her, and she backed him up, claimed he was telling the truth. She didn't want to press charges, and neither did he. It was written up and filed."

An unreasonable knot of anger had stuck in her throat and was squeezing. She glared at him. "That's it? A misdemeanor twenty years ago? Why would you scare me like that?"

"That's all I *found*. If there was anything while he was a juvenile it would be under seal. And yeah, it's a misdemeanor, but he could have gotten up to a year in jail and a fine. He got lucky."

"It would be lucky if he was guilty," Claudia said, indignant. "But if the D.A. didn't want to file on him, he wasn't guilty. And why would an incident report be on file when it went nowhere?"

"Think of it like this," Joel said in such a reasonable way that it irked her further. "You have a call out where no one wants to press charges, so you get whatever information you can and run it for warrants, etcetera, and you clear the parties—no charges filed. Then, let's say, three weeks later one of the parties involved in the call unexpectedly drops dead, and it's from an undiagnosed injury that she—or he—suffered in the fight three weeks earlier."

Seeing her opening her mouth to respond, he raised his hands in a calming gesture. "Don't get excited, babe, you asked the question and I'm just giving an example. In this scenario, we have a baseline for a homicide investigation. Besides which, with the police report, any surviving family members have documented proof that the incident occurred."

"Fine, I get it. They could pursue a wrongful death lawsuit." Claudia could not sit still. Still huffy and defensive, she slid out of the breakfast nook where they were sitting, snatching the food waste off the table and tossing it in the garbage. "And I'm not a skittish cat; don't be condescending."

"Wouldn't dream of it. I'm just telling you how it *could* go down." He leveled a stern glare at her—the one she most hated. "You might want to remember; I was risking my ass to look at him at *your request* for a background."

"I know," she said, at once chastened, "and I appreciate it. But I don't like where this is going."

"Neither do I. Listen, I know better than to advise you to watch yourself with this guy, but..."

"Right. Got the message, thanks for checking. Seriously, though, Matt would have been in his early twenties, and if you didn't find anything else—"

"How sure are you that he didn't have a hand in that Valentine girl's disappearance?"

No matter how hard she glared at him, his expression remained impassive, which ratcheted up her ire another notch. "You have to be joking. He was sixteen at the time."

"And you don't think sixteen-year-olds do bad things?"

"Matt's not like that. He's not violent."

"Except for the domestic battery call?"

"Detective Jovanic, you are starting to piss me off. Do you *always* have to be a cop?"

He grinned then, with lips still shiny from the chicken he had just eaten. "Do you know how cute you are when your dander is up? It's that red hair."

Her hand went up to push her hair back. "It's not red, it's auburn."

"Come here and kiss me."

"With those greasy chicken lips? I don't think so." She danced away, but slowly, so he knew that she wanted him to follow.

Joel dashed a napkin across his mouth and ran up the stairs after her.

Chapter thirteen

Tuesday, October 10

According to Matt, Rachel Thomas, the mortician, had told him she was swamped. She was preparing the bodies of five victims for burial after a horrific hit and run accident that killed everyone in the vehicle; she would not be available to speak with him for a week or more.

"I've put a note in my calendar to call her when things calm down. Meanwhile, we move on to the next on the list," Matt relayed in a phone call. "I've made an appointment to talk with the detective who originally worked on the case."

"There was only one?"

"Only one who's alive and kicking."

"Does that mean we're going back to Edentown?"

"Nope. He's retired and moved to Hemet."

"Hemet's no closer than Edentown," Claudia pointed out.

Eighty-five miles east of Los Angeles in the Inland Empire, many retirees moved to the growing town, where they found they were able to stretch their dollars further. Former Orange County Detective Louis Radnor was one of them.

"It's not going to be an issue. The only way he agreed to meet with me is if we do it on Zoom."

"It's too easy for people to hide their body language behind the screen. And detectives aren't best known for telegraphing what they're thinking."

"Believe me, I tried to talk him into seeing me in person, but he flat out refused," Matt said. "Hey, with gas at more than five bucks a gallon, maybe it's not so bad."

"That's looking on the bright side. Am I invited to sit in?"

"If you're free tomorrow at the crack of dawn. He wants to meet at seven-fifteen, before he heads to the golf course."

Inwardly, Claudia groaned at the early hour. But this was one interview she did not intend to miss. "Send me the link, I'll be there."

Louis Radnor was already on the screen with Matt when Claudia joined the call on the dot of seven-fifteen. He looked to be in his mid-seventies with thinning flyaway white hair and a grizzled beard and moustache. More than ten years into retirement, his mien held not a speck of softness. In the unsympathetic scowl, she fancied she could see the accumulated atrocities he had dealt with; the inhumanity and downright evil he had chased in his thirty-five years on the force. She saw the beginnings of that look on Joel's face too. It made her want to beg him to find a different career.

Tough, cynical, sharp, insightful. Those were the words that came to Claudia's mind as they introduced themselves. Impatient, too. Giving Matt no chance to say anything, Radnor started on the offensive.

"You got some steel balls, Macedo, trying to make it look like we didn't do our job on this case."

Oh, right. This is the guy who tried to implicate Matt in Lucy's disappearance twenty-six years ago.

In his Zoom square, Matt's own hostility burned bright as fire. It must have taken a supreme effort to keep his tone mild. "That's not why I'm doing this, Detective, though you guys screwed with *my* head, big time." A pointy sliver of hostility snapped off and shot across the ether like an arrow. "I was *sixteen*, man. You had to know I had nothing to do with whatever happened to Lucy."

It isn't easy to skewer someone through a computer screen, but the detective's hard eyes made Claudia shiver. Radnor's lip curled into a sneer. "Or, we just couldn't make anything stick."

It had been a long time since Matt had found himself under that scrutiny.

What if the detective was right?

Despite what Joel had told her about Matt's early arrest, it didn't fit with the guy she had dated in high school. Nor what she had seen of the man she knew now. Surely, for someone to have made Lucy disappear, and to cover it up so thoroughly that no one ever located her, it would have taken some skill. And if Matt had any involvement in Lucy's disappearance, why make a film about it now? She was left feeling bothered, and she couldn't put her finger on the source.

Matt got hold of himself. "Thanks for talking to us, detective. I'd rather not use the short time you have available to rehash nonexistent evidence."

"I shouldn't even be talking to a suspect in an open case," Radnor said. "I've got an eight-fifteen tee time and a twenty-minute drive to the links. What is it you want to know?" He used the same words Troy Valentine had, but without the younger man's more cooperative spirit.

"You already know my interest in the Lucy Valentine case," Matt said crisply. "What can you tell me that I won't read in the file?"

The detective was the picture of indifference. "Nothing else to tell. All our leads came up empty. We got *bupkis*. We talked to the dad in Chicago in case he was harboring her. He barely remembered her name. No love lost there."

"You were convinced that he wasn't faking it to cover up?"

"That's right. You learn to hear what's true or not. It's in the voice."

"My husband says the same thing," Claudia said. "He's a homicide detective."

Radnor's head swiveled in her direction. "Yeah? And what's your role in this?"

"Claudia's a handwriting expert," Matt said, speaking for her the way he had at Troy's.

"I'm hoping to examine the note you found in Lucy's room," she said, taking back her presence. "Do you happen to remember whether it was authenticated by your in-house document examiner?"

"There didn't seem to be any question that she wrote it," Radnor said gruffly. "The girl's mother didn't dispute it."

Maybe because she was so terrified about her daughter, she didn't pay attention, Claudia thought but didn't say. He already believed they were attacking his investigation. She had no desire to antagonize him any further.

"I'm hoping to see the note," she said, keeping Troy Valentine's involvement out of the conversation.

"It ought to be in the file."

"It's not in the file I was sent," Matt said.

"In the original file. If you didn't get it, they're holding it back in case there's ever an arrest made." There was that significant look again, as if he was waiting for Matt to break down and confess.

"We heard there was something 'strange' or 'odd' about the note," Claudia said. "Can you talk about that?"

The scowl was back. "Where'd you hear that? In fact, how did you even know there was a note?"

"Nothing nefarious, Detective. I was in Lucy's class too. When she disappeared, her brother's babysitter told people about it. I expect she heard about it from Mrs. Valentine, or Lucy's little brother."

Radnor's lips tightened in disapproval. "Did you ever hear the saying, 'loose lips sink ships?' Talking about the contents of the note could compromise a case if it went to court."

"Is it realistic to think there might be an arrest after so many years?" Matt asked.

"You never know, Macedo. Cold cases get solved all the time. Say a victim is found and has the perpetrator's DNA on them. With current methods they can identify it down to the billions. A buddy of mine caught a killer like that. The DNA was a ninety-nine percent match. Bitch is in prison for life." For the first time, Radnor smiled, but it was not a pleasant smile. More like a lion licking its chops after eating a zebra.

"I guess you never found out who else Lucy was dating," Matt said.

"You mean the phantom 'new boyfriend'?" Radnor drew sarcastic air quotes around the words. "That was a figment of your imagination, Macedo. I remember the interview with her gal pals like yesterday. There were two of them, and they both insisted they never heard her talk about anybody but you. In fact, they didn't mind saying that she didn't think *you* were 'all that.' There *was* no new boyfriend. Here's a thought—if she did tell you there was someone else, maybe it was just her way of letting you down easy? That's it, kids. That's all I got for you."

Radnor reached out a finger to click on the Leave Meeting button. His screen disappeared as completely as Lucy Valentine, leaving Matt and Claudia looking at each other in dismay.

"Sonofabitch." Matt was breathing as heavily as if he'd run a mile. His jaw worked furiously. "He's the same jerk he was in 1998."

"He still suspects you," Claudia said, perplexed by the detective's attitude. Again, she had the feeling that something wasn't adding up.

"Ya think?" He shook his head, like a dog shaking off water. "That was a total waste of our time. You can cross him off the list. I'm gonna call—"

Claudia cut into his eagerness to go on to the next thing. Something had been troubling her ever since he had told her about being a person of interest in the case. "It's not reasonable for them to pursue you just because she broke up with you months earlier." Gazing at him through the lens of the web cam, it was impossible to know whether he was looking directly back at her. "There's something more that you're not telling me, isn't there?"

Emotion flickered across his face and disappeared; pain, perhaps. Distress, certainly. "Matt?" Her intuition was knocking hard.

He lowered his gaze and she could no longer see his expression. Then he exhaled, a long breath of capitulation. "I don't want you to think badly of me—"

"What is it, Matt?" What she had learned from Joel about the twenty-year-old domestic incident report beat at her like a drum. She thought of the hours she and her friends had spent searching for Lucy. She thought of Lucy giving Matt her virginity. And a few months later, Claudia had done the same. Her voice hardened. "If you don't tell me the whole truth right now, you can count me out. I'm off the project."

His head jerked up. "All right, all right, I'll tell you, but..." His wild-eyed dread was a warning. "It's just that it's not what it's gonna sound like."

"You've got three seconds to spit it out. Three. Two—"

"Okay, wait—Lucy was pregnant."

Chapter fourteen

Claudia frowned. His announcement, which was not at all what she had expected to hear, had left her feeling off-kilter. "How is that 'not what it sounds like?'" she demanded.

Matt tugged on his beard, scratched his head. Stalling.

Coming up with a good story?

"Because if it was true, it couldn't have been mine. Even at that age I wasn't totally stupid. I used protection."

"Oh, a condom has never broken before?"

"Hey, I didn't know anything about it until Radnor used it to try and pin Lucy's disappearance on me. I don't trust him as far as I can spit. He claimed that one of those girls—her friends—told him that Lucy had just done a home pregnancy test and it was positive. That was three months after we'd last been together. And she *did* tell me she had another boyfriend. I didn't make that up."

"Just because she waited three months to do a test doesn't mean it wasn't yours, Matt. Maybe it just means she waited."

He looked so miserable that Claudia might have felt sorry for him. But he had withheld this devastating information from her, and Lucy had gone missing right after telling one of her closest friends. No wonder the cops had been on him on him like a tick on a dog.

Would Lucy have been so scared of her mother's reaction that she had run away, rather than confess that she was pregnant? Or had something far worse happened to her?

"You're not positive the baby wasn't yours, are you?"

"The condom didn't break, Claudia. I can't be more positive." He squared his shoulders and pulled himself together. "I've got to find out what happened to her. Please don't pull out on me now."

"Too bad *you* didn't pull out when you had the chance."

"That's not funny." He looked at her with dawning comprehension. "Wait, are you mad because I had sex with her before you and I—"

"Don't be ridiculous," Claudia retorted. But if she told the truth, it did sting. Thinking back on it now, she didn't remember him coming out and saying it was his first time; it was just implied. It was ridiculous to be humiliated about it so many years later, wondering whether Matt had viewed her any differently because he was her first real lover. Or because she had given in to his coaxing.

She was not going to share with him what had happened to her when she was much younger—abused by a neighbor—another reason moving to Edentown had been a dream come true for her. She had finally escaped the pedophile next door.

It had taken some persuasion to get her into the backseat of Matt's '95 red Ford Taurus. He'd danced around it for a couple of weeks until one night when they got into the 'heavy necking and petting' her mother had warned her against. Claudia tried to ignore his hints that it was time for the next step. The move from first base to a home run had been so fast, she'd hardly had time to catch her breath.

She blushed even now, remembering the awkward fumble: getting out of her Levi's in the cramped space, and rushing back into them when the floodlights of a police car lit up the Taurus. She was supposed to be staying over at Kelly's house, not having sex in the parking area in the woods behind the high school—the same woods where she and her friends had unsuccessfully searched for Lucy the previous year.

The two teens had hurried to straighten their clothes before the patrol cop got out of his car. Lucky for them, the cop took his time sauntering over. She had never forgotten the name on his badge—Officer George Agnew. He had looked old to her, but was younger than her parents. And after a stern talking to and a warning, he left them with a broad wink to let them know he remembered what it was like to be a sexually charged seventeen-year-old.

Afterwards, she had been mortified and angry—angry at Matt for talking her into it when she didn't feel ready—and herself for letting him. It made her wonder whether it had been the same way with Lucy, who had been a year younger when they dated.

"I have to go," she said. "I'll talk to you later."

"Wait, Claudia" Matt pleaded. "You do believe me, don't you?"

"I don't know what to believe. I'm feeling confused right now, and to tell the truth, I feel betrayed. Not because you had sex with Lucy and she ended up pregnant—whether it was your baby or not. You didn't tell me the truth. I can't work on a project where I don't know if I'm getting the whole story. I can't trust you."

"You *can* trust me. I promise, there's nothing else to tell. The reason I didn't tell you about her being pregnant was because I was afraid it would muddy things. It didn't change the truth. Don't listen to Radnor. I swear to you, I had nothing to do with her disappearance."

"I'll have to think about it," Claudia said, and shut down her Zoom window before Matt could get any further into her head.

"You aren't telling me you believe this guy, are you?" Joel's skepticism radiated off him like an untreated sunburn. They had finished cleaning up after dinner and were on their way upstairs to Claudia's home office to relax.

"His credibility is shot with me right now, but I'm trying to be objective and look at it from all angles." Claudia dropped onto the comfy old sofa and took the bottle of Stella Artois that he handed her. She tossed back a long swallow of beer, thinking over her conversation with Matt.

"On one hand, I can understand that he would want to avoid implicating himself with what looks like incriminating information and may not be. On the other hand, *if* he's guilty—of something—we don't know what, but it would have to be bad—I want nothing to do with him. I keep coming back to the big question: if he did something to Lucy, why in the world would he start a project that could lead the cops back to him?"

Joel set his bottle on the floor and stretched his length out on the sofa, laying his head in her lap. "Criminals do stupid things for all kinds of reasons, babe, you ought to know that by now."

"And if you're a hammer, everything you see is a nail. Not everyone who acts sketchy once in a while is a criminal, Detective." She combed her fingers through his hair, massaging his head with gentle pressure until he moaned with quiet pleasure.

"If you keep doing that, I won't be responsible for my actions," he promised.

"That's what I'm aiming for."

"It might take a little while to recharge my batteries. Meanwhile, what are you going to do about Macedo?"

"I'll rag on Kelly and make her tell me if she knew anything about it. Too bad Rachel is unavailable—I think she was the one closest to Lucy. Maybe I'll talk to some of the *Echo* staff 'kids' who knew Matt back then too; they might have something to say."

"The *Echo* was the school newspaper?" Joel asked.

Claudia nodded. "I won't tell them anything I know about him. I'll just probe around and see what shakes loose."

His grin had a touch of the devil in it. "They don't stand a chance with my devious wife on the job."

Claudia gave his hair a tug, just hard enough for him to feel it. "Tools, Columbo. Use what you've got. Isn't that what you always tell me?"

"Doesn't sound to me like you're planning on backing out."

She deflected the question behind the comment. "I should ask Matt for his handwriting. I'll have a better idea then what he's all about."

"You mean you didn't get it when you were dating him?"

"Don't be silly, of course I did. But if he hasn't changed any since he went off college, that's a problem in itself." She looked down at him. Her husband the detective; her lover, her friend. He didn't always agree with what she chose to do, but he was always on her side. "We don't have much to go on," she said.

Joel stretched his chin to look up at her. "Want me to see if I can get anywhere with the original case file?"

"You'd do that?"

"I might." He reached up and undid the top button on her shirt, and then the next. "Mind you, there will be a price, and it won't be cheap."

She gave him a slow smile. "Can I afford it?"

"Maybe not." He unbuttoned the next two, and let his fingertips drift down her skin, tracing the lacy cup of her bra, slipping inside it. "But I'm happy to work out an installment plan."

Chapter fifteen

Wednesday, October 11

The next morning, Kelly was in court. Claudia left her a voicemail to call when she was out of session. Her perky ringtone played during the judge's mid-morning break.

"I have a custody hearing to schedule with Judge Herring," Kelly said. "Then I'll be out of here. Meet for lunch?"

"Sure. Where? It's on me."

"Ah, you want something from me."

"Now that you mention it, I do."

"Well, since you're feeling generous, *Kemosabe*, I'll come to you. Cowboys at one?"

"You do know that word is Apache for 'idiot,' right?"

Kelly snickered. "One o'clock it is. See you there."

That left most of the morning for Claudia to ignore Matt's several voicemails and texts, which consisted mainly of apologies, and pleas for her not to give up on the film project. She knew deep in her gut that she was not going to give it up. Lucy's story had hooked her ages ago. Now that she had an opportunity to work on the case, she was in it for the long haul. Even if she had to go rogue and conduct her own investigation.

Leaving Matt uncertain about what she was going to do was a minor act of revenge for his perfidy—not a word she would normally use but fit in these circumstances—whether it was intentional or otherwise.

Cowboys was their go-to place in Playa de la Reina. The low-key restaurant and bar was a mile from where Claudia lived. She climbed into Levi's and a clean shirt, laced up her sneakers, and walked down the steep hill.

Long ago, before the present owners had knocked down walls to make two dining rooms, it had been a California Craftsman house with peaked roof, wood siding, and porch. The furnishings were plain wrap and basic—square laminated cafeteria tables and chairs. The aromas that came from an old barbecue smoker on the deck could not have been more tantalizing.

They bypassed the bar and went straight to the back room, where bookshelves lined the walls and a sign informed customers that they were welcome to take a book and return it or donate another. The room's sole occupant was a senior citizen in a blue Pendleton shirt, engrossed in an old Ludlum spy novel while he waited for his lunch order.

Claudia and Kelly took a table in the corner. Having eaten there countless times, they knew the menu by heart. Kelly ordered a Calamity Jane—grilled chicken breast with Swiss on a bun. Claudia's order was her usual—Cowboys burger with cheddar, hold the onions. A mountain of steak fries in a plastic basket was more than enough to share.

Kelly wanted to talk about last weekend's reunion. Her eyes lit up with the memories. "It was so much more fun not having to suffer the high school angst."

"Except for the part where I found Mr. Dickson dead," Claudia came back. "That was not much fun for me."

"Well, yeah, except for that," Kelly said. "I saw you sitting with the *Echo* kids at the banquet. *That* was fun, wasn't it, being with your old compadres?"

Claudia shook her head. "Not so much. They just wanted to talk about Dickson."

"That's too awful to think about. So, let's not. Were you surprised the cheerleaders were as clique-y as ever? *Not.* I can't believe I used to care whether or not they accepted me."

"You were ninety-five times better than they were."

"Only ninety-five?"

Claudia grinned. "I had to leave a little room for error."

"I guess that's reasonable. Except I'm a hundred times better than Natalie Parker."

"A hundred and ten. At least. I apologize."

"Thank you. She did her best to totally dominate the table. She always had to be in the spotlight. Can you see her as mayor?"

"Oh, yes, I can. She's been a political animal forever, and she sure married the right guy for it. Tom is a good ole boy who knows all the right asses to kiss."

"Plus, she's still got Andie to pick up the slack."

"Wanna know what I think? Andie is the real brains behind that outfit. She's not as soft as she was in high school." Claudia took a deep breath and exhaled gustily. Kelly was not going to like the reason she had called this meeting. "In case you're wondering why I bribed you with lunch—I mean, what I wanted to talk to you about—has to do with Matt, and Lucy Valentine."

"Lucy again?" Kelly eyes narrowed with suspicion. " I don't have anything else to say about—"

"I suppose you knew she was pregnant when she went missing?"

Kelly's head jerked as if she had been hit with a stun gun. "What the holy hell—"

"Should I take that as a 'no'?" Claudia said dryly.

"A *big* no. So, *Matt*—"

"Says it couldn't have been his, but, the lead detective on the case doesn't believe him—we talked to him this morning."

"Wait. The cops knew about it, and they didn't arrest him?"

"If they'd had any solid evidence, they would have. He was their sole suspect. The way they operate, I doubt they looked any further once they set their sights on him."

"How the hell did they know she was pregnant?"

"It seems that Rachel told them."

"That bigmouth bitch; she never told *me*. Do you think it's really true?" Kelly was more indignant at being left out of the loop than the fact of the declaration.

"Matt swears up and down that he's innocent of anything to do with Lucy's disappearance, and he says it couldn't be his baby because they'd stopped seeing each other two or three months before she disappeared. But why couldn't it be? He admits they were having sex—which I could have happily gone without hearing."

Kelly turned her eyes heavenward. "Get over it. Boys at that age are oversexed and permanently horny."

"Yeah, thanks, like I never knew that—" Taking a moment's pause, Claudia tried out various scenarios in her head. "She wouldn't have known for sure until she took the pregnancy test, and that could have been long after conception." She looked around for the waitress. Having not eaten since dinner with Joel last night, and after getting up early for the meeting with detective Radnor, she was starving. "What are the chances

Rachel would make up something like that? What would she have to gain?"

"To hurt Matt would be my guess. Rachel was jealous when he and Lucy started hanging out."

"Wait, what? Rachel liked Matt, too?"

"No, not that. When Lucy and Matt got together, it meant she had less time for Rachel. You know she's gay, right?"

"I didn't know for sure. Are you saying Rachel was jealous as a friend, or was it more personal than that? Did she have a crush on Lucy?"

"I don't know. I'm just saying, maybe that's what happened."

"But would she kick him to the curb like that?"

"She might. She and Lucy used to be tight before Matt. They were friends again later, but it was never the same."

Things were starting to add up. "She's the one who told them about Matt to begin with," Claudia said.

"Damn, that's harsh."

"Let's assume Lucy *was* pregnant and it wasn't just a story Rachel told the cops. Matt claims he couldn't be the father because he used protection. Then, if both things are true, whose little baby seed was it? According to Matt, she broke up with him because she liked somebody else. She could have already had sex with the new guy. In which case it could have been his."

The food arrived. Kelly dragged a French fry through the ketchup and maneuvered it into her mouth, thinking out loud. "Assuming there *was* a new guy, who could it have been?"

"And why did she feel like she had to keep the boyfriend secret?" Claudia had not known Lucy well enough to be certain of anything, but there were not many alternatives to pick from. She attacked her burger, pondering the question some more before taking a stab at it. "Maybe because it was a guy her friends—you and Rachel—wouldn't approve of for some reason."

Kelly's sandwich stopped halfway to her mouth. "You mean like somebody married? She was fifteen—that would be illegal."

"I wasn't thinking a married guy—that would be sick. More like, I don't know, an outlaw type. Remember that guy, Gerry Polson, who got expelled for doing heroin? I could see her going for him, couldn't you?"

"I don't know, he was one scary dude. I think he ended up in a motorcycle gang."

"Okay, so not him. Who would she be worried about?"

Kelly thought about it for a while. "Lucy was supersensitive. She acted like she didn't care what anyone thought of her, but it wasn't true. People's opinions affected her. A lot." She squeezed her eyes shut, going back through time. "Remember how she dressed goth—everything black—fingernails, and she dyed her hair, too? I did, too, but I didn't give a rat's ass what anyone said about me. Some of the girls on the cheer squad started dissing us, Nasty Natalie included. They were talking smack about Lucy's outfit—giggling, calling us Goth Girls. Basically being hateful little she-devils. They slunk away when I yelled at them, but Lucy was on the verge of tears. Afterwards, she refused to talk about it."

Claudia felt a new rush of sympathy for the missing girl. "That old 'sticks and stones' adage is crap. When you're sixteen, words *can* hurt you. They can be devastating."

"The point being, her sensitivity about what people thought of her. Who was a guy that other people at school would make fun of?" Kelly's eyes narrowed, then widened. "Omigod, Claudia. What if it was Vince Ramsey—oops, I mean *Vincent?* Everyone would have laughed at her for sure if she was with him."

"Because in their opinion, he was 'weird,' and they went after him for his red hair? He wasn't weird, he was brilliant. They envied his straight A's." Claudia mused on the possibility for a few moments. "The bullies would have loved it. But what would have attracted her to someone like him? They were opposites in looks—her so tiny, and him so tall. And opposites in personality."

"Opposites attract? They were both loners."

They stared at each other. "This is crazy. Did you ever see any evidence of him and Lucy being even the slightest bit friendly?"

"No, but isn't *that* the point? She kept the new boyfriend secret." Kelly arched one eyebrow. "Can you imagine, Vincent Ramsey, a baby daddy? The mind reels. Though look at that hot chick he brought to the reunion. I never would have expected—"

"I wonder if he would talk to me," Claudia said. "I was nice to him at school. He never acted like he noticed, but maybe it sunk in."

"He was reasonably polite to us at the reunion," Kelly agreed. "Polite for Vince, that is."

"But something this personal—what can I say to him? Did you impregnate the girl who disappeared in our junior year? Did you make her disappear?"

"If it *was* Vince, maybe she told him about the pregnancy and he freaked."

"And did what? Killed her? That's what the cops think happened with Matt. Can you see either one of them as a stone-cold killer?"

"I'm an attorney, remember. I've seen it all."

"You're a *family* attorney."

"Well, you know what families can be like. Anyone can be a killer under the right circumstances."

"So we've made the leap to assuming Lucy is dead?"

"We're just kicking around possibilities."

"You know what I hope? That she ran away and is living her best life."

"Of course we want that for her." Kelly set half of her sandwich in its plastic basket and wrapped it in paper. "Go for it, Claud. Call him. If you can get past his gatekeepers. For sure, he'll have a bunch, seeing that he's a bigshot business mogul—which I am having trouble comprehending."

"I can do better than that." Claudia got out her phone and tapped through screens. "Cathi Soden had everyone's info for the reunion. Vincent's cell phone has to be on the list."

Kelly nodded approval. "I like the way your mind works, grasshopper."

"Oh yeah? Last night, Joel called me devious."

"And he was so right." She finished off her beer and reached for a cold French fry. "Be sure to keep me posted."

"Hang on, I'm texting Cathi right now."

Cathi Soden's return text popped up four minutes later with Vincent Ramsey's private cell phone number.

"Got it. Cross your fingers and toes that I can set up a meeting with him. It's better to talk in person, rather than on the phone." She heard herself repeating the comment she had made to Matt about Louis Radnor. It occurred to her then that Matt's texts had started coming further apart. He must have gotten the message that she would not talk to him until she was ready.

Until he has been punished enough? A snarky voice said in her head.

She dialed the number Cathi had sent her. Vincent Ramsey's voicemail came on, and she kicked herself that she had not planned ahead and come up with the message she would leave him.

"Um, er, hi Vincent," she stammered. "This is Claudia Rose. I mean, um, Claudia Bennett—from high school? If you remember, we spoke at the reunion registration table last Friday? Would you please give me a call back. There's er, something I'd like to talk to you about. It's, er, urgent."

Kelly was giggling as she ended the call. "Er, um, uh, er. You sounded like a nervous teenager calling him for a date."

"That's about how it felt."

"Let me know the minute you hear back from him. The suspense will be killing me."

"I'll be glad to put you out of your misery. Wish me luck."

"Knock him dead, grasshopper."

That afternoon, Claudia was in her office when a text came from Matt.

> Troy found the Lucy box.

Chapter sixteen

He answered her callback without preamble. "Are you in?"

"Did he find the note?" Claudia asked, not giving him a straight answer.

"He didn't say. He just mentioned the box."

"When are you going? I can meet you there."

"I'm on my way right now. Do you want to get together ahead of time and talk about it?"

"No, I think we're good."

He must have picked something up in the way she said it. "Are you still pissed at me?"

"I don't know, Matt," Claudia answered coolly. "Are there going to be any more disastrous surprises?"

"Not from me, I promise." His sigh gusted across the miles, a hurricane of regret. "You know everything I do about this case."

"Then I have a question for you." She weighed her words with care. "Is Vincent Ramsey on your list of people to interview?"

"Vincent Ramsey?" Matt said. "Hadn't occurred to me. Why would it?"

"Kelly and I were talking, and his name came up. I just wondered whether he might know anything about the case."

"You think he had something to do with Lucy? Doesn't seem her type." He paused. "Hey wait, you don't think he could be the guy—"

She heard incredulity in his voice, mixed with hope. "I have no idea. We were trying to figure out who she dumped you for."

"Ouch, Claudia. It's not bad enough that she dumped me, but for *Vince Ramsey?* Is that what you're saying?"

"May be worth checking out. I've already left a message for him to call me."

There was a pause, then he said, "Yeah, he might talk to you. He did have a soft spot for you."

"What are you talking about? He totally ignored me, even when I spoke to him."

Matt huffed a chuckle. "That's the thing with Ramsey. He never said anything, but I used to see him looking at you when you weren't paying attention. More than once."

"*Looking* at me? What's that supposed to mean?"

"What do you think it means? *Looking* at you. Like he had a crush on you. I bet if you and I hadn't been dating—"

"I think you're imagining things," Claudia said. "But *if* it's true, that would shoot our theory to hell."

"Not necessarily. I'm talking about senior year. Lucy was junior year. She was already out of the picture by then."

"Guess I'll find out if he calls me back."

"That sounds like an awkward conversation—one that can happen outside of my presence."

"Who said you were invited?" Claudia said tartly. "See you at Troy's."

It was the middle of the afternoon when Claudia entered the 405 North to Studio City. For once, traffic on the normally congested freeway did not live up to its "Carmageddon" reputation. Things slowed near the Getty Museum and picked up again when she merged onto the 101 East. Exiting at Laurel Canyon, she made her way through winding roads to Troy Valentine's home.

Matt had arrived first. He was in his car, working his phone as she drew to the curb. Claudia greeted him with enough of a smile that he knew she had decided to let him off the hook—as long as he didn't give her any further cause to distrust him. It wouldn't do the film project any good to be unfriendly with the producer.

"What a gentleman," she said half-mocking when he opened the door for her.

He smiled back. "Boy Scout, remember?" He held up his hand in the Scout sign. "Ready to go in?"

"Let's go."

Troy must have been keeping an eye out for them. They crossed the street to find him waiting at the front door to welcome them inside.

"I can't tell you how excited I am." He ushered them into the living room and thrust a sheet of paper at Claudia. "Here's my handwriting. Tell me the truth. I don't care how bad it is, I want to know *everything.*"

He isn't wasting any time.

She took the handwriting sample and began to look it over. "I'd like to spend some time looking it over in my office." Seeing Troy's crestfallen face, she amended that to, "Here's what I'll do. I'll tell you a few things now, and I'll write up some notes and email them to you. Is that okay?"

He shrugged. "Sure, if that's the way you do it." Then, eagerly, "What can you tell me?"

His handwriting was large and sprawly, taking up most of the space on the page. Yet, it was well organized with a left margin that was larger than the right one. The spacing between the words and lines was clear.

There were extra loops and flourishes, tasteful, not overdone. Claudia took several seconds to gather her thoughts. It was harder to verbalize on the spot than take the time to think about it and write down her thoughts before sharing them with the person whose writing she was analyzing.

She took a breath and said, "Considering what you've gone through, it's quite remarkable. You are a deeply emotional person, but you have learned to keep your emotions under control—for the most part. There are times when you're under pressure and they flare up unexpectedly. Scares the hell out of people around you. You get restless and bored quickly if there's not enough going on to keep your interest. What's most important to you is that life have plenty of excitement."

"Oh. My. God," Troy declared when she had finished. "This is *amazing*. Go on. Tell me some more."

"You're multi-talented and highly creative. When it comes to pleasure, if there's something you want, you aren't the type to deny yourself. You do what feels good." Claudia glanced at Matt, who was looking at her with admiration, then back at Troy. "You said tell you 'everything.' Do you mind if I get personal?"

"Not at all. Say whatever you wish. I'm an open book."

"If you say so. This part is not surprising. You do your best to avoid feeling any negativity or pain. You want to stay optimistic whenever you can, and you'll do just about anything to distract yourself when difficult feelings or situations come up."

"Distract myself, how?"

"Your handwriting can't tell me specifically how. It could be anything, from throwing yourself into work, or shopping, or an addiction, or..."

"I don't do drugs," Troy broke in. "And I hardly drink anymore. Not with the kids. Well, except for when they're not home. I confess—don't tell anyone—we indulge in a little ganja once in a while." He mimed smoking a joint. "I mean, it's legal, right? But we don't want the boys to be exposed until they're old enough to know what it's all about. What else do you see?"

"Mmm, I'd say you have what I call 'star quality.' To me, that means you have a high opinion of yourself and your abilities—well deserved. But it's hard for you to see your flaws. You're not exactly given to introspection."

"Oh, my. I'd need to think about that for a bit." He laughed at his own joke. "Not that I disagree, but as you said, I don't like to admit it." He handed her a second page. "This is Dennis' handwriting."

"How about I look at this one later?" Claudia said, hiding her dismay. It would be too easy to get far into the weeds and never get to the real purpose of their visit. Like paying a deposit, she had given Troy something to chew on. The balance—her analysis of Dennis—would come later.

He made a face, giving in. "Okay, I get it. You can't wait to see Lucy's note."

"That *is* why we came to see you," Matt said. "But I'm glad you got to experience Claudia's skills, so when she examines the note, you'll know that she's the real deal."

"Oh, I already knew that." Troy threw Claudia a wide grin. "I googled you, Ms court-qualified 'well-respected around the world' handwriting expert. Yes, I read all about you, and I have every faith you'll do right by my sister." He gave Matt a sidelong glance. "I googled you, too, Mister, and I know you're no slouch, either. But *she's* the reason I decided to work with you on this."

Matt looked surprised, but not displeased. "I promise you, Troy, you're making the right choice. If there's any way to find out what happened to Lucy, we'll find it. I appreciate your help."

Troy snorted. "Yada yada; enough ego stroking. Now, *suivez-moi.*" He started to walk into the kitchen with a glance back over his shoulder. "That's French for 'follow me. On TV, the detectives liked to see evidence *in situ.* Stand by, kids, we're going to the garage."

He led them through the kitchen and out the back door, past a late model Camry to a detached two-car garage, which he opened with a remote. The door rose almost silently on well-oiled hinges, revealing the tidiest garage Claudia had ever seen. She was positive that no car ever parked in this space.

The floor was shiny clean black and white tile, the side walls lined with shelves of neatly labeled bankers boxes and plastic boxes and moving boxes. On the topmost shelf, a large gap between two boxes looked like a missing tooth in a smile. In the middle of the floor was a large box. A sheet of newspaper had been laid out next to it.

Troy crouched over the box, looking up at them. For the first time since their arrival, he became deadly serious. "Today is the first time the contents of this box will have been seen in—God, I don't know how many years." He tore away the packing tape and pushed back the flaps so Claudia and Matt could see inside.

Holding her breath, Claudia looked at the visible top layer: a teddy bear, what looked like folded up flannel pajamas with tiny red hearts on them; a pair of Winnie the Pooh socks, and books—*Goosebumps, Harry Potter.* She swiped at tears that swelled in her eyes and threatened her mascara.

"These are the things Mom most wanted to save—things she felt were most connected to my sister—the things she couldn't bring herself to let go of."

Troy knelt on the garage floor and started removing the keepsakes. Despite his earlier assertions that he and Lucy were not close, there was something reverent in the way he placed them on the newspaper.

Claudia noticed a folded sheet of paper stuck flat against the inside of the box. She leaned in to look closer. It looked like notebook paper. "What's that?"

Troy removed and unfolded with a strange expression on his face. He looked at her. "This is it! Like I told you, it's weird. You're the expert. I hope you know what it means." He handed over the note.

Reminding herself that twenty-six years ago a desperate girl had written the words she was about to read, Claudia took the paper from him with the same reverence. She looked at the short note with a jolt. She had not taken Troy literally when he said it was "weird looking," but she had to agree.

The body of the note was comprised of three short lines, handprinted in pencil in a moderately large and shaky hand. The letters were malformed in such a way that she could not believe they had been written with a normal writing hand.

Why?

"Was your sister right- or left-handed?" Claudia asked Troy.

He rubbed his chin, frowned, and said, "God, I don't know; is it important?"

"It could be."

He squinted his eyes and frowned, thinking about it. "I think she was right-handed. I can picture her eating cereal and the spoon is in her right hand." He opened his eyes, eyebrows raised. "Does that help?"

"Mmm, maybe, maybe not. A lot of lefties do everything besides writing with their right hand. Apparently, your mom accepted this as Lucy's handwriting?"

"She never said anything to me about it not being hers. She just kept asking what it meant, and why Lucy would do a thing like that—leaving home and not saying why."

Claudia handed the note to Matt. He read it aloud under his breath, frowning; halting at times to decode a word that was difficult to make out.

> Mom
> I need space.
> Don't go looking for me. You won't find me.
> I'll be back when I can.
> Your daughter, Lucy

"What mother would read this and take it at face value?" Matt said. "No sane person would allow a sixteen-year-old to just disappear and not look for them."

"Obviously not *my* mother," Troy snapped. "She called the cops the same night Lucy left."

"Hey, man, I didn't mean any disrespect. I was just thinking out loud. I meant that Lucy must have known your mom wasn't going to listen."

Troy ignored Matt. "What are you thinking?" he asked Claudia.

"Besides the content not making a lot of sense, something is off with the handwriting. The first problem is it appears to be written with the unaccustomed hand. You said you think Lucy was right-handed, so if she wrote this, it was with her left hand. But why would she need to do that, unless her writing hand was injured? There could be chemical influence, too—drugs or alcohol, or both. What I need is some of her known, authentic handwriting, to compare. Is there anything else in the box—homework, or anything we can be sure that she wrote?"

"Let's keep looking. If there is anything, this is the only place it would be." Troy reached into the box and removed a rose pink wool crocheted baby blanket edged with satin ribbon. "My mom made one of these for each of us when we were born. Mine was blue. Obvs. I guess when she was on maternity leave and didn't have to work her butt off, she had time for stuff like this."

He laid the blanket gently on the newspaper and continued to unpack items from the box: a christening gown, frilly little dresses, and knit hats to fit a toddler. Sheets of colorful unicorn and dolphin stickers. A nearly bald baby doll, and a frayed wedding Barbie with matching groom Ken.

"Mom completely lost her mind when Luce got into the Goth scene. She didn't want to keep any of that 'junk,' which is what she called it, even if it was Lucy's. And omigod, when she dyed her hair black—Mom was about ready to kill her." Troy huffed a regretful chuckle. "When she saw what Luce had done, it was already too late. That was one screaming match I'll never forget. The bathroom sink was splotched an icky grey color from the hair dye, and stayed that way from that day on." His face contorted into a comical grimace. "Crap, I hope my kids never get that mad at me."

Claudia could have described plenty of similar screaming matches between herself and her own mother. Not because she had gone Goth. She had asserted her independence in other ways. "I remember Lucy wearing dramatic makeup," she said. "Very pale skin—powdered, I think—with thick black eyeliner and eyebrows."

Troy nodded agreement. "That was my sis."

"She took pride in getting people to look at her, even when the attention she got wasn't especially positive" Matt mused. "I think she liked to shock them."

"But she didn't like it when they talked about her," Claudia said, reminded of what Kelly had told her about Lucy's sensitive nature. Kelly had also said Lucy's handwriting was tiny. She looked at the note again.

"I may have asked this the other day, but aside from the pot that you found, was Lucy into drugs or alcohol?"

"Not that I know of. You have to remember, though, I was just a kid of eleven. I wouldn't have known what to look for."

Matt seemed doubtful too. "In the short time we dated, I never saw evidence of it. She was, kind of, uh, experimental, but—" He darted an uncomfortable look at Troy, and Claudia understood that he was referring to his sexual experiences with the missing girl. *Awkward.*

She changed the question. "Do you remember whether anything had changed in her behavior around the time she went missing?"

"Well, that's something I was asked about a thousand times, so I can tell you it's stuck in my mind. She had gotten more and more quiet and, well, angsty. If I tried to talk to her she'd bite my head off."

"Did you know she was pregnant?" Claudia asked.

Troy's eyes bugged like a treefrog. "What? *No!* Pregnant?" He swung on Matt, but before he could hurl an accusation or a question, Matt raised a hand and shook his head. "Don't look at me, man."

"Who, then?"

"No clue. She broke up with me because she was seeing someone else at the same time. It was her best friend, Rachel, who told the police she was pregnant. They're the ones who told me."

Troy was shaking his head. "I guarantee you my mom didn't know she was sexually active. She tried to be strict and make all the rules that parents are supposed to make, but she was never home to enforce them. We did pretty much whatever we wanted."

"Let's get back to the note," Claudia said, not wanting the conversation to go too far off track. "*If* Lucy wrote this, the quality of the handwriting suggests that she was under the influence of *something,* and/or under extreme stress. From the text of the note, and from what we know—or think we know—we're safe in assuming that it was the pregnancy that she needed to get away and handle—maybe have an abortion?"

"But she was a minor," Troy protested.

"In California, a minor doesn't need parental consent to get an abortion. As far as I know, that was also true in 1998."

Matt handed the note back to her. "Are you saying that because she was under stress it affected her handwriting like this?"

"Not necessarily. I need to compare it to something she wrote in normal times, but I have strong doubts about this handwriting. Why don't you look in the box some more, Troy, and see if you can find something with her handwriting. You never know, maybe she sometimes used her left hand like this. I'd like to be able to rule it out before I reach any definite conclusions."

He knelt beside the box again and dug through the remaining items until he came to a spiralbound notebook with a shiny black cover, which he took out. Flipping through it, he nodded. "This is as good as we've got. It looks like her English Lit homework. I hope you find what you need in here."

Claudia took it from him, her hopes rising. This was her first glimpse of handwriting they knew for sure to be Lucy's. She had written her name inside the front cover of the notebook. During the time she had used it, she had been a diligent student. She had made careful notes on how to write an essay, notes on style, structure, subject matter. She had made a list of books in the eleventh-grade curriculum—fiction, nonfiction, poetry, drama. Claudia, who had sat in the same class with her and done the same work, remembered them all.

She had written the date at the top of each page. The handwriting was as Kelly had described it: tiny and cramped, leaning to the left, with large spaces between the words. A pattern of space formed as the writing progressed down the page. These patterns were known to handwriting analysts as "rivers" because they literally formed a river of space.

With more than two decades of experience in the field of personality analysis behind her, Claudia had no trouble recognizing what she was seeing: the reflection of a lonely teenage girl who felt isolated and unable to emotionally connect to the outside world. The handwriting indicated that early in her life, Lucy had not received the nurturing she needed that would have helped her to form deep emotional bonds—possibly due to the absence of her mother, who had to work, and even more due to the absence of a father figure in her developmental years.

There were indications of depression. From what she knew of Lucy, Claudia believed that her classmate's attraction to the Goth subculture was a way of acting out feelings that she could not easily verbalize. "I don't remember any kids at school besides Lucy and Rachel who did the whole Goth thing, do you?" she asked Matt.

"As far as I remember, it was just them."

"They sometimes used to show up in costume—nineteenth century style clothes—Steampunk maybe. Most of the time, though it was more or less regular clothing. Either way, you could count on it being black."

Matt nodded. "Yeah, dark, sort of morbid. That pale, pale makeup, and black lipstick. Like she wanted to look dead. Sometimes she'd paint thick black tears under her lower lashes."

"She spent a lot of hours cultivating that look," Troy agreed.

As if a lightbulb had gone off in his head, Matt snapped his fingers. "Hey, wait you guys. I just remembered, there *was* a dude who used to wear one of those long, dark overcoats, and the same type of makeup the girls wore. I didn't know him, but he was kind of an outcast too. Maybe she hooked up with him. We need to find out who he was and talk to him."

"I don't remember anyone like that," Claudia said. "I'll ask Kelly if she knew him."

"I'll ask around too."

"That's all well and good," Troy said. "But what about the handwriting? What do you think?"

She didn't want to tell him her conclusions about Lucy's personality yet. The item of first importance was to establish the authenticity of the note. Claudia looked down at the notebook and back up at him. "I need time to study it, but at first glance, my preliminary opinion is, it's highly unlikely that Lucy wrote that note."

Chapter seventeen

An hour later, after Claudia had said goodbye to both Troy and Matt, Troy phoned her. She was in the car, driving on Jefferson, crossing Lincoln, a scant two miles from Playa de la Reina, and home.

"Oh, Claudia," Troy trilled. "You'll never guess what I found after you took off."

"Put me out of my misery; tell me quick."

"Keep your hat on, girlie, and get a load of this—when I was repacking the box, I dropped *Harry Potter and the Sorcerer's Stone*—which my sister loved, by the way—on my foot. Lemme tell you, that is one heavy mutha. Well, after I stopped dancing around the garage and made sure my toe wasn't broken, I saw that something had fallen out of it..." He left the sentence dangling.

"Troy! No more dramatic pauses. Do I have to beg?"

He chuckled, then swiftly cut himself off. "I shouldn't laugh. What I have for you is not even a little bit funny. It's something Lucy wrote to herself, poor kid." Troy's voice trembled with emotion. "I wish I could time travel and give her a big, squishy hug right now."

The light at Pershing turned red and Claudia hit the brakes. "Would you please take a photo and email it to me?"

"Already did. Let me know what you think of it."

"I will. I'm almost home."

"Don't forget."

"As if."

"I'll send it to Matt too. I'll be waiting to hear from you. Ciao."

As promised, Troy's email was waiting in her inbox. The attachment showed a high-resolution photo of a piece of paper that had been ripped out of a notebook similar to the one Troy had allowed her to bring home.

The handwriting was consistent with the writing in the English Lit notebook, and bore no resemblance to the writing in the note left for her mother. On the note Troy had sent, the text was decorated with darkly drawn doodles around the text—thick black boxes separated into compartments with x's drawn through each section—a symbolic segmenting of parts of her life, perhaps. The x'ings might reflect the desire to literally cross herself out.

Although it was not possible to tell from a digital copy how hard the pressure was on the page, from what she saw on the screen, Claudia believed it was heavy.

As she read the words, her heart burst with pity for the girl who had written them.

> *They hate me. I can feel it the way they look at me. They talk about me behind my back, sneering and picking me apart, calling me 'Goth Girl.' It's not like I'm blind and deaf. I can hear their snarky giggles. They know it, too, and they don't care how much it hurts me. They smile with their lips, but their eyes are ice cold, like stone.*
> *I don't even want to be part of their dumb squad. Today in class I got that itchy feeling on the back of my neck. It's like*

hairy spider legs crawling all over my skin. I know they were whispering about me again. I have to walk on eggshells all

the time and act like I don't care.
Why do they have to be so mean and hateful? I cry myself to sleep just about every night. The only time I feel good is

when I get stoned. I can hardly wait until tonight.
I wish I was dead.

Claudia called Troy. "This is deeply disturbing. Do you think the police saw it?"

"Not if it was in that book, which it has been all this time. It's thanks to Harry Potter that I found it, and let me tell you, if I hadn't been such an oaf and dropped it on my toe—"

She interrupted the steady flow of words. "I sincerely hope your toe survives, Troy, but it's a good thing you did drop it."

"Yeah." There was a long pause and a sniff. "When I read what she wrote—it sounds like—like—do you think it could be a suicide note? Could that be why we never heard from her again?"

Claudia had already had the same thought, but at this point, there was no way to know for sure. "Saying she wishes she was dead isn't the same as saying she's going to kill herself. And if she did, chances are, someone would have found her long ago." She felt less confident than she sounded. Suicides sometimes aren't discovered for decades if the death occurred in some remote location. The alternative was one she would rather not verbalize to Lucy's brother—if she had been taken by some degenerate, there was no telling where she had ended up.

"Are you going to give it to that detective?" Troy asked. "I haven't forgotten how he treated me like I was suspect. Like in the Jon Benet

Ramsey case, where they tried to blame her brother. He was nine years old for fuck's sake. I was eleven."

"There was no question Jon Benet was murdered, and they apparently looked at everyone. But I agree, a kid that age does feel like a stretch. As for giving it to Radnor, I'll talk to Matt about it." An idea struck her. "How about this—I can show it to my husband first. He's a detective at LAPD. I can see what he advises."

"Married to the mob, Claudia? I had no idea."

"Uh, not the mob. He's a cop."

"Kind of a mob. Nowhere near as exciting. That would be fantastic, thank you. Keep me posted."

"I will."

They ended the call and she texted Matt.

Claudia studied the spatial arrangement and the letter forms and the writing movement. The same signs of depression and feelings of alienation were evident that she had identified in the notebook. If she could get her hands on earlier samples of Lucy's, it might be possible to determine when those negative feelings began to manifest.

Her phone rang. "Anonymous." Not Matt. Expecting it to be a spammy call, Claudia answered cautiously and was surprised to hear the clipped tones of her classmate.

"Claudia Bennett. This is Vincent Ramsey. You left me a voicemail yesterday. I was in meetings and couldn't call back until now."

"Hi Vincent, I appreciate you getting back to me so quickly."

"What can I do for you?"

"Vincent, this might sound like a strange question, but I was wondering if you remember when we were in the eleventh grade, one of our classmates disappeared?"

Vincent went silent for a prolonged moment. "Why wouldn't I remember? It was a significant event."

"I think you knew our classmate, Matt Macedo? He's a filmmaker, and he's making a documentary about the disappearance. I'm helping him gather information, and I thought you and I could meet, maybe for lunch, and talk about it."

"Why do you want to talk to me about that girl?" Suspicion colored Vincent's tone.

"We're talking to several classmates who knew her. We're looking for anyone who remembers anything about Lucy or what happened that might be interesting for the film."

"But why are you calling *me?*"

"Oh, uh, I thought maybe you knew her."

"Because we were both freaks?" He sounded more curious than angry.

She could not very well say "yes," so she reached for a softer truth. "I never saw you as a freak, Vincent; I hope you believe that."

Again, there was a hiatus. It was part of the speech pattern she remembered. She waited him out until he had processed what she said and prepared a response.

"You were nice to me," he said at length. "I noticed it, even if I didn't say so. Or maybe act like it."

"I'm glad to hear that."

"I've learned some social skills since then. Learned to recognize—" he broke off mid-sentence.

When it became clear that he was not going to continue, Claudia said, "Kids can be heartless, as you know." She paused to give him a chance to respond. When he didn't take it, she said, "Matt—and I—are hoping to find out what happened to the girl who went missing—Lucy Valentine. After she disappeared that year, there was never any sign of her ever again. The police weren't able to get anywhere back in 1998, but it's still an open case."

"I'm willing to see you and talk to you. But that girl. Lucy. She was one of the heartless ones. She made fun of me like the rest of them did. She just did it in different ways when no one was looking."

"That's a shame," Claudia said, disappointed. "I was hoping if nothing else, maybe the two of you were friends, and—"

"*If nothing else?*" Vincent said, as sharp as a broken bottle. "What does that mean?"

"Nothing. I just thought—"

"No, I get it," he said, speaking across her. "You think I had something to do with her running off the way she did and you're trying to pin it on me."

"No, Vincent, wait, that's not—"

"I guess it was too much to think you called me for a kind reason. I know that I have difficulty communicating sometimes, but that doesn't mean I'm stupid."

"Please don't think that. You are the least stupid person I ever met."

"I have nothing to give you, Claudia Bennett."

"Wait, Vincent—"

She was pleading into a void. He had disconnected.

Chapter eighteen

Wednesday, October 11

"So, Columbo, what sage advice can you give me to pass along to Matt?" Claudia took two cold bottles of Stella Artois from the refrigerator and handed one to Joel, who was lounging in the breakfast nook, his long legs stretched out.

"You want to know what to do with new evidence related to a twenty-six-year-old case? You've already got a good copy of it on the computer, right? Someone needs to contact the agency that handled the case back in 1998 and find out who the current detectives are. Then, Macedo should get the original writing to them."

Not what she expected. "Oh. I thought you would say we should hand it over to Louis Radnor," Claudia said.

"The retired detective? He's gonna be the one with some of the best insight on it. No reason not to give him a copy, but it's whoever sits at his old desk that you guys need to contact. That person would have inherited Radnor's cases, and that's who is going to pick up any pieces in the cold case and look into it—*if* they're interested and have time."

"Why wouldn't they be interested?"

"Some of the younger D's only want to work the fresh, new cases. You won't know until you talk to them. Either way, the actual evidence—the physical piece of paper that Lucy wrote on—has to go to the current case agent to be added to the file."

Claudia over. "I need to go back to Edentown anyway and talk to Lupe Garcia—she was the editor of the school paper, and she's the current editor of the last newspaper in town there. She knows everyone and everything that's going on in Edentown. Since I'll be there anyway, I could stop in at the police department and talk to the new detective."

"Want me to call Edentown PD and find out who's on that desk?" Joel asked. "Smooth the way for you?"

She smiled at him. "I confess that it pains me to need help, but that's an offer I refuse to refuse."

Matt said he would meet her in thirty minutes at Tyler's Coffee House at the bottom of the hill from her street, almost next door to Cowboys.

Claudia was waiting for him with coffee and an almond croissant, and the additional material he could use in the film. He was pleased with her news, but the content of Lucy's note to herself troubled him too. His reaction was the same as Troy's. "It sounds like a suicide note to me."

"I'm not so sure about that." She had printed a copy of the note after spending some time studying it. Taking it from a manila envelope, she showed it to Matt. "This is her normal handwriting. It's basically the same as the handwriting in her English Lit notebook—the style, the size, the spacing. There are signs of depression and loneliness, but there's no such thing as a 'suicidal writing' per se. And the thing is, once someone decides they're going to end it all, we generally see *some* changes in the handwriting, though not every time."

"Changes like what?"

"All sorts of things are possible. Some people make the decision and feel excited, maybe even elated, knowing there's going to be an end to their suffering. That's why people complete suicide, right? They can't see another way out. They think there is no solution to their emotional pain—I'm separating this from the pain of physical illness."

"You mean, the 'Kevorkian solution.'"

"Assisted suicide is a whole other topic," Claudia said. "Sticking to *emotional* pain, the handwriting of someone who had decided to kill themselves would likely reflect the change in attitude from misery to elation. For example, the writing might get larger, and the writing line—the baseline—might rise significantly. The movement to the right—towards the right side of the paper—gets more intense, with a stronger right slant and higher velocity—which means it's written faster. Here's the thing: the right side of the page represents the future. If the handwriting goes all the way to the edge of the paper, leaving almost zero right margin, it was as if the writer was rushing into the future—and in the case of a suicidal person, hurrying up their death."

"You said, 'might' mean," Matt said. "How does that help?"

"I'm just giving you one possibility. It's hard to generalize because it's all about context. You can't form an opinion without considering the whole picture of a specific handwriting, and the circumstances under which it was written. A feature like a narrow right margin means something in one handwriting, but in a different context it could be tweaked to mean something else. To be accurate, you can't separate out just one feature, like a margin, or slant, or anything else, and interpret it without seeing how it fits into the whole. All the parts work together."

"Sounds like a lot of complicated B.S."

"It *is* complicated, but it's *not* B.S. People used to think handwriting analysis was a parlor trick. It's based on scientific principles, and there's an art to interpreting the findings. It's getting better recognition these days."

Matt put up a hand. "Okay, I'm good with that. But you have a specific handwriting right there in your hand—Lucy's. You have the context. What do you see? Was she suicidal?"

"All I can tell you is, from what I've seen, *this* note is consistent with her handwriting in the notebook. In other words, there's nothing unusual about it—nothing that draws my attention and says 'suicide,' except that it slants somewhat more to the left."

"What does that mean?"

"When she wrote this—and the content supports it—she was pulling away from others. She was going inside herself for comfort. We know she had a mother who loved her, but who wasn't around to show it. Lucy needed to have that love reflected back to her in a way that she could receive it and believe in it—to let her know she was loved and lovable. Troy told us that her father wasn't around to do the job, and then his father—her stepfather—defected too. She had a hard time socially in school. She may have imagined that if she tried reaching out to her peers it would make her more vulnerable. In other words, she was afraid of being rejected, so she was the first to reject."

"You think that's why she dressed the way she did, and acted so aloof?" Matt asked.

Claudia nodded. "She wanted to stand out as unique, to be seen and she wanted to be understood. She needed someone who she could talk to, confide in, but my guess is, she was afraid there was nobody who could understand her. So, she shut them out before they could get close. Like she did with you."

"You're right. She was starting to open up to me, but the moment we seemed to be getting closer, she pushed me away, hard."

"What do you think changed?"

"The last time we were together—before she broke up with me, I mean—she had started talking about how much she missed her dad, and how it killed her that he had a new family in Chicago. She believed he'd forgotten her."

"Unfortunately, from what Radnor said about her dad, she was right."

Matt stared into his empty coffee cup. "When she said that, I didn't know what to do. I wanted to make her feel better, comfort her, but I was a bumbling sixteen-year-old with my own issues. I tried to put my arms around her, and she jumped up and locked herself in the bathroom. I felt like an idiot—stupid and confused. She wouldn't come out, just yelled through the door that I needed to leave. So, that's what I did. I laid awake all night, worrying about what I was going to say to her the next day. I shouldn't have bothered. She didn't come to school for the rest of the week. The next time I saw her was when she told me she liked some other guy."

"I expect she felt like she'd exposed too much of herself to you," Claudia said. "She didn't know how to deal with it. And, oh, by the way, Vincent Ramsey was not the new guy she was seeing. He called me back today."

"Yeah? What did ol' Sideshow Bob have to say for himself?"

Claudia summarized the phone call. "It sucked that the call ended with him thinking we were trying to use him. And what's even worse, we *were* trying to use him. I feel bad about that."

Matt glossed over her regret. "He convinced you that he wasn't 'the guy?'"

"More than that—he said that Lucy was one of his tormentors. We can cross him off our list."

"Consider him crossed," Matt said with a dissatisfied grunt. "Next up..."

"My husband has offered to call Edentown PD and get the name of Detective Radnor's replacement and give us an introduction if you want."

"That's nice of him, thanks." Matt hesitated. "I'm not going to be available to work on Lucy for the next few days."

"Oh. Work calling?"

"Yeah, I have some actual paying work that'll help bankroll the documentary until I get a deal with a studio. It's a commercial to shoot in Palm Springs, and it starts tomorrow, which means I can't go to Edentown this week." He cleared his throat, looked a little twitchy. "Not that I meant to imply you don't have work to do, too, but if you don't, and you wanted to get started on the legwork—"

She waved her hands, dismissing his concerns. "Chill, Matt, I'm flexible this week. I can go to the E'town police station tomorrow. But you will need to swing by Troy's and pick up the original note. Joel says it has to be handed over to the detective who's got the case now."

"I'll make a run over to Studio City right now, and drop it off to you tonight." He reached over and gave her hand a grateful squeeze. "Thanks, Claudia, it's a deal."

She gave him a crooked smile. "You had me way back at 'handwriting.' I'm all in now."

"Lucky for me, and I know it."

"I'm going to call Lupe Garcia and see if she'll meet me, seeing as I'll be in town."

His eyebrows went up. "You think Lupe might know something?"

Claudia started gathering up her cardboard cup and napkin. "If anyone knows anything, it's gonna be Lupe. She was forever hip deep into everybody's business. And from what I saw at the reunion, that hasn't changed any."

Chapter nineteen

Thursday, October 12

With Lucy Valentine's original note safe in an acid-free protective plastic sleeve, Claudia aimed the Jaguar south and prepared to go back in time once more. That was how it felt, heading to Edentown. Despite the fact that few things had remained the same where she had grown up, with each mile she drove, it was as though the years were rolling back to 1999.

She had phoned Lupe Garcia and told her about Matt's documentary. Lupe had jumped at the invitation to meet her, and suggested the Original Pancake House for a late breakfast.

The A-frame building with its brick façade looked exactly as it had for as long as Claudia could remember—there was something heartening in that. The 1950s-style sign towered over the driveway as it had during the myriad occasions she had eaten there with her family, and as she grew older, with friends. As she drove into the cramped parking lot, she had a feeling that apart from the prices keeping pace with inflation, she could count on the menu being not so different from those old days.

Entering the back door ten minutes early, she found Lupe already at one of the maple wood tables, steaming black coffee in front of her in one of the restaurant's signature handcrafted ceramic mugs. Lupe glanced up with a crooked smile, pert in a pixie haircut—shaved in the back, fluffy on top. In a stylish two-toned blazer and skinny jeans with tan suede boots, there was no better way to describe her than trim and well turned out.

Claudia dropped into the chair opposite Lupe and picked up the menu. "I thought I was early."

Lupe shrugged. "Finished my first meeting sooner than I expected. I've already ordered. Veggie omelet."

Having noted Claudia's arrival, the waitress sauntered over with a coffee cup in one hand and a pot in the other. "Coconut pancakes, please," Claudia said with a smile. "A million carbs, but I'm not here to count calories."

Lupe snickered. "Good thing. You might want to hit the gym after you leave."

"We can't all be itty bitty sprites like you and Lucy Valentine," Claudia said, already wondering whether this was going to be an hour she would regret.

Lupe's eyebrows went up. "Okay, then. Let's bypass the chitchat and get right down to it, huh?"

"You're a busy woman, and as I recall, one who likes to cut to the chase. But we can spend some time talking about the weather and the traffic if you like." Claudia heard herself being snippy. Lupe had always brought out the worst in her.

"You're right," Lupe said. "I am busy. So, what is it you want to know that you think I can help with?"

"Anything at all you can remember about Lucy. She didn't seem to have many friends. Since you agreed to meet with me, I'm assuming that you knew her."

"We lived in the same neighborhood for elementary and middle school. When we got to high school we had some classes together. Yes, I knew her, but that's not to say we were always bosom buddies." Lupe glanced away, her lips pursed, seeming to reflect. Her eyes traveled around the restaurant, landing briefly on the other diners and moving on. "When we were little kids we used to play together. Took our baby dolls around the neighborhood in their strollers—girly stuff like that. Lucy was a regular kid until around third grade, maybe fourth."

"What do you mean, a 'regular kid?'"

"Like I said, playing with dolls. Then her father had an affair and moved away with his ho. Her mom also got remarried not long after that and had another kid—" She seemed be searching for a name.

"Troy," Claudia supplied. "He was eleven when Lucy disappeared."

"Right. Troy. After her family split up, Lucy changed—more or less stopped talking. It was like—like she became a shadow of herself. No more play dates. She never wanted to hang out anymore." The waitress came with an armload of plates. When she was gone, Claudia said, "It sounds like that was hurtful."

Lupe shot her a sharp glance. "Don't go psychoanalyzing me, Claudia. I'll never let you see my handwriting."

Claudia grinned, "No problem. I'd have to charge you a big fee to analyze it."

The grin defused the spurt of tension, and Lupe gave her a faint smile. "What I meant was, when she wasn't there anymore it made a major splash at first because of the sensational nature of her disappearance. But after that there was barely a ripple. Nobody noticed she was gone because she was already like a ghost."

"I get what you mean. What were people saying when she first disappeared? There must have been talk about what happened to her. Being the *Echo* editor back then, you knew everything that was going on."

"What makes you think I'd tell you if I did have some insider scoop?"

Claudia considered the woman across the table. The lines on her attractive face were starting to etch her skin the way it sometimes happens in aging women who have spent years working off every extra ounce of fat. It made her look pinched, dissatisfied. "What's up, Lupe? You're successful. You married a good guy. Are you still holding it against me that Matt and I—"

"Don't flatter yourself. I could have had Matt if I'd wanted him."

Old grudges died hard, Claudia thought, knowing that Matt had never been attracted to her. "Then, is there something else that's making you act like I'm dirt on the bottom of your shoe? Or is 'resting bitch face' your standard attitude?"

To her surprise, Lupe gave a burst of laughter. "I like you, Claudia, I really do. If I didn't, I wouldn't have met up with you."

"You agreed to meet with me because you were curious."

"Yeah, whatever. Have you talked to Rachel Thomas about Lucy? They were chummy, and your old *amiga*, Kelly Brennan too. Hasn't she told you anything?"

"Rachel hasn't been available. Overloaded with work, she says."

"An unexpected glut of dead bodies?"

"Nice way to put it. I'll call her while I'm down here, see if she can get together. And if Kelly had something to tell, I'm sure she would have."

"Is that so?" Lupe's sideways squint said more about her skepticism than words. "You know what I find interesting? Lucy's only two gal pals are unavailable and have nothing to say. And yet, they were both with her on the last day she was seen."

"What are you talking about? We were all in gym class when Lucy left early. "She said she was going home. The media—"

Lupe stopped her with a delicate snort. "'The *media*?' You do know I'm part of the media, right? Well, in case you don't know this, I can promise you, you can't count on the media to tell the truth."

Claudia couldn't resist rolling her eyes. "I've been misquoted enough times to have learned that."

"I have it on good authority that Lucy hung around school until lunch, then she met up with Rachel and Kelly. They snuck out and went to her house with her."

"And?" Claudia asked, wondering why Kelly had never told her this.

"And that's as far as my intel took me. I heard that afterwards, neither one of them would say what was really going on."

"Did anyone tell that to the police?"

"Claudia! Are you shitting me? We were teenagers. We didn't trust the cops as far as we could spit."

"They both got interviewed by the cops."

"So?"

"Did you know Lucy was pregnant?"

"Where did you hear that?" She tried to play it off as if it was no big deal, but the shock in Lupe's eyes gave Claudia her answer.

Their waitress came back to refill their coffee and bring takeout boxes. Claudia shoveled half of her meal into one for Joel and folded the flaps closed. She looked at Lupe in the eye. "I can't divulge my source, but it was Rachel who told the cops."

Lupe's eyes opened wider. "Holy shit, Claudia. That's a ! I wish I'd known at the time. It would've made a fantastic headline in the *Echo*."

"As if Ada would have let you print it," Claudia scoffed, referring to their faculty advisor, Ada Brown, whom they had regularly disrespected behind her back.

"Truth. That old battleaxe was constantly on my case. I don't think I ever wrote one headline that she didn't toss out." Lupe put on a silly voice, imitating Ada's German accent. "'Zat is too *zenzational*. You *must* change it!' Hell, sensational is what sells news." Behind her eyes, it was easy to see the wheels spinning. "Being pregnant and scared to tell her mom could be plenty of reason for Lucy to run away."

"Do you believe that's what happened? That she ran away?" Claudia showed her a copy of the note Troy had retrieved from the Harry Potter book. "Her brother just found this. It isn't dated, so it may not have anything to do with her leaving, but it does sound like she was being bullied. Not that it was called that back then."

"No, we called them 'mean girls.'" Lupe read the note and flicked a finger at it. "You know she's talking about that bitch Natalie Parker, right?"

"How sure are you that Natalie was one of the girls Lucy is referring to?"

"Sure sure. I used to hear Nat talking shit like this whenever Lucy was around. Besides, Nat was out in front of whatever was going on—she always was—still is," Lupe's lips twisted. "The other day there was a story in the news about a kid who was being bullied at school and hung herself. Maybe Lucy—"

"In Lucy's case, no body was ever recovered." Claudia reminded her, repeating what she had said to both Troy and Matt. "And a sixteen-year-old girl who kills herself is most likely to do it at home. Even if she didn't—if she went into the woods or someplace like that, you'd think a hiker would have tripped over the body at some point."

"So, what, then? You're in the 'she was kidnapped' camp?"

"It's the most feasible explanation to me."

Lupe stopped her. "Wait, wait, go back. If she was pregnant, who was the guy?"

"The cops heard she was dating someone at the time, but they never could find out who it was. Kelly didn't know about it, either."

"She was such a loner. Who the hell could she have been dating? Somebody outside of school?"

Claudia said nothing about Matt, keeping his confidence. Lupe scrunched up her face, searching the databank she kept in her brain until she found what she was looking for. "Maybe it was that weirdo who used to wear a black raincoat to school every day. What was his name?" She thought some more. "Darnell Trent. Did you know him?"

"I didn't have any classes with him, just saw him around campus. People talked about him."

"He used to slouch around by himself with a stupid pout on his face; never talked to anyone. Half the time he was asleep at his desk, and always in trouble for not turning in homework and flunking exams. He got sent to his guidance counselor more times than he was in class." She nodded. "That'd be the perfect guy for someone like Lucy. She was the same type."

Lupe was talking about the same person Matt had mentioned. Now she had a name, Claudia was already taking out her phone. She googled "Darnell Trent, Edentown, California."

"Don't get excited," she said, reading from the article she found. "'Darnell Trent, 22, was killed in action, fighting the Taliban in Afghanistan.'"

Not ready to be dissuaded, Lupe insisted, "That doesn't mean he didn't get with Lucy back in 1998. What if she told him she was pregnant and he didn't want to be responsible, so he got rid of her?"

"That's so extreme, Lupe. You have absolutely nothing to base it on."

"Now that you tell me she was pregnant, you've got me intrigued. If there was a pregnancy, there had to be a guy. Who was it?"

"It's more reasonable to think she was grabbed off the street by a pedophile."

Lupe's eyes sparked with speculation. Already leaping ahead in her mind, she was no longer listening. "As soon as I get back to my office, I'm going to start looking through the '98 yearbook. We have copies of all of them in case of local obits. I'm gonna figure out who the father was."

Claudia called for the check. "When you figure it out, you let me in on it, okay?"

"Are you picking up the tab for breakfast?"

"Yes, I am."

"Then you will be the first to know."

Chapter twenty

The Edentown Police Department was housed in a twenty-year-old two-story building with all glass fronting, which seemed curiously insecure.

Detective Heather Watson, who met Claudia at the front desk, was in her late 40s or a healthy early 50s. Solidly built, with stylishly blonde-streaked brown hair, she wore a navy blue trouser suit and sensible shoes with chunky heels. After a bone-crushing handshake that would have done a quarterback proud, she led the way to a cramped interview room that contained a metal table and chairs, and a side table. A camera aimed at the table was mounted near the ceiling.

Watson stood aside for Claudia to precede her. She gave a nod at the camera and said, "Don't worry, it's not running."

"I'm not worried." Annoyed to find herself feeling like a suspect, Claudia took a seat at the table. She had expected to be taken to the detective's cubicle, and being in an interview room made her nerves jump the way being on the witness stand to testify in a trial did. It was the part of her job she liked the least, and it did not take long for her to figure out that was the detective's hidden motive. No doubt a habit from interviewing suspects in this room.

Watson took a seat and took immediate control of the interview. "Right after Detective Jovanic called me, I got in touch with Louis Radnor. He said you'd already spoken to him—you and Mr. Macedo." She did not try to hide the sneer in the way she said Matt's name. The verbal sparring had begun with a thrust.

Claudia parried. "Yes, we did. I understand that he continues to view Mr. Macedo as a suspect—which is interesting, considering Matt is the one who is interested in re-investigating the Lucy Valentine case. I hope you can put that aside for now. I'm sure you'll want to take an *objective* look at the new evidence that's come to light and reach your own conclusions."

"I'm disappointed you would think we might do otherwise," Watson countered, and Claudia had no doubt that a layer of sarcasm lurked under her deadpan expression.

"I understand the case officially remains open?"

"Yes, it was never solved. There's no statute of limitations on missing persons."

"I see. When did anyone last do any work on it?"

The detective had brought nothing with her into the interview room. In order to answer the question, she would have had to familiarize herself with the contents of Lucy's file. There was a pause. "It's been a while," she temporized. "You've gotta remember the case is more than twenty-five years old. People work on cold cases when they're not busy with new ones. Serious crimes happen every day that need our immediate attention."

Claudia flinched as though she had been slapped. "What I'm hearing you say is, nothing is going to happen."

"Believe it or not, urgent cases take precedence. That's how it is. Now, why don't you show me what you've got. I'll grant you, I'm curious to see this 'new evidence' you've uncovered."

Claudia took a transparent plastic sleeve from her briefcase and handed it over. She had placed the original note in it for protection. "This isn't directly related to the note that was left for Lucy's mother, but since it was something new and relevant, we thought you would want to see it."

Watson took it and leaving it in its Mylar sleeve, looked it over. When she finished, she said much the same as everyone else who had read it. "Could be a suicide note."

"It's possible," Claudia conceded. "But if she killed herself, where was the body?"

Watson gave her a patronizing look. "As you know, Mrs. Jovanic, just because a body wasn't recovered, it doesn't mean there wasn't one."

"Jovanic is my husband's name," Claudia corrected her, irked that she was not being taken with any degree of seriousness, especially by another woman. "My last name is Rose. Does the file show whether any sex offenders were interviewed at the time Lucy disappeared?"

Annoyance crossed the detective's face. "That would have been part of our normal procedure."

"I'm not questioning procedure; I'm curious. Have you even looked at the file?"

Watson's eyes went stone cold. "I wasn't on the department at that time. But I can assure you Detective Radnor had, and still has, an impeccable reputation as an investigator. I have every confidence that whatever he did was strictly by the book."

"In other words, the answer is 'no,' you haven't bothered to look at it. At the time, it was the general feeling in the community that the police believed Lucy was a runaway and she would come home by herself."

Heather Watson's jaw tightened. The unspoken implication that the police had not done all they could was not lost on her. "Regardless of what you think you know, *Ms. Rose,* we take missing kids seriously."

"I'm sure you do." They were getting nowhere. Claudia decided to wrap up the meeting with a final pointed question. "Just so I know, are you going to pursue this note at all?"

Watson gave her a chilly fake smile. "I repeat, Ms. Rose, this is a cold case. We'll check out your 'evidence' as we have the time. Meanwhile, please feel free to continue to supply us with anything else that comes to light during your, er, 'investigation.'"

Claudia could just about see the air quotes around the words. As loud as a Sunday church bell, she heard the subtext of what Detective Watson was telling her: the note would go into the file and sit there for another twenty-six years unless she and Matt could uncover something more that would give Watson a specific direction to take. She picked up her briefcase and got to her feet. "Thanks for your time, Detective." She did not offer her hand.

"Glad to help," Watson said without a trace of irony. "I'll take you out to the front."

They walked in silence along the empty corridor, each woman deep in her own thoughts. They were nearing the exit when an office door opened and a man stepped out, his head bowed, reading the contents of a sheaf of papers in his hands. They started to pass each other, and Watson said, "Hey, Sam."

The man glanced up, raising his free hand, absent-mindedly acknowledging her. "Detective Booker," Claudia said, recognizing him. His head jerked up, his focus sharpening as he looked at her. "Er, it's—Ms. Rose, right?"

Surprise moved across Watson's face. "You two know each other?"

"We met at the Edentown High Reunion recently," Claudia said.

Samuel Booker nodded slowly. "That's right. I interviewed you about Joshua Dickson."

Watsons look of surprise increased. "Dickson. The drowning victim?"

"Ms. Rose here is the one who found the body in the school swimming pool."

"No kidding."

"Mr. Dickson was my driver's ed teacher back in 1999," Claudia hastened to explain. "It was my bad luck to be the one who found him. Of course, his luck was far worse than mine."

"So, what brings you here today?" Samuel Booker asked.

"Ms. Rose brought in some information on an unrelated cold case," Watson said.

"You don't say." Booker looked pleased. "That's an interesting coincidence. I was just about to contact you with some follow-up questions on the Dickson case. Since you're already here, you can save me the trip up to L.A."

"What kind of follow-up questions?" Claudia asked. "I'd like to get back on the freeway before rush hour, and I have another stop to make first."

The two detectives exchanged a significant glance. She wondered what it meant.

"Er, I'll leave you in Detective Booker's capable hands." Heather Watson was already turning away. "Thanks for stopping by, Ms. Rose. I'll get in touch if anything comes out of the note."

Even as Watson spoke, Claudia felt certain she would not be hearing from her again.

"Let's find a place to sit down for a few minutes," Booker said. He gestured her back the way she and Watson had just come—back to the same interview room they had vacated.

"How long is this going to take, detective? I told you everything I knew."

"I'm hoping that with your experience and your connections, you can help me."

"Help, how?"

Booker gestured with his papers, and she caught a glimpse of the printed line drawing of a nude male body. Notes had been scribbled around it that she knew would have been written by the medical examiner.

"This is the autopsy report on Joshua Dickson," he said.

Behind the offhand words, Claudia had a premonition that something unpleasant waited to pounce on her. She looked at him for a long moment, her lips puckered with growing suspicion. "Okay. What does it say?"

He paused just as long as she had. "Mr. Dickson experienced blunt force trauma to the head."

"He must have hit his head on the concrete when he fell into the pool."

"No, Ms. Rose," Booker said with something that sounded dangerously like satisfaction. "He was hit on the head *before* he fell in the pool. The medical examiner concluded that the victim died from blunt force trauma-induced drowning, exacerbated by alcohol consumption."

She wanted to deny it the way she had when she first saw Joshua Dickson's body in the pool, but she couldn't. "Someone deliberately—?"

"Joshua Dickson's death was not an accident."

She saw it all again—the body floating at the bottom of the pool; his hair drifting like octopus tentacles ... "You're saying someone—" Claudia could not bring herself to say it.

"The cause of death was murder," Detective Booker filled in for her.

"But, why? Who?"

"I'm sorry to give you the bad news. I'm sure it's upsetting. But you were the person to discover the body, so—"

"But, how could it be? Who would do such a thing? Everyone loved him."

"Apparently not everyone," Booker said. "We don't know yet what happened—whether he went outside with someone and got into an argument, perhaps, or someone followed him out there with intent to harm him."

"It wouldn't have been anyone from my class. Maybe someone else who knew he was going to be there. Or, a case of mistaken identity..." Something he had said just registered. "You said blunt force trauma. Did you find a weapon?"

"Unfortunately, we did not."

"I don't remember seeing any blood in the water."

"There was no external bleeding. The medical examiner found a hairline fracture at the base of his skull. It caused a hematoma—a blood clot in the tissues. If it had been treated right away it likely wouldn't have been life-threatening. But if he was pushed into the pool right after taking that blow, as I suspect, he was left to drown. His death came close to passing as an alcohol-related drowning. The amount of alcohol in his system was 1.08, well above the legal limit, which is—"

"Point oh-oh-eight," Claudia supplied, struggling to absorb what she had just learned. "He must have been totally plastered, unable to defend himself."

"Yes. Our ME is very thorough. Someone else might have missed the hairline fracture."

She knew Booker was observing her closely, but she could not meet his eyes. Her last encounter with Josh Dickson was replaying in her head. He had been so lighthearted; his old self. Who would have wished him harm? The thought ended at a blank wall.

"The weapon could have been anything," the detective was saying. "A bottle would be easy to dispose of in the nearest trash can. If that was the weapon, considering how many bottles of beer and wine were served that night, there would be no way to prove who had used one of them to clock the victim."

Claudia stared at him. "You're saying someone almost got away with the perfect murder."

Booker nodded. "Even if there were fingerprint or DNA matches, they could easily be explained. 'Yes, officer, I was holding that beer bottle, so what?' Nobody would think anything of it."

"How do you think I can help?" Claudia asked, knowing that the offer was expected of her, although she wanted no part of it.

"I was thinking maybe some of your classmates would be disposed to talk more frankly to you than to a cop. This isn't something I would ask of just anyone, but you have experience as an expert witness, and I believe you said you're married to a detective. Maybe if you get the opportunity, you could ask around. You told me that Mr. Dickson was seen arguing with someone that night."

"Sue Goldman," Claudia said, trying and failing to imagine her well-put-together English teacher beaning Josh Dickson with a bottle. "When I was in high school, they were good friends. They ate lunch together practically every day. They were the two youngest teachers in the school—only a few years older than we were. We spent far too much time speculating on their relationship. Honestly, detective, I have no clue what they might have argued about. Or if it's even true that they were."

"I spoke to his wife," Booker said. "They moved back East in 2001. She said he was here to settle some family business and thought it would be fun to attend the reunion since it was happening during his trip."

"Yes, that's the same thing he told me at the cocktail party."

"Do you think that with his wife thousands of miles away, he might have felt free to rekindle an old flame with Ms. Goldman and something went wrong? Maybe she wasn't into one-night stands?"

"And what? She hit him over the head with a bottle and pushed him into the pool?" It was Claudia's turn to be skeptical. "Not sure how you think I can answer that, except pure, meaningless guesswork. I saw them from across the room talking together. There didn't seem anything noteworthy in their body language or manner that caught my attention. *I'm* not the one who saw them supposedly arguing. That was Lupe Garcia, she was—"

"Lupe Garcia, the managing editor of the Gazette?"

"Oh, you know her? I had breakfast with her this morning. She was our school newspaper editor. Lupe never met a scrap of gossip she didn't love. I bet she would be delighted to talk to you."

"When you saw her this morning, did you discuss Mr. Dickson's death?"

"There was no reason to. It was all talked out at the reunion banquet. I came to Edentown to talk to Detective Watson about a missing person case from 1998. A classmate from my junior year. Trying to get her to give a good goddamn about it."

She looked up and read the conjecture in his eyes. "I'm helping a friend do some research for a documentary he's making," she added. "We came across some new evidence that I thought Detective Watson would want to see. Turns out I was off base."

"1998 is a long time ago," Booker said. "I'm sure Detective Watson will give your new evidence all the attention it deserves."

"You have more faith in her than I do," Claudia said. "If there's anything to be found, we will find it."

He gave her a wry look from under lowered brows. "I have no doubt you will."

"I'm sorry I don't have more to offer. If I hear anything that might be of use, I'll give you a call."

"I appreciate that, Ms. Rose. With so many people attending the reunion, anything you can do to help us narrow things down, the better."

"Understood, but honestly, I'm having trouble seeing Ms. Goldman doing anything violent. I imagine it would take a lot of force to hit someone hard enough to cause a skull fracture."

"Maybe not as hard as you'd think," Booker said. "Let's assume the beer bottle scenario. Considering how thick those bottles are, and depending on where the blow landed—in this case the back of the skull— it might not take more than one or two swings to knock him unconscious." He paused for breath.

"Like I said, if the internal bleeding could have been stopped quickly, the likelihood that he could have survived is good—even an ice pack on the wound could have helped. But as intoxicated as he was, and then getting pushed or rolled into the pool ... well, that suggests premeditation."

Detective Booker hauled himself to his feet, signaling an end to the interview. He held out his hand to her. Claudia could not tell what he was thinking, but behind his detached gaze she could see that a lot of speculating was going on. She rose and took his hand. He caught her eyes. "For a guy everyone supposedly loved, somebody sure had it in for him."

Chapter twenty-one

Claudia sat in her car in the police department parking lot feeling ill. She gripped the steering wheel to steady her hands, which were shaking.

Why would anyone want to kill Josh Dickson?

She phoned Rachel Thomas from the road and asked for a meeting. Judging by her unwelcoming manner when Claudia identified herself, she guessed that her classmate would not have answered the call had she recognized the phone number.

"I can't take a break," Rachel grumbled when she heard the reason for the meeting—that Claudia wanted to get her comments about Lucy Valentine for the documentary. "I already told Matt Macedo I'm on my own this week. What's so urgent?"

"I'm in town and was hoping to talk to you while I'm here. It's easier to talk in person."

"Easier for who?" Rachel heaved an aggrieved sighed. "You'd have to come to the mortuary and talk while I work."

"I can do that. And I promise not to take a lot of your time. I want to get on the freeway before it gets late."

Grudgingly, she agreed to meet if Claudia could be there in thirty minutes. Claudia could. "I hope you're not queasy about seeing dead bodies" Rachel added.

"I guess you forgot I recently saw one."

"It's different up close and personal. Sure you're up for it?"

Thinking about Josh Dickson, and some other corpses she wished she had not seen, Claudia made a face at the rearview mirror. "I guess we'll find out."

The Eternal Peace Mortuary and Funeral Home was situated in a large, two-story dwelling in old Edentown next door to an ancient cemetery. Ancient by California standards, anyway. It had been established in the mid-1800s.

A discreet wooden sign with its name edged in fancy scrollwork stood in front of the house under an ancient oak whose branches spread across the entire front yard.

Claudia had no idea how long the place had served its current purpose—certainly longer than she had been alive. Back in the 90s, walking past it on her way to school, she had been happy never to have occasion to venture inside the slate blue and white painted clapboard walls.

It was mid-afternoon when she parked on the street and walked up the steps to a wraparound porch that looked more like the South than Southern California. The wide front door stood half-open on a large, old-fashioned foyer with polished floors covered by a red Persian rug. The homey type of place you would want to go if you needed to arrange a funeral, Claudia decided, entering the silent entrance hall.

A tasteful flower arrangement stood on a table in the middle of the foyer. The flowers might account for the floral fragrance that seemed to perfume the air. Or, perhaps more likely, the scent came from an accumulation of countless such arrangements that had lived and died here over the years.

She saw no one, heard no one. To the left of the front door, a staircase with snowy painted newel posts led up to what Claudia guessed was the living area.

She called out "Hello," and checked the place out while she waited. Rachel, who had been disinclined to make things easy, had simply told her to look for a door at the back of the foyer, and take the stairs down to her work area. Claudia strolled to the white-paneled wall at the back and looked it over, not seeing a door.

There were, however, two sets of oak double doors off the foyer, both closed. Curious, she opened one and peeped inside. Rows of chairs were set up facing the front of the room. A polished bronze casket stood on a green-draped trestle, the upper lid open, ready for viewing. A portrait of a sixtyish man—its occupant—was displayed on an easel next to it.

Claudia backed out and was closing the doors behind her just as a teenage boy came rushing down the staircase, skateboard in hand. Seeing her, he skidded to a halt. "Hey, I didn't think anyone was coming for Mr. Sanchez until—"

"I'm not here for a viewing. I'm here to see Rachel."

The kid's eyes went to the doors she had just closed. He threw her a cheeky grin. "You're not gonna find her in there."

"Yeah, I noticed Mr. Sanchez was alone."

"You got an appointment?"

"She's expecting me. She told me to look for a door in the back wall and go downstairs, but I didn't see a door."

"You sure she wanted you to go *downstairs?* Visitors aren't usually allowed down there."

"I'm not a client, I'm a friend." That was stretching the truth—she had never been fond of Rachel—but it seemed to do the trick.

"Got it," the boy said, "Jack to the rescue."

He went to the rear of the foyer, where she had already looked, and beckoned her to follow. Rachel must have known she wouldn't have found the door on her own, neatly hidden in the paneling as it was.

About four feet from the left wall, approximately where you would expect a doorknob on some other entrance, Jack put his hand flat on the wall and pressed.

A piece of paneling slid aside like something out of *Clue*, revealing a landing and a service staircase that led down to a basement or cellar. Unlike the handsome staircase in the foyer, this one was utilitarian—unpainted, undecorated, and uncarpeted. Claudia had read enough Patricia Cornwell books that she could imagine the rationale: easy cleanup of any leaked fluids. The coconut pancakes lurched in her stomach.

For a second or two, she teetered on the landing, having second thoughts about descending the steep, poorly lit staircase. But she had promised Matt, and she had no intention of returning home and confessing to Joel that she had chickened out. With a thumbs up to her young rescuer, she moved onto the first step. "Thanks, Jack. You're the best."

"When you get to the bottom, turn left at the end of the hallway," Jack said with a nod and a friendly grin, then closed the door behind her.

With a quiver of misgiving, Claudia descended to the mortuary level, reaching the bottom more than a little pleased to have made it without falling and breaking her neck. There appeared to be just one direction to take, and she moved along it as Jack had directed. At the end of the L-shaped hallway was a sharp turn, and a sudden cold breeze chilled her skin. For a millisecond she thought, *"Ghost."* Then she got a grip and realized the cold air must be coming from the outside—likely, a loading area where a van would park to make a delivery, or a hearse could pick up a casket headed to the cemetery. Before the turning at the L was a door with a window, and a printed sign on the wall next to it:

WARNING – LIMITED ACCESS AREA

The prep room where Rachel the mortician worked her magic. She had notified Claudia on the phone that all visitors were required to sign a waiver. "To keep the funeral home and our license safe from being responsible for any harm you might suffer. Like, from anything you witness in the embalming room." She had recited the warning smugly, as if daring her to take the risk.

Claudia knocked, and bracing herself against anything she "might witness that could be harmful," she opened the door and entered. At first glance, the brightly lit room looked like any surgical suite. Typical hard-surfaced counters and cabinets. What made a stark departure from the familiar were the positioning hooks, the body lift suspended from the ceiling, the embalming machine, fume hoods, and ventilation system, the floor drain. A not unpleasant, but faintly astringent chemical odor caught her nose and made her eyes water. She sniffed, reminded of vinegar and burnt matches.

"Embalming fluid," Rachel informed her without turning around. Clad in blue scrubs, her long black hair scrunched in a messy bun on top of her head, she was hunched over a stainless steel wheeled table. A second table held a sheet-covered corpse. The third was unoccupied. "The waiver is on the desk," she said. "Sign it quick, or you'll have to leave."

Claudia made her way to a messy desk at the back of the room and found the waiver and a pen on top of a stack of file folders. She ran her eye over it to see what she was signing, scratched her signature on the printed line. "Thanks for talking to me when you're so busy," she said, looking around for a place to stand where she would not be in the way, and also to avoid looking at the occupied tables.

Not looking up, Rachel jerked her head to a spot at the head of the empty table. "Over there."

Positioning herself where the mortician had indicated, Claudia could see that she was painstakingly applying a pink-toned lipstick to the mouth of an elderly woman who could have been peacefully sleeping. A sheet covered most of the body, stopping just short of the neck. The snowy white hair had been coiffed and styled as thoroughly as if she had been to an expensive salon.

"You have real artistic talent, Rachel. She looks so natural."

"As long as the family can say, 'wow, that looks like her,' and her spirit doesn't tell me that what I did sucks, I'll be happy."

"Her *spirit?* Do you see them?"

Rachel swiveled around on her stool, her dark eyes owlish behind black framed glasses and a surgical mask. "Yeah. Sometimes."

"Like—?"

She pulled the mask down under her chin. Her expression relaxed into something less stern. "Like the little angel I worked on last week. She was three. The family got T-boned—a DUI. You can't imagine what they were going through."

Claudia stopped herself from saying that she could imagine it all too well. Her sister-in-law had been killed by a drunk driver, leaving behind a grieving husband and twelve-year-old daughter. Rachel wasn't listening anyway.

"That poor baby needed a whole lot of reconstruction." Her gaze softened. "Little ones like that are always the hardest. Here was this precious child at her own funeral, seeing her parents crying and wailing, trying to understand what was wrong with them. I saw an older woman spirit with her, holding her hand. Grandma, I'd imagine. She was fine on the other side, but her people didn't know it."

"You saw her at her own funeral?" The concept was not new to Claudia, who had a friend who was learning to be a medium. But down in the basement prep room, it took on a new reality.

"The dead are often taken to their funerals. Mostly it seems to be the ones who need closure for some reason," Rachel said, then added nonchalantly, "Sometimes they show up when I'm working alone down here in the middle of the night. That's always interesting."

"That sounds damn scary."

She shrugged. "Death isn't scary, but it can be startling when an apparition shows up."

Her casual comment tempted Claudia to look over her shoulder. Aside from the clients on the tables, she was reassured to note that the two of them were the sole occupants of the room. That she could see, anyway.

As if she had caught herself being too friendly with someone she wanted to keep at arm's length, Rachel's black eyes hardened again, and she pulled her mask back up over her mouth and nose. "Your boyfriend already called me a couple of times," she said curtly. "I told him I was too busy for this crap."

"Matt hasn't been my boyfriend since high school. I have a husband, remember? I'm just helping him out with some research for the documentary he's making about Lucy Valentine. Since I was down here at the E'town Police Department, it seemed like a good opportunity to see you."

Rachel flicked a curious gaze at her. "What were you doing at the PD?"

"Talking to the detective who is in charge of Lucy's cold case."

"Then why do you need to talk to me?"

"Because you were Lucy's friend and they're not interested in reinvestigating it."

"Like they don't have current crimes to deal with."

"That's what the detective said." But the other detective, Samuel Booker, had requested her to talk to her classmates. Claudia thought for a moment about how to share the shocking news. "Before we talk about Lucy, while I was at the police station, something else came up that was, um, unexpected, to say the least."

"What do you mean?"

"There was some news about Mr. Dickson."

"Poor Mr. D. Wasn't that sad?" Above her mask, Rachel's brows knit into a frown. "And you were the one who found his body."

"Unfortunately, yes. The detective who interviewed me told me that the medical examiner has ruled that it wasn't an accident."

Rachel twirled around on her stool, her eyes wide and startled. "Not an accident? He killed himself?"

"No. Somebody did it for him. He was murdered."

"*What?* I thought he fell in the pool and drowned because he was so drunk. That's what they said on the local news."

"During the autopsy, the medical examiner found a hairline fracture at the back of his skull. They think he was hit with something hard and was pushed into the pool and left to drown."

"Omigod, I can't believe it. Look at my hand, it's shaking." Rachel laid her hand flat against her chest and said nothing for a long moment before she shook her hand a couple of times as if flinging something off it, and reached for a makeup brush from the standing tray beside her.

"That was my reaction too. I almost threw up when the detective told me."

"I wonder where they'll take him." Rachel sounded a little wistful as she picked up a small clay pot of powder. "If it was here, I would take good care of him."

"No doubt. But I'd expect once the police are finished with him, they would ship his body back east to his wife."

"Probably." Apparently done with the topic of Joshua Dickson, Rachel began to brush a pink-toned blusher on her client's cheeks with light strokes. "I don't know why you guys have to keep hounding me about Lucy. Like I told Matt, I've been working day and night since the reunion. I've been called out in the middle of the night to pick up bodies every night this week. And yesterday alone, I had three decomps to embalm and restore. *Three*. Do you have any idea what that's like? One in a couple of weeks is more than enough to cope with. I had to embalm all night." Her volume was increasing and becoming strident. "I've had to grab what little sleep I can on the couch up in the attic. My phone is never off; I'm on call all the time—"

As the tirade ran down Claudia felt her face burn from the heat of Rachel's vented spleen. "I'm sorry," she said. "You must be exhausted."

The mortician gestured at the woman on her table. "This is the one time all week I've had a chance to sit and do something peaceful, and—" Once again, she cut herself off. "What is it you want, Claudia?"

"To talk about your friendship with Lucy. As I understand it, you and Kelly Brennan were her only real friends."

"So?"

"I heard that the three of you left school together on the day she went missing. Where did you go?"

Fear, unmistakable, flared in her eyes. "Who told you that?" she breathed. What did Rachel know about Lucy Valentine to make her look so afraid?

"You know I can't say. Is it true?"

"What the hell difference does it make? She left and never came back."

"If you know something about it—"

"I don't know jack." She put the brush and pot on the tray beside her with a clatter, and Claudia could see that her hands were shaking again.

"What can you tell me about how she was in those days before she disappeared? Her mood. Did she seem upset, or scared, or—"

Rachel threw her hands up in exasperation. "You think I remember something that happened twenty-six years ago when I was sixteen?"

"I don't know. Do you? It was a major event in all our lives, and she was your close friend, wasn't she? You were one of the few interviewed by the police. Seems like something you might remember."

Unexpected tears brimmed in her eyes. She pulled off a glove and removed her glasses and mask, swiped the heel of her hand across her face. "Don't you get it? It's not something I *want* to remember."

In the silence that followed, Claudia noticed for the first time that soft music was playing—wood flutes and singing bowls. Spa music. She glanced around, seeing the underground room for what she believed it was for Rachel—a cozy nest to insulate her from the outside world—if you could call working with human remains cozy. To some extent, she had been an outcast like Lucy. But unlike Lucy she had lived to outgrow it and create a successful career for herself.

Or *had* she outgrown it? Who knew what was going on inside her? Did that teenage outcast rent space in her head even now?

"What did you three do that day?" Claudia asked, not expecting an answer.

Rachel surprised her. "Lucy was going through something—something major," she said haltingly. "She had some problems and she needed to talk. She felt desperate. So, Kelly and I cut afternoon classes and we all went to my house. I knew my mom would be at the restaurant where she worked. My stepdad was out of town, and the kids were in school and daycare." Her shoulders slumped, perhaps in surrender—throwing in the towel on a lifetime of keeping the story to herself.

"The other kids were way younger than me. I never fit in with them. That was something Lucy and I had in common—the second family shoving the first one out—maybe not physically, but in every other way." She huffed a sardonic laugh. "It was worse for her, though. My mom didn't make me babysit like hers did. Her dad moved away. Mine died when I was four."

Her eyes slid far away, and Claudia remained silent, loath to pull her back and risk losing whatever chance she had to learn what Rachel knew.

When she began speaking again, Rachel's voice was soft, as if thinking aloud. As if she had forgotten that she was not alone. "We sat in my room and smoked dope. Kelly and I kept asking what was wrong, but Lucy didn't want to tell us. Then I got this idea to play the Ouija board—that it would be fun to ask it some questions. We were stoned by then. Lucy got excited and wanted to do it, but not Kelly—she said it was going to bring in 'lower spirits' that could do us harm. Lucy told her we were going to do it and if she didn't want to join in, she could get the hell out. So, Kelly left in a huff, and it was just the two of us. When we were alone, Lucy told me what was going on with her."

"What did she tell you?" Claudia asked.

"I'd rather not say."

"I know she was pregnant."

Rachel gasped as if she had been punched. "What the—who told you that?"

"I'd rather not say," Claudia threw her own words back to her. "So what happened?"

"I was shocked, but she wanted to go ahead with the plan. We closed the curtains. I lit some candles and set up the board on the floor in my room."

Rachel gave a soft laugh. "Lucy had never played Ouija, but she put her fingers on the planchette like a pro—do you know what a planchette is?"

"It's the little heart-shaped plastic piece on wheels. Each player touches it and if a spirit is present, it's supposed to move around the board when you ask a question," Claudia said. "I have played before."

"Good, then you know how it goes. I said a little prayer and put my fingers on it, too. Then I started asking if there was a spirit that wanted to talk to us. Right away, like immediately, the planchette started moving. I've never seen it go so fast."

An eerie frisson ran down Claudia's back. "What did it say?"

"It moved to 'yes.' I asked the spirit's name, and it spelled out 'Charlie.' I asked if it was my cat Charlie, who had died that year. It moved back to 'yes' again. We both thought it was awesome that my cat showed up to give us advice."

Claudia prided herself on being openminded, but she wasn't too sure about the spirit cat. She took care not to scoff. "What did Charlie have to say?"

For a time, Rachel was silent. Then she said, "Lucy asked if her problem was going to get solved." She raised her eyes, and what Claudia saw in them made her shiver.

"And?"

"The answer was 'no.'"

"Just 'no?' Well, crap. What then?"

"She asked why. It spelled out 'danger.'"

"Seriously? You really believe it was a spirit doing that?"

"It was." Rachel's expression could not have been more grave.

"Lucy started crying and she couldn't stop. She said her mom would kick her out and she didn't know what she was going to do. I tried to tell her it was just a game and that it was me who moved the planchette, but she knew I was lying.

"She started freaking out and getting paranoid. I tried to get her to calm down, but she grabbed her backpack and took off running." Rachel closed her eyes as if she couldn't bear for Claudia to see what was in them.

"It was you who told the cops she was pregnant, wasn't it? You were the only person who knew her secret."

"Yes, I told them. I thought they should know, in case she'd—you know, hurt herself."

"Did Lucy tell you who the father was?"

"She didn't tell me *anything* else. I didn't know she—"

Whatever Rachel intended to say was cut short by the prep room door being opened. A swarthy man in a black suit poked his head in. "Are you about done with Mrs. Emory, Rache? We need to bring her upstairs." He caught sight of Claudia. "Oh, sorry, I didn't know you were with someone."

The short break gave Rachel time to gather herself. "You're fine, Darius. Yes, Mrs. E. is ready to go." She stood up. "You can take her. This lady is leaving now."

Claudia wanted to argue that she needed to stay and hear the rest, but there was nothing to do other than say "thank you for your time" and make her way back upstairs.

Where had Lucy gone after that Ouija board session? If she was to believe that the spirit of Charlie the cat was manipulating the board as Rachel claimed, what did 'danger' mean? Not something Claudia could take to Detective Booker, even though the prediction had proved unfortunately true. Had the answer influenced Lucy to harm herself?

She climbed into the Jaguar, puzzling it all out. Rachel had said they were all stoned. At the tender age of sixteen, Lucy must have not understood the effect cannabis would have had on her developing fetus—or maybe she knew and didn't care.

Lucy had left Rachel's house, had gone home and—left her mother that note? No. The note was not her handwriting, Claudia was quite certain of it.

Then who wrote it? Had Rachel lied just now? Had she gone home with Lucy and written the note for her, disguising her handwriting? But for what purpose? Maybe she had helped Lucy run away, and kept her secret until now.

It wouldn't do any good to analyze Rachel's current handwriting to compare to the note. It would have been affected by her life experiences over time, and changes in temperament as she aged. But if she could get some of her handwriting from high school—

That was when Claudia had a lightbulb moment.

Chapter twenty-two

Joel phoned while Claudia was on the road. He had been called out to a homicide and expected to be home late, which left her evening free.

As keen as she was to get back to Playa de la Reina, the stop-and-go traffic on the 405 from Edentown was the worst Claudia had ever seen—unrelenting all the way. It was dark when she climbed out of the Jag after the four-hour nail-biting drive, too many miles of it facing directly into the sun. Ten minutes from home, she ordered pizza delivery, and fell through the front door after six o'clock.

She exchanged business attire for comfy old sweats and opened a bottle of Pinot Noir, savoring the slow uncoiling of tight muscles that had hardened into blocks of concrete. When the pizza arrived, she ate two slices of pepperoni with extra cheese—the coconut pancakes of the morning were a distant dream—while her mind ticked through the plan that had formed while she battled gridlock.

Claudia covered the pizza for Joel, went in search of her folding kitchen ladder, and lugged it up to the office.

Her yearbooks from middle school and high school were in two stacks on the top shelf of the closet. She reached for the *Edentown Pioneers 1999* and pulled it down. The title and a cartoon image of the school mascot were embossed in gold foil on the royal blue faux leather cover.

Like rewinding a video, the last day of high school replayed in her head. The same as the last day of every year of school. With no regular classes scheduled, students scribbling notes in each other's books; exchanging goodbye messages with friends and classmates who would be leaving for college in the coming weeks or months. All those kids were in their early forties now. Like her. Fewer than half of them had attended the reunion.

Claudia carried the thick book over to a long folding table that she kept standing for occasions when extra space was needed, like now. Shoving aside a stack of file folders and pile of books, she set the yearbook on it and opened it out flat. She flipped through the pages, stopping to read some of the notes.

"2 cool 2 B 4 Gotten"

"H.A.G.S." It took a minute to remember the meaning of the initials: "have a great summer."

"The sweetest girl in school"

"Hoes be winning"

"Y2K coming—end of the world as we know it" *Yeah, we all know what happened with that.*

A large portion of the real estate on the inside front cover was taken up by Kelly's hopeful message—starry-eyed plans for their future written in blue ink—not so different from what Claudia had written in hers, though she had long since forgotten the specifics.

Next came Matt's declaration of undying love that had lasted until the end of summer, when he left for university. Skimming through the teachers she paused at Josh Dickson's smiling face with sadness. He and Sue Goldman both looked so young and happy, unaware that twenty-five years later he would meet such an appalling fate. Murder, Detective Booker had said. Just the thought of it made her stomach flip.

She came to the message Lupe had written down the left edge of the page that held her class photo: "It was a blast working with you on the *Echo* this year. Have a fun summer. Laterz, Lupe Garcia"

Vincent Ramsey had scrawled his illegible signature at a diagonal slant across his photo, nothing more.

The other reporters on the *Echo* editorial team had each penned a few words.

"What's up, Claudia? Stay outta trouble! Bill Spencer"

"No more homework, no more books. No more teachers dirty looks, haha. Luv ya, Joe Martin"

"Listen to Mr. D—dont drink 'n drive!!! Your the best. ." Being reminded of the lousy speller Teri was made her smile.

Since Lupe had pointed the finger at Natalie Parker as the ringleader of the girls referred to in Lucy's note to herself, Claudia searched out a message from her, and for good measure, Bethany Grainger, another of the girls who had hung out with Nat and Andie that year. She couldn't find an entry from either Bethany or Natalie, but Andie had written, "Dearest Claudia, stay as sweet as you are. Your friend, Andrea Adams."

Rachel Thomas, instead of writing a message, had chosen to draw a clever self-caricature, depicting herself with a long nose and heavy black bangs that covered her eyes. She had signed her name across the cartoon face, not her class photo as Vincent had done, and had written the pessimistic misquote, "good girls finish last" in black marker pen.

Claudia snapped photos of the various handwritings in the book using her iPad camera, then emailed them all to herself. At her desk she woke up her PC and launched the graphics editing software she used in her document examination work.

Her plan was to compare each of the handwritings of the classmates she had selected to the handwriting in the note that had been left for Lucy's mother on the day of her disappearance. She would not be looking at personality traits. What interested her were the basic letter designs, characteristics, and features, so she could familiarize herself with the way they each wrote naturally. It was a long shot, but if any of them had written that note for some reason, she might be able to identify the writer.

Claudia enlarged the images on the monitor, one at a time. Loading up the printer with matte photo paper, she printed out the samples that warranted further analysis.

When they were all printed, she spread them out on the table and began to look closer at them. When she felt that she had a good grasp of the writing patterns in each, she inspected the enlarged copy of the note again.

> Mom
> I need space.
> Don't go looking for me. You won't find me.
> I'll be back when I can.
> Your daughter, Lucy

The deformed character of the writing was such that she was convinced it had been written by someone's awkward hand—the one not used for writing. Unless the person had an injury to the hand or wrist, switching hands would normally be done in an attempt to disguise the identity of the actual writer. It didn't add up for the girl to have written it that way herself, though it was signed "Lucy." What reason could there be for her to disguise her handwriting and then sign her own name? And why write "Your daughter?"

Something Rachel had said came back. She and Lucy had been smoking dope that afternoon, which would have an effect on handwriting. But *this* effect? Claudia had read about cannabis in teens being linked to depression, and depression tended to reduce the size of handwriting—like Lucy's everyday writing. The handwriting in the note was large. Alcohol tended to increase the size of handwriting. Rachel had only mentioned pot, not alcohol.

She pushed that aside and went on to her comparisons of the other students with Lupe's handwriting. Lupe, the *Echo* editor, had used a thick, rust-colored felt-tip pen to write in the yearbook, printing her message in an upper case style, which fit her confident, chin-first personality type. She was right-handed. Could she have produced those forms in the note using her left hand?

Claudia, who was right-handed, dug out a felt tip pen from her desk drawer and a sheet of paper from the printer. Using her left hand, she attempted to copy the note.

The results were less than beautiful, and the felt tip distorted the writing to a laughable degree.

Setting aside Lupe's writing, she picked up the photo of Matt's message. His protestations of innocence aside, just because he was making the documentary was not a good reason to exclude him. In fact, reminding herself that people who received anonymous notes were often found to have been the author themselves, it was a good reason for inclusion.

Matt's printed handwriting was well organized and balanced in every respect. If he had done something to Lucy and was desperate to send everyone in a different direction, fear would have had a strong effect on his writing. But *this* effect? As much as she did not want to find anything incriminating, she had to be honest with herself. One or two letter forms were in some ways similar and made her want to look at it further, but they did not meet the criteria to make an identification. Then there was the question of how he would have gotten the note into her room.

He would have known about the door to the outside.

Rachel's handwriting was an upper and lower case mixture of print and cursive style with a high degree of tight angles. There was nothing consistent with the note that Claudia could find, which had more rounded forms.

Andrea Adams—Andie—was last. Her cursive writing had more curves than angles and was compact. The emphasis was on the middle zone—the vowels and some other letters. The upper extensions, on letters such as l and h, and lower extensions on g, j, y and z were short and cramped. She could not imagine Andie writing that crazy-looking note. She had been a good girl to the nth degree; someone who desperately wanted to please, not just her cousin Natalie, but everyone. Chances were, her parents had tried to shield her from any kind of pain, which meant she never learned to soften the blows of everyday life. Parents who didn't do their kids any favors. She had grown into a follower who had trouble making her own decisions. Nat, on the other hand, had been ready and willing to tell her what to do. Too bad she didn't have Nat's handwriting in the yearbook.

An hour into her examination, Claudia had to concede that the handwriting samples were too short to provide the information she was looking for. The few similar features she had come across that made her wonder—like what she had noticed in Matt's message—did not contain enough letter combinations to allow her to make any firm conclusions.

Then it hit her.

Lucy Valentine had disappeared in 1998, the year *before* their class graduated. She was looking at the wrong yearbook. The writing in the *Junior* yearbook might be somewhat different. She felt like doing a face palm.

A second trip up the ladder. Another examination of the handwritings of the same students in the earlier yearbook with disappointing results. Their handwritings were, as she had expected, less developed, less mature than the ones they had penned in their senior year, but basically, they were the same.

Bottom line, none of the handwritings she had examined could be easily matched up with the writing in the note. *Damn.*

There was one new handwriting to add to the pile of prints: Natalie Parker's. In Claudia's junior yearbook, she had written a typically narcissistic message: "I hate that you're so tall. You're a nice girl, but why can't you be shorter?" She had drawn a gigantic heart and written her name on it, followed by "VOTE FOR NATALIE JANE PARKER FOR PRESIDENT!"

As usual, the world revolved around Nat, even in her yearbook message.

Claudia sank into the chair behind her desk and topped off her glass from the bottle of wine. A wave of disappointment crashed over her. The evening had been pretty much a bust.

Chapter twenty-three

Friday, October 13

Joel was already up and moving around by the time Claudia opened her eyes to raindrops pattering at the window on a grey, drizzly morning. He had gotten home late the night before. Worn out after the long day and more wine than she was accustomed to drinking, she had fallen asleep early, and it barely registered when he crawled into bed and spooned against her. She was just conscious enough to scoot back against him, and to hear his soft snores begin faster than she could blink.

No more than four or five hours later she reached out a hand and found the sheets cold on his side of the bed. Unable to properly wake up, and fumbling with an unpleasant sluggishness that left her feeling dopey, she listened to him in the shower, then getting dressed. And then he was gone, his goodbye kiss lingering on her lips.

Her scalp throbbed as if thumbscrews were being tightened all around her head. She sat up and perched on the edge of the bed, regretting that she had not gone downstairs with him for the few minutes it would have taken to brew a pot of coffee and make toast.

She scrabbled in her nightstand drawer for a bottle of ibuprofen to ward off the iron helmet of a hangover headache, shook out two, and swallowed them with half a bottle of water. Last evening, she had convinced herself that she deserved to relax with a "couple" of drinks. Rarely did she drink more than two glasses of wine in a sitting. That she had polished off the entire bottle was testimony to her frustration.

The lack of sufficient handwritten materials for her examination continued to gnaw at her like a rat on a rope. Short of calling each of the people on her list of possibilities and asking for any old handwriting samples they could give her, her efforts were scotched.

"Did you happen to keep any of your 1998 homework?" was unlikely to produce anything more helpful than a look of "are you stoned?" or worse.

The sound of her cell phone was an icepick against her temple. The Edentown area code was familiar, but not the phone number. She let the call go to voicemail and flung herself back on the pillow. There was no one she wanted to speak to in her hometown until she was more alert and her head wasn't throbbing.

Matt had to be brought up to speed about her trip south—the results of her visit with Lupe and the two detectives, and Rachel. She would not mention her misgivings about his handwriting and its possible similarities to the note Lucy's mother had found. But it was lodged firmly in the back of her mind and refused to budge.

She drifted on a cloud for a while as the icepick started to soften its blows against her head. And as she drifted, something niggled in her brain that didn't want to be puzzled out. She let it go, and was dozing off when the phone rang again. Kelly.

Claudia tapped the answer button with a groan. "What?"

"What's up chickadee? Anything new on the freezing cold case of Miss Lucy V?"

"Do you have to be so frigging cheerful?"

"Oh, my; who peed in *your* cornflakes this morning?"

"Pee—*no* Noir," Claudia answered sourly. "I was trying to sleep it off, but the damn phone keeps ringing."

Kelly snickered. "I get the hint, but I'm going to ignore it. Who else called you at o'dark thirty besides me?"

"E'town area code. Lupe, is my guess. I haven't listened to the voicemail yet, so your curiosity will have to go unsatisfied."

"Lupe Garcia? Did you meet up with the dirty laundry queen yesterday? That woman would do well to use a glue stick in place of lip balm."

"You do have a way with words."

"That's one reason you love me forever. How'd it go?"

"How did it go?" Claudia yawned and peeled out of bed, grabbed her robe from the chair where she'd left it and headed downstairs, shrugging into it as she went. "Aside from the worst drive home ever?"

"Yada yada, L.A. traffic, what else is new? I'm waiting for the Lupe deets."

Kelly's courtroom skills were legendary because she was bloody-minded enough to never give up. There was no point in trying to put her off sharing the particulars, so Claudia didn't bother to hedge. "Yes, I did see Lupe, and I learned one important new thing from her."

"You did? Tell me..."

"She told me that you were with Rachel and Lucy the day Lucy disappeared."

She heard a sharp intake of breath, then a long silence. "Well, shit, Claudia. That wasn't her business to spread. And where did she get it from?"

"She didn't say."

"Damn. What else did you do on your fucktangular fact-finding mission?"

"Is that a new word? Fucktangular?"

Kelly affected a prim, librarian voice. "Fucktangular: A situation that's complicated and messy in multiple unpleasant and difficult ways."

"Ah. Well, yes, it is that," Claudia agreed. "I also had the dubious pleasure of chatting with your personal friend Rachel Thomas while she was painting the face of a corpse."

"Ewww."

"She actually did a very nice job on a lady my great-grandma's age."

"Your great-grandma is dead."

"There you go."

"What did you expect to get from Rachel?" Kelly asked, and something in the way she tried, and failed to sound casual, perked up Claudia's attention.

"What I *expected* to get was some background on Lucy's attitude around the time she went missing. What I got was filled in on some of the details about the actual day. More than I ever got from you, my alleged 'BFF.'"

"What did she say?"

"She confirmed what Lupe told me. Why didn't you ever tell me that the two of you were with Lucy after she left gym that day?"

The silence went on long enough for Claudia to count to five in her head. When Kelly spoke again, the chirpiness had gone out of her voice, leaving her curiously subdued.

"It was too traumatic to think about," she said softly. "I wanted to block the whole thing out. I mean, you're with someone and they just vanish into thin air a few hours later. Poof."

"Yes, it was traumatic, and worse for you, being closer to her. But it's not like you to keep something of that magnitude from me."

"Yeah, I know, I know," Kelly muttered. "I wanted to tell you. It's just, every time I tried to talk about it, it felt like I was choking. The words wouldn't come out. Then, after that detective questioned me—the guy you talked to—"

"Radnor?"

"Yeah, him. After he let me go, I kept telling myself that if I didn't talk about it, it never happened."

Claudia was not one to nurse hard feelings, but she felt the sharp thorn of resentment scratching at her. She and Kelly had propped each other up since kindergarten through countless highs and lows, and the lie by omission had happened too long ago to hold a stupid grudge, but right now, she was not quite ready to forgive and forget.

"How about you tell me about the Ouija board," she said.

"Christ on a bicycle. I never thought of Rachel as a backstabber. Guess I'll have to change that opinion. She has no subtlety at all. She's a goddamned front stabber." Kelly sucked in a breath that could fill a balloon, then exhaled it into the phone.

"There's not much to tell. There was Lucy, being all miserable and morose. She kept telling us that she had this major problem, but she wouldn't say what it was. We had no idea she was pregnant—not that there was anything we could have done for her if we *had* known. I mean, if *I'd* known, I would have been all over her. I would have made her tell who knocked her up. As it was, I just felt stupid and helpless. Helplessly stupid. And then, out of the blue, Rachel decides she's going bring out the Ouija board and ask the spirits for help, which scared the pants off me."

"And don't forget the part where you were all smoking dope, which I'm sure made you paranoid, too." Claudia said, not caring that she sounded smug.

"Omigod, is there anything she *didn't* tell you?"

"I don't know, Kelly. *Is* there?"

"No. I swear to God, there isn't. When Rachel got out that witch board and closed the blinds and started lighting candles, I hightailed it the hell out of there. I was definitely not into summoning up spirits of the dead. I got plenty of that creepy shit at home. I wasn't about to be doing it at Rachel's house. Of course, it wouldn't scare me now. I *might* even play it if—no, Claudia don't you dare suggest we do it."

Claudia had forgotten the factoid about Kelly's mother being into the occult for a time. She mainly associated Georgia Brennan with hanging out in bars and bringing home a string of strange men—which was why most of Kelly's teen years were spent at the Bennett home.

Kelly laughed. "Remember when my mom was into that ridiculous black magic phase?"

"Yes, I do remember." Claudia felt a stab of sympathy on Kelly's behalf. "Omigod, you were so humiliated when she started threatening to put spells on some of those guys when they got tired of her."

"She scared that one guy shitless when she started sticking pins in a voodoo doll and told him she was going to—" Kelly interrupted herself and returned to the topic at hand. "Never mind that. Rachel didn't know what to do with Lucy. She was trying to distract her with the board. I never talked to her about it, so I have no idea what happened afterwards."

"The board didn't have good news for her," Claudia said, and summarized what Rachel had told her.

Kelly laughed, a loud guffaw. "Come on, dude, you can't mean she took the spirit of Rachel's *cat* seriously?"

"It's so not funny, Kel. Lucy was a desperate sixteen-year-old looking for help. The question is, what happened after she left Rachel's house?"

"What do you mean? We know she went home and wrote that note for her mom and—"

"No, she didn't."

"What—how do you—?"

"That note wasn't written by Lucy, if for no other reason than first, it's completely incompatible with her handwriting, and second, there would be no point in disguising her writing and then signing it with her real name."

Kelly started to speak, but was cut off by the beep of an incoming call. Claudia glanced at the screen and saw the same number she had ignored earlier. "I need to see who this is. I'll keep you posted. Later." Leaving no time for argument, she switched over.

The female voice that spoke was older than she remembered it, but Claudia recognized it right away.

"Is this Claudia Bennett? Sue Goldman here; Ms. Goldman, from Edentown High School? Your English teacher? Why the *hell* would you give my name to that detective? Booker? Detective Booker. He left me a message that he wants to talk to me about Josh Dickson because *you* said he should call me? Why does he want to talk to me about Josh?"

Damn Booker. Rachel had nothing on his *big mouth.*

The angry spate of words fizzled, and Claudia hunted for an explanation that would not inflame Sue Goldman any further. In the end, she chose the truth. As it had with Josh Dickson, it felt strange to be talking to her teacher as a peer.

"Detective Booker is talking to a lot of people who were at the reunion, Ms. Goldman, not just you. At the banquet, someone mentioned to a group of us that you and Mr. Dickson had what they thought looked like an argument, and they were concerned about it. Any of the people at our table might have mentioned it to Booker, and yes, I did say he should talk to you."

"Who said there was an argument? You tell me right now who said that, Claudia. I have a right to know." She made the demand in such a firm tone that for a second or two, Claudia was back in AP English being chastised for passing notes in class with Andie Adams.

She kicked Lupe to the curb without compunction. "It was Lupe who said it. The detective wanted to know if she was right, and there *was* an argument."

Goldman sounded bewildered. "Even if we did have an argument, why would the detective care? How is it even his business?"

He wants to know whether you're a suspect... No, that was not the way to go. "Er—he wanted to know in case it had something to do with Mr. Dickson's death," Claudia said.

"I don't understand. Wh—what—why would it have anything to do with his death?" Ms. Goldman's voice cracked with emotion.

Double damn you, Booker.

Hit with a pang of regret, Claudia dropped the news about her teacher's old friend, maybe lover. "I'm truly sorry to be the one to tell you this, Ms. Goldman, but the autopsy report showed that it wasn't an accidental death. Mr. Dickson was murdered."

"No! No! That can't be right."

The teacher's agonized cry tore right through Claudia. If she'd had any questions about Sue Goldman's feelings for Josh Dickson, they were answered in her anguished wail. She let the seconds tick past until Goldman was calmer and could speak coherently. Her first question was whether there had been an arrest.

"No, they haven't caught the killer yet."

"But the news said that he drowned." Goldman's voice began to rise. "What really happened to him? Oh, poor Josh."

Claudia hesitated, reluctant to cause her further distress. "The medical examiner found evidence that he was knocked unconscious before he was pushed into the pool."

"Oh. My. God. He was mugged? Oh my—"

Before she could unleash another wail, Claudia interrupted. "What makes you say that?"

"What else could it have been?"

Interesting. Rachel had assumed suicide as an alternate scenario, and Goldman assumed mugging.

Claudia said, "Detective Booker didn't say anything about a mugging. He believes that someone either went outside with him or followed him out there."

"It wasn't a crime of opportunity? You mean—are you saying it was deliberate? That someone *intended* to—to *kill* him? Oh, my good lord, as if it wasn't bad enough that he's dead, but, oh God, you're saying someone *killed* him..."

She could hear Sue Goldman start to hyperventilate. Then the line went dead. Goldman had ended the call without signing off.

There was something distinctly off about her old teacher's reaction. Was the lady protesting too much? And what *had* their argument been about?

Chapter twenty-four

Claudia met Matt for coffee and sandwiches at Tyler's Coffee House. The rain was coming down too hard for a walk, and even the short dash from the car left her drenched. Shaking the wet out of her hair, she brought him up to speed on what she had learned so far. When she had wrapped it all up with the phone call from Sue Goldman, his brows were furrowed, but not for the reason she expected.

"You've really accomplished a lot," he said. "You're not going to let this Dickson thing distract you, are you?"

"This *'Dickson thing?'*" she repeated, hardly able to restrain the spate of anger that blew through her. "I shouldn't get distracted by our high school teacher being *murdered?* No, Matt, I'm not going to be distracted. I just need five minutes to process it before leaving it behind. *You* didn't hear Ms. Goldman wailing on the phone like I did."

Matt had the grace to look embarrassed. "I'm glad I didn't have to hear that. Hey, I'm sorry if I came across unsympathetic. I'm not. At all. It's a stunner for all of us—and her more than anyone." He shook his head. "You don't expect someone you knew and liked to be murdered, even when you haven't seen them in twenty-five years. I'm sorry, Claudia, I'm just totally focused on the film project."

"It's *your* project, Matt, but I did make a two-hundred-mile round trip yesterday and interview, let's review it again: Lupe. Detective Watson. We'll set aside Detective Booker, as that was the 'other' case I'm not going to let distract me. Oh, don't forget my chat with Rachel in an embalming room—"

Matt's face reddened. "Would you stop? I get it, I get it. I'm a total moron. I can't tell you how grateful I am—"

"Cut the crap, Matt. I'm not fishing for compliments. I just want you to recognize that while you've been busy with your other project, *something* has been happening."

"I don't take your efforts lightly," he protested. "I'm serious about that. What you got from Rachel is invaluable. It's gonna add something significant to the film." He brightened and she was reminded again of what had attracted her all those years ago. Like the film director he was, he spread his hands in the shape of a frame. "I'm seeing a re-enactment with the Ouija board scene—Kelly freaking out and running off, leaving the other two girls bent over the board, the candle flickering in the dark—"

"One man's tragedy is another man's documentary," Claudia murmured dryly.

Matt winced. "You know what, Claudia? Sometimes, you can be downright cruel."

She grinned. "Takes one to know one, right?"

He bit into his turkey on sourdough and chewed thoughtfully. "Now that you and Sue Goldman are besties, maybe you can pave the way for me—us—to talk to her about Lucy. What do you think—get a teacher's point of view?"

"We're hardly besties, especially with me dropping the bomb on her. Plus, she's not happy that I gave her up to Booker," Claudia said, relenting. "But I could give her a call tomorrow and see if she's up for an interview—one that's not about Mr. D—though I don't know what she could add…"

"You are the best!"

"You just said I was cruel."

"You are, but you redeemed yourself."

"Redeemed myself? That makes me want to slug you." She said it as a joke. Matt did not need to know that her mind was already turning over excuses she could use to get their former English teacher to agree to an interview for the documentary. And to reveal the subject of her supposed argument with Joshua Dickson.

The niggling feeling from earlier that morning had dug in like a tick and was scratching at Claudia' temporal lobe—the part of the brain that controls memory—the hippocampus, where new memories form, and the amygdala, where old memories go to hide. It tickled like an untriggered sneeze all afternoon.

After she and Matt went their separate ways, Claudia went home and spent some time catching up on emails she had neglected. An inquiry from a public defender's office in another county, asked if she would take on a case that involved a threat note. She responded in the affirmative and two minutes later she received PDF files of the documents.

She was often appointed by judges in criminal cases to assist in the defense of an indigent client who could not afford her standard rates. In this case, the client was charged with bank robbery, and the enhancement of making a terrorist threat. He had been caught on camera entering a bank and handing a teller a threat written on a generic deposit slip. The question was did he write the threat?

> I HAVE A BOMB – DO what I say anD we go HOme in one piece. Put the money in the bag. Don't put no dye.

Along with the note, which the client denied writing, the attorney had included a grainy black and white bank photo of him handing it over—which would not influence her examination of the handwriting.

A first glance at the exemplar samples showed both similarities and differences to the threat note. Looking closer, Claudia began to see tiny peculiarities that were apparent in both the questioned and the known handwriting. He wrote it.

As she worked on the case, the memory sneeze moved closer to the surface. Doing her best to ignore it, she wrote her declaration for the attorney—it would not help the guilty client but would demonstrate that the public defender had done due diligence in preparing his client's defense.

Joel had promised to be home at a reasonable time, and Claudia had promised to cook. Grandma's meatloaf and mashed potatoes—the perfect meal for the rainy evening.

She diced the onion and bell pepper and mixed them in a bowl with the ground beef, then added ketchup, mustard, egg, milk—the perfect relaxing, mindless activity. She was kneading the crushed Ritz cracker crumbs into the mixture when her brain pulled the trigger on the sneeze.

"Sweet Jesus!"

Claudia washed the muck off her hands and shoved the bowl into the fridge. Something more urgent was calling than meatloaf.

Checking the weather from the service porch door, Claudia ran down the back steps without bothering to search out an umbrella. It was nippy outside, but the rain had slowed to a drizzle. She unlocked the person door to the garage. It had been many weeks, maybe longer, since she had last been inside. The garage was for storage; their vehicles sat outside the rollup door.

As though all the stale, frigid air had collected over those weeks, a blast colder than the outdoors hit her when she opened the door, penetrating her fleece sweats. Shivering, she flipped on the light switch and surveyed the mess in dismay.

When they got married two years ago, Joel had given up his apartment and officially moved into Claudia's house. Pieces of furniture he had hung onto, boy's toys, miscellaneous sports equipment. He had stacked his belongings in front of the shelves that held her boxes. Theirs was not the worst garage jumble she had ever seen, but neither did it come anywhere close to competing with Troy Valentine's *uber*-neat space.

No question, this was a job for two. She turned out the light and hurried back upstairs, glad for an excuse to get back to the warmth of the house.

Joel arrived home at the promised time. The meatloaf and mashed potatoes were ready, and when they sat down to eat, they both agreed that it was the best she had ever made. They exchanged their news of the day, and when she described her brief incursion into the garage, Joel volunteered to help.

"It can wait until tomorrow," Claudia protested weakly. "You look tired."

"It's the weekend. I can sleep in." He gave her a penetrating stare. "Am I wrong in thinking you're itching to get into that box and to search for old handwriting samples?"

"Well, no, but..."

"Okay, then. Let's do it."

They cleared off the table and left the dishes to soak in soapy water. Then, bundled into warm jackets, they went down the back stairs.

The condition of the garage had not magically improved in the hours since Claudia's visit. Joel surveyed the clutter in front of him. "Shit, I never realized I'd left such a mess. After Pete and I shoved it all in here, I never gave it another thought. As you can see."

Claudia laughed. "I never claimed to be Felix Unger, but you make a good Oscar Madison."

"You're comparing us to *The Odd Couple?* C'mon, I'm not that bad, am I?"

She laughed. "I plead the fifth."

Joel scratched his head in resignation. "I can see what I'll be doing on my next couple of days off—making a trip to the dump with half this crap."

"Maybe Pete will be nice and let you use his truck. It's brother-in-law duty."

"Good idea. Where do we start?"

Claudia indicated a plastic-wrapped queen-sized mattress that stood in front of the shelving. "The box I'm hoping to find should be behind the mattress on the top shelf. If we can slide it aside—"

"You mean after we move all the bins that are blocking the mattress? How sure are you that it's there?"

"*Fairly* sure, but I need to see."

Joel shucked his bulky jacket and, ignoring the cold, began hefting the plastic tubs and bins, stacking them off to the side. There was not enough room in the cramped space for both of them to work, so Claudia stood aside and relished watching his well-toned muscles bulge and ripple in his short-sleeved T-shirt. Her heart squeezed with love for every molecule, from his short salt-and-pepper hair down to his running shoe-clad toes. It made her want to jump him right then and there in the garage. She reminded herself why they were there and reined in her lust.

A few minutes later he had opened up a path to the mattress. Getting into position on each side, she pushed, he pulled. Moving the cumbersome thing and its box springs left them both out of breath.

"This is definitely headed for the dump," Joel grumbled.

"Oh, but think of all the happy hours we spent romping on it," Claudia said. "Hey, there's the box I need."

Joel liberated a box marked "CARDS, ETC" that she pointed to, and carried it all the way upstairs to her office. The moment he set it on the floor in front of the sofa Claudia dove in and began to explore its contents. At the door, Joel half-turned back. "I think a shower is called for after that archaeological excavation. Wanna come scrub my back? I'll scrub yours—"

Buried deep in old school papers, Claudia raised her eyes with an absentminded smile. "Oh, I do want to. But I'm not going to let you distract me. My brain has been working overtime on this all day, and now..."

"Never mind. I require your full attention. I'll wait until I can get it."

"I'm sorry, really I am, but—"

"Just remember, Grapholady, you owe me."

Fighting the temptation to jump up and follow him anyway, she said, "Put it on my tab. I promise, I'm good for it. And by the way, thanks for the help."

With a salute and a nod, Joel disappeared into the hallway.

The box was the repository of every greeting card Claudia had received over the years and wanted to keep. There was no filing system, just a pile of cards. She dug through them, pausing to read those that had special memories attached. It did not take long to find the one that had triggered the earlier mental sneeze. A Valentine's Day card from Matt. On the front was a cartoon drawing of a saltine cracker and a triangle of cheese, and the printed words: "We go together like Cheese & Crackers!"

Inside the card, he had written, "We are better together. All my love, Matt"

She could still feel the excitement that had fizzed through her veins the night he had handed it to her, along with the traditional bouquet of red roses and a box of See's chocolates. He took her to The Homestead, Edentown's nicest restaurant. Her heart had been pounding hard enough to leap out of her chest. In fact, she had been left breathless, and had to break off their kiss and come up for air. He had wrapped it all up in a metaphorical bow that made her think they would be together forever.

And then, four months later when they graduated, after tearfully telling her how hard it would be to leave her, Matt announced that he was going to school on the East Coast. He didn't even ask her to wait for him or promise to write.

You broke my seventeen-year-old heart, you bastard.

That had been the one and only Valentine's Day they had together. She set the card to one side and continued her search. She kept digging for the Christmas and birthday cards he had given her, which must be somewhere in the pile.

There were letters in the box as well. She read through some of them, reminded of events in her life, good and bad. Sweet letters from her grandmother from childhood on. High school laments from Kelly, typically when she was going through one breakup or another, and sometimes delirious ones about new crushes. There were other notes from other school friends. Homework. And finally, the sample a twenty-five-year-old Joshua Dickson had written for her to analyze.

She recognized it right away and recalled him volunteering it when he heard she was newly studying handwriting. He had said he was curious to know what she could find out about him.

Back in those days, she hadn't known what she was doing, but she gave him a list of personality traits that seemed to impress him. His approval had left her beaming.

Since she had been too inexperienced then to keep a copy of what she had given him, she was viewing what he had written with fresh eyes. She read the silliness Dickson had written for her to analyze.

"Dear Claudia,
Why didn't Han Solo enjoy his steak dinner? It was Chewie.
Why don't you ever see elephants hiding in trees? Because they're so good at it!
I've never had my handwriting analyzed. I can't wait to see what you find out about me.
Joshua M. Dickson, EHS Class of 92"

Despite what she had learned about him from Kelly, Claudia did her best to view his handwriting from an unbiased angle. It wasn't easy. Red flags jumped out at her from the mostly printed writing—too-heavy pressure. Capitals and jump-up letters in the middle of words where they didn't belong. Sinuous movement across the unlined paper. Letters slanting in every direction with no consistency in size. The personal pronoun "I" squeezed and angular. Letters bumping up against each other, which suggested a problem with boundaries. T-bars crossed at the baseline—a sure sign of self-defeating behavior. The knots in the lower zone were the kicker.

The upstrokes on the "g" and "y" were tied in a knot that twisted around the stems of the letters—a characteristic identified with victims of sexual abuse who were unable to talk about it. That gave her pause.

The redeeming feature was the spatial arrangement, which was fairly well organized. She had learned that, even if all other aspects of a handwriting sample were interpreted negatively, with a decent picture of space the writer could function well in the world.

In 1999, with enough knowledge to be dangerous, she would have copied her list of "this means that" traits from her books. The wavy baseline and changing size and slant probably translated to "whimsical," or "flexible." The heavy pressure "intense." The lower zone knots "willing to try new things." Those traits might have been true to some degree, but properly putting them in the context of the big picture produced a far more accurate interpretation.

Josh Dickson's story depressed her from start to finish. In the end, though, whatever he had done died with him. Putting his handwriting sample back in the box and continuing her search, Claudia wished he had been called to account and held responsible for his actions.

Her eye landed on a half-crumpled flyer for some long-ago school dance. She smoothed out the paper and saw a handwritten few lines:

> *"Claudia, I need you to write an article about me in the* Echo *for my Prom Queen campaign. I know you're writing one about Amanda Miller, even though you know she doesn't stand a snowball's chance. Will you do it? Pretty please. Natalie Parker"*

Typical narcissistic Nat. Claudia started to toss it back into the box, stopped by a subliminal *ping*. Claudia reached for the flyer again, and took a closer look at Natalie's handwriting. *Huh.*

Using the same procedure she had followed with the handwriting samples from the yearbook, she photographed the handwriting on Matt's card and Natalie's on the flyer. After emailing them to herself, she enlarged them on the screen and studied them, then printed them out and compared each in turn to what in her mind she called the "mom note."

In Natalie's handwriting the curved bottoms on the lower zone letters—the y's and g's, and the unusual form of the letter k had attracted her attention. There was an intriguing similarity to some of those forms in the mom note. It was insufficient for an identification, she told herself. The forms were not common, but neither were they unique to Natalie. Besides, why would she have written the "mom note?"

Matt's handwriting in the Valentine's card was no easier to match than his yearbook writing had been. The same was true of his handwriting on the other cards she eventually dug up. Regardless of how much she wanted to, Claudia could not allow herself to rule him out.

When there was nothing more to be done, she set it all aside and flipped off the office light. She slipped into bed beside her husband, who welcomed her by relieving her of the short nightie she had just wriggled into. A mere two years of marriage qualified them as newlyweds in her book.

Chapter twenty-five

Saturday, October 11

The next morning, the doorbell rang while Claudia was scrubbing the meatloaf pan.

Kelly, arriving unannounced, stood on the porch with a bag of warm almond croissants and a cardboard Starbucks cup holder containing two tall cups of coffee with a heavenly aroma.

The rain had abated, leaving behind a bank of dirty grey clouds that kept the day as gloomy as it had been all week.

"Have I forgotten something we were supposed to be doing this morning?" Claudia asked, casting a side eye at Kelly as she came inside.

Her friend handed her the bag and put a finger to her chin. "Mmmm, I can't think of anything."

"Then you're either apologizing for something, or you want me to do something, or ... what exactly is it you're doing here?"

"Can't I just drop by to bring my BFF her favorite breakfast food?"

Claudia read the brilliant smile Kelly turned on her as entirely manufactured. "Almond croissants are welcome anytime, and so are you, but I happen to know that on Friday nights you're usually having a no-pajama party with your latest dude, and you don't get up until noon on Saturday." She pointed at the kitchen clock. "It's barely nine-thirty."

"What can I say? It was a slow week for sex. Speaking of, where's your hunky hubs?"

"At the gym, so we have an hour for—whatever this is." Claudia found plates for the croissants and slid into the breakfast nook where most of the important conversations in the house happened. "Sit down and spill it."

"Honestly, Claudia, you're so suspicious."

"That's because I know you too well. Go on, I'm waiting."

"Okay, fine." Kelly took the bench on the opposite side of the table and pushed one of the coffee cups across to her with a half-hearted huff. "After you slapped me upside the head with all that dope you got from Rachel the snitch, we left things hanging. Remember, you got a phone call and never called me back? I'm sure you just forgot, right? So, I thought we could finish our conversation over a friendly pastry."

"Translation: you want to know whether it was Lupe who called me yesterday, and if so, what she said. Am I right?"

"And—was it her?"

"No, it was not." Claudia gazed at her friend, saying nothing, stretching out the suspense until Kelly was ready to pop with curiosity. At last, she told her. "It was Sue Goldman."

"Sue Goldman our English teacher? What did she want?"

"She was miffed because that day I told Detective Booker—the one who interviewed me after I found Dickson's body—what Lupe said about seeing him and Sue arguing at the cocktail party."

"Why the hell would you tell him that?"

"Because our dear Sue might have been the last person to see him. But he ratted me out to her, so I'm miffed too."

"I don't see the relevance. What did she say about it?"

Claudia opened the lid of her cup and blew across the surface of hot coffee. "She didn't deny the argument, just asked why Booker would care."

"Oops. Did you tell her someone whacked him over the head?"

"Well, not in those exact terms." Claudia felt the sting of remorse, remembering Sue Goldman's shriek of pain. "I wish I hadn't told her anything. She reacted like someone who was in love."

"Reacted like what? Screaming and crying? That's what I would do."

"That's about right." Claudia's phone sent her a news alert. She picked it up and checked the screen. "Crap. The police just announced it. It's the big headline, look." She pushed the screen toward Kelly, who said, "Holy crap," and read aloud:

> ### MURDER AT THE REUNION
> *"What appeared to be an unfortunate accident has been confirmed by the Orange County Medical Examiner as homicide. Fifty-year-old former Edentown High School teacher Joshua Dickson was found dead in the school's swimming pool during the recent reunion of the Class of '99. A popular driver education teacher and part-time assistant coach during the late 1990s, Dickson moved out of state in 2000, but was attending the reunion while visiting Edentown. Dickson was remembered fondly by members of the class and his fellow teachers at the school. No arrests have been made. Police are seeking any and all leads, and ask for the public's help."*

Kelly handed back the phone. "I wonder if Ms. Goldman has seen it."

"I feel so bad for her. Think how hard *we* took it, and we didn't even have a personal relationship with him like she did. At the very least they were close friends. Probably more than that."

Kelly picked at croissant crumbs, pushing slivers of almond around with the tip of her fingernail. Her mouth was making sounds that didn't quite get off the ground. "Uh...hmmm, uh—"

Claudia pulled apart a piece of the flaky croissant and popped it into her mouth, watching her friend and waiting to see what she was going to say. She chewed and swallowed, and the silence went on until she lost patience. "What are you 'hmmm'ing' about?"

Kelly blew out a breath big enough to flutter her lips. "This is filed under 'things I promised myself I would never tell.' But he's dead and it's about a hundred years later, so I guess it doesn't matter anymore."

"What doesn't matter? You're starting to scare me. What happened?"

"Nothing happened. Well, not exactly."

"Then, what *almost* happened?"

"Yeah, that's more like the right word." Kelly's eyes darted around the kitchen. "Is it too early for a stiff drink?"

"Uh, yeah it is. It's coffee and croissants too early."

"Oh, you know what they say; it's five o'clock somewhere…"

"Quit stalling and tell me what's making you want to drink. Now, please."

On the other side of the breakfast nook, Kelly fidgeted. Her gaze jumped from one thing to another, anywhere but at Claudia. "It's just—um, remember that thing you said a minute ago? About us not having a personal relationship with him…"

"We didn't. Did we? Did *you*? What the hell, Kelly?"

This time Kelly's sigh filled the room. Conflicting expressions warred on her face as she brushed away tears that brimmed and threatened to spill over. "Back in school, did you ever hear the rumors that Dickson used to keep a blanket in the back of the driver's ed car and invite girls to 'go for a ride' with him after classes?"

"We all heard that, I'm sure we talked about it." Claudia studied her oldest, closest friend, wondering how many important pieces of information she had withheld over the years. "It was just one of those stupid rumors ...wasn't it?"

Refusing to meet her eyes, Kelly shook her blonde head. "Unfortunately, not."

Horrified, Claudia inhaled and held it, unable to let the breath go. "And you know this, how?"

"The first time he stuck his hand up my skirt I yelled at him, 'what the fuck?' He tried to play it off like it was an accident. The next time, I stabbed him in the leg with a sharp pencil. That was the last time he tried it on me because I never got in a car with him again. And I never wore a skirt to school again, either. I wish I'd stabbed him in the nuts."

All at once, Kelly's coolness towards their driver's education teacher at the reunion made perfect sense.

"Some of the other girls thought it was exciting and fun," she said in a watery voice. "I was angry and hurt. Mostly, I was disappointed that he would be such a creep. Before—before he did that, I was like the rest of them—thought he was cute, and fun. But the truth was, he was no different from those assholes my mom used to bring home who tried to put the moves on me, even when I was a little kid." Her lips twisted in bitter self-contempt. "I should have known better with *Dick*son. It was just so freaking unexpected."

Kelly's words rang in Claudia's head. What their teacher had done made her want to puke. *"I* was one of those girls who thought he was cute and fun too," she said. It came out as a confession.

"I doubt anyone ever reported him. Or maybe they did and he moved back east because someone told on him. He might have been warned or even fired."

"I feel stupid for not knowing," Claudia said. "I'm so sorry that happened to you."

"I'm just glad he didn't pick on you too." Kelly got up and went to the worktop. She tore off a paper towel from the roll and wet it, dabbed it around her eyes. "If you think about it, he was like any predator. I look back at myself as a potential victim, and do you know what I see? So typical, so *fucking* cliché: emotionally needy girl with a shitty opinion of herself, starved for attention."

"Starved for attention from a male role model," Claudia added. Her face blazed in shame. She had been too wrapped up in her own teenage angst to pay attention to her best friend's distress.

"I wish I'd called him out on it at the reunion. I wanted to, but I couldn't quite get up the guts, even then."

Claudia was quiet, thinking about it. The neighbor who had stolen her innocence had threatened her to keep silent. But she had been a lot younger than high school age. "I wonder how many of them he tried it on with, and how many took him up on his offer. How did he get them to keep quiet about it?"

"I don't know how many, but I can tell you this: after the, er, pencil stabbing incident, he cornered me and said if I told anyone, that they wouldn't believe me. He said he would go to the authorities and say I had come on to him and had threatened to lie about him. He was right. He was a well-respected, well-liked teacher, and I was, well, not exactly an A student. I know I don't have to remind you how often I got suspended for skipping school, or smoking pot, etcetera, etcetera. He could easily have set me up to take the blame if I reported him." Kelly shook her head. "The stupidest thing is, I *did* flirt with him, I admit it, but I never expected—"

Claudia slid out of the breakfast nook and went to put her arms around her friend. "Don't you dare take responsibility. He was the adult and you were a child in his care." She hesitated, then blurted out what she was thinking. "Maybe he got what was coming to him."

Chapter twenty-six

Monday, October 16

Claudia gassed up the Jaguar and headed south once more. She had spoken to Sue Goldman, who was newly distraught after seeing the news about Josh Dickson in the media. It had taken some arm-twisting, and in the end, she agreed to meet and talk about Lucy Valentine if Claudia would come to Edentown High at lunchtime.

Promising to bring lunch with her, she left Playa de la Reina at a time designed to avoid the worst of the rush hour and get to the high school ahead of the lunch bell. For security reasons, during the week the campus was closed to unpermitted cars and street parking was restricted on Mondays for trash pickup. She found a place to leave the car several blocks from the school where she would not get a ticket and dashed up the front steps of the administration building, red-faced and winded.

Passing through a metal detector at the front doors—something they had not needed in her school days here—Claudia headed to the office. She told the bored work-study student who checked her in and gave her a visitor's pass that she was an alumnus from the class of '99. The girl's shrug said she could not have cared less.

Climbing the familiar worn staircase to Ms. Goldman's classroom on the second floor, Claudia wondered whether it might have generated a flicker interest if she'd told the girl that she was the one who had found the former teacher's body in the swimming pool.

The upper floor hallways were quiet, the classrooms deserted. As Claudia entered the classroom with a knock, the English teacher glanced up to greet her. She sat behind her desk in her empty classroom, her eyes red-rimmed, the skin around them shadowed. More than that, her face appeared to have aged a decade since the night Claudia had glimpsed her at the reunion cocktail party. In the company of Josh Dickson she had looked happy, her smile sparkling.

Claudia handed over the bottle of water and plastic box she had picked up at Goldie's, a familiar deli near the high school. To her delight they were still open and doing a brisk business. "I hope chicken salad is okay."

Sue Goldman accepted her offering with a listless hand. "Thank you. I can't say I feel like eating, but please, you go ahead. Pull up a desk."

From behind the building, the muted sounds of a pep rally penetrated the windows. The noise was loud enough for the entire student body to be in the quad, demonstrating their school spirit, joining in the same old cheers to the thumping of drums.

"Teamwork, teamwork, that's our dream work!" and "Pioneer spirit knows no limit!" Claudia went to the windows and looked down at the cheer squad on the concrete stage below—girls being launched high into the air, tumbling, landing, and jumping up and down while the audience roared their support.

"Some things never change." She stowed her purse in the metal basket underneath the desk. Setting her own box of chicken salad on the desktop, she crammed herself into the molded plastic seat. "I seem to remember these things fitting better."

Goldman managed a fragile smile. "Students come in all shapes and sizes. The desks remain the same." Her navy blazer and leopard-print blouse were not much different than what she had worn when a younger, slightly slimmer Claudia had sat at one of these desks, learning to interpret theme and meaning. "Where do you live these days?" Goldman asked.

"Playa de la Reina. Have you heard of it? It's a tiny beach town north of here, right next to LAX. More of a village than anything."

Goldman looked skeptical. "That's a long drive for this conversation. I told you I don't have a lot to say about Lucy."

"Anything you can contribute might be helpful to Matt. He wants to make this documentary something special and important. It's not meant to be about the disappearance of just one girl." Claudia paused. "Do you remember Lucy?"

"I remember her very well. She was a bright girl academically, but lonely. She spent a great deal of time in my classroom after school, writing stories and chatting. On the surface, she was doing it for extra credit, but there was more to it than that." Goldman's lips flattened in disapproval. "I believe she needed adult company. I tried to provide a role model. There was such potential there, but it was buried under a poor ego."

Hearing about Lucy from a different perspective from that of her brother and her two girlfriends, Claudia felt a budding excitement grow in her. "I heard that her personality changed quite a bit after her father left the family and moved away when she was in fourth grade," she said.

"I wouldn't know about that. I didn't have her as a student until she got to eleventh. After you phoned yesterday, I went back to look at the 1998 yearbook, her junior picture."

Sue Goldman's eyes softened and lost focus, as if she were seeing Lucy as she had been then. "She was so young. I believe the way she presented herself—the all-black clothing and fingernails painted black, and all that—it was a desperate cry for attention—especially at a school where it was not popular, as it was at some other schools. Two or three others dressed up like that, but Lucy was the student I remember. It made her stand out, and not in a positive way."

"You're right about that," Claudia agreed. "Some of the girls used to make fun of her for her 'goth' look."

Goldman nodded regretfully. "I was aware of that. I tried talking to her mother about it at parent-teacher conference night, but I got the feeling that she wasn't paying attention. It felt like her mind was elsewhere—as if she was here because it was the right thing to do, not because she wanted to come, or because she had any interest in the good work Lucy was doing."

"Lucy's brother told Matt and me that their mother had a job that took up most of her attention."

"That's not an excuse to shirk your parental responsibilities." That Ms. Goldman was offended was clear. She might as well have "Tsk'ed."

"It must have made quite an impact for you to remember it for so long," Claudia said.

"There are some students you never forget. And in this case, Lucy's disappearance made it impossible to forget her."

Claudia had already decided not to bring up Lucy's alleged pregnancy. It was unlikely the girl had confided in her teacher, who would have been obligated to report it to her guidance counselor—that would have opened a very smelly kettle of fish. Instead, she took a different direction. "You said she wrote stories. I heard she wanted to emulate Poe."

That brought a fond smile to the teacher's face. "She did write horror very well. She worked hard at it, and she would have got an A in my class if—" the smile faded. "I have often wondered what happened to her."

"We all have," Claudia said. She had gotten what she wanted about Lucy; it was time to turn the conversation to the other topic that interested her. Unexpectedly, Sue Goldman broached it first.

"I wanted to ask you, Claudia, is it true that you were the one who discovered..." she did not finish her sentence.

"Yes, I'm sorry to say it is true."

"What a ghastly thing that must have been for you."

"Yes, it was. It was even worse to find out that someone had deliberately killed him." Claudia went for broke. "Since then, I heard something else about him that was very upsetting. It made me wonder—"

"You know about the drugs?" Goldman said in a faint voice.

"Drugs?" Claudia echoed, bewildered. "No, I didn't know anything about drugs."

"Oh." The teacher's hand flew up to cover her mouth as if she could stuff the words back into it. "What, then?"

"It was about him taking girls out in the driver's ed car after school."

All color drained from Goldman' face. "Holy Mother of God," she whispered. "I thought the drug thing was the worst—"

"Take a couple of deep breaths," Claudia said, opening the water bottle and handing it to her, worried that the teacher would start to hyperventilate the way she had on the phone. "Sip some water."

Goldman closed her eyes and took her advice. When the color returned to her face, she said, "I thought you were talking about the conversation you told the detective—"

"The argument Lupe Garcia mentioned?" Claudia asked when Goldman said nothing more. "Are you saying it had something to do with drugs?"

"I wouldn't call it an argument. Like I told Detective Booker, it was more of a 'heated discussion.'" Closing her eyes again, she filled her lungs, and let out the air in a rush. "About five years ago, my younger sister and most of her family were killed flying their plane to Colorado. They ran into some unexpected bad weather in the mountains. The baby was the sole survivor. Livvy suffered a catastrophic brain injury that requires round-the-clock care." Goldman paused for another long breath.

"I refuse to put her in a facility. I'm her godmother and I owe it to my sister. You can imagine, home care is very expensive, even with the insurance settlement." Her shoulders drooped. She scrubbed her hands over her eyes. "Who am I kidding? I've always been single, and the debt is crushing me. As for Josh, we kept in touch, and saw each other every year or so."

"We used to wonder about you two," Claudia interjected, hoping Sue Goldman would put an end to the speculation, one way or another.

"He knew I was struggling," Goldman said, leaving her curiosity unsatisfied. She fiddled with the lid of her food container, snapping and unsnapping it. "At the reunion, he told me he had a proposition that would help me out financially."

It didn't take a psychic to see where this story was going. Even before she heard the rest, Claudia felt punched in the heart. She wanted to yell and protest, but she kept her mouth shut and let Goldman unspool in her own time what had happened.

"He said he had a deal going with teachers at several schools in New York where he lived, and a couple of other places too. These teachers identified certain 'susceptible' students and were selling them drugs that Josh supplied." Her face flushed to a dull crimson. "He was suggesting I could supplement my income to help with Livvy. At first I thought he had to be joking—he was always joking around. He must know there was no possible way in hell…" She paused to catch her breath.

"When I understood that he was serious, I was repelled in a way I can't even describe. Then I got furious—absolutely livid. First, that he would ever think to do a thing like that to school children, and second, that he would try to involve me in his criminal and immoral activities. If he hadn't been drinking so much, he would have known better than to ever make such a foul suggestion."

Goldman met Claudia's gaze and her eyes widened. As if she had just realized that she was saying the words out loud, she exclaimed, "I don't know why I told you all this. Please don't use anything I've said…"

"You said you've already told Detective Booker," Claudia assured her. "There's no need for it to go any further. It has nothing to do with Matt's documentary."

"Thank you for that. The detective said he would get in touch with the DEA so they could implement a proper investigation." There was something pitiful in the gratitude that lit Sue Goldman's face. Just as suddenly, her expression darkened. "I hope they catch every teacher who is involved. There's a special place in hell for someone who would abuse the trust of a child that way."

Added to what Kelly had said, Dickson had been a Jekyll and Hyde of the worst kind. Claudia wondered whether his wife was aware of his double life, and whether Sue Goldman had been his only side relationship. From what she had learned about him it seemed unlikely.

"Honestly, Claudia, I don't see why Detective Booker cared about whether we argued, or had a discussion, or…"

Claudia met her eyes. "Because it gives you motive to kill him."

Sue Goldman looked back at her with a long, pensive gaze. "Oh. I guess it does."

Chapter twenty-seven

Claudia left her former English teacher in a puddle of tears. It pained her to see her in that state, but Sue Goldman had made it abundantly clear that she wanted to be left alone for a while before the bell rang for fourth period.

She sat in the Jaguar, weighing her next move: head for home, or interview someone else while she was in the area. Joel's ringtone, the theme from *COPS* startled her out of her woolgathering.

"I gave Booker a call," he said.

The announcement took her aback. "What did you say to him?"

"That since my wife was the one who discovered his homicide victim, and he was the investigator in charge, I wanted to check in and see if there was anything I should know. A courtesy call."

"And did you get anything new out of him?"

"Yeah, I did. Booker interviewed the bartenders who worked the cocktail party. One of them saw someone follow Dickson in the direction of the back door to the gym. Unfortunately, the description wasn't any use."

"Nothing? How about gender?"

"Nada, just dark hair, dark clothing—jacket and pants, not a dress. Booker said even getting that was like pulling teeth. Out of the four bartenders, only one noticed anything at all. And she wasn't even sure the person was following him, just that they were going in the same direction."

One word roused her attention. "She?"

"The keen-eyed bartender was female."

"Not so keen-eyed if she was that vague in the description. Since she noticed it well enough to mention, what was it that made her notice Dickson leaving the party?"

"If Booker asked her that, he didn't tell me. Too bad there were no security cameras by the back door."

"Did he happen to mention the name of this not-so-helpful bartender?"

"No, and this is the part where I remind you that it's a police investigation and they don't need your interference."

"Because I'm 'just the wife?'" the question had a keen-edged blip of annoyance at the implied need to protect her, combined with gratitude that he had taken the trouble to talk to Sam Booker.

"You know better than that. Should I remind you that I didn't have to call him?"

"I appreciate that you did. Truly, I do."

"I'm serious, Claudia—you need to keep your refined nose out of it."

"Refined? Is that a nice way of saying I have a big nose?"

"Only if you stick it in police business." She heard his sigh of surrender. Joel was too smart to ask for a promise he knew she would never keep. He must know that her mind was already spinning through a list of the people she might be able to reach out to and get contact information for the bartender. Since Kelly's revelation, and the conversation with Sue Goldman, her interest had transferred from Lucy Valentine to Josh Dickson. For the time being, she had invested all the energy she was going to on Matt's behalf. Those investigations were about to be suspended in favor of learning more about her driver ed teacher's demise.

"What time will you be home?" Joel asked. "We can go out for dinner—our favorite place."

Claudia laughed. "Trying to distract me with fine dining, detective? Sometimes you're so transparent. How about a raincheck? I'm going to get a hotel room at the Hilton and come home in the morning. I can't face the afternoon traffic again."

"Is your movie producer gonna be there, too?"

"Oh, sure. 'I'm ready for my closeup, Mr. Macedo,'" Claudia teased. Then, in case there was a tinge of genuine suspicion behind his joke, "You never have to ask that question, Columbo. I don't want anyone but you keeping my bed warm."

"I just like to hear you say it." The satisfied grin in his voice made her grin, too. "I'll miss you tonight," he said.

"I'll miss you too. Call me when you're turning out the light so we can say goodnight. Love you."

"Love you."

They ended the call and Claudia texted Cathi Soden:

"How can I get the name of the female bartender from the reunion cocktail party?" Thirty seconds later:

"That's easy. She's an ETH alum. Randi Quinn. Here's her number..."

Claudia dialed the number.

"Yeah, I did talk to the cop," Randi Quinn said. "Is there a problem?"

"Not at all. The guy whose death he's investigating was my driver's ed teacher in high school. I'm the one who found him. I'm just wondering why anyone would want to kill him."

"*Kill* him?" Randi echoed. "If you want to meet for a drink, I get off work at five. I'll tell you what I know—which isn't much."

That was easier than she expected. "Love to," Claudia said. "Where should we meet? I'll be at the Hilton where we had the reunion banquet."

"Meet me in the bar there at six. I'll text you a photo of me. You do the same."

"Will do. See you then." She texted a link to her LinkedIn profile. Her phone pinged with Randi's photo.

After reserving a room at the Hilton, the afternoon stretched in front of her. She spent some time at the local Macy's, purchasing sleepwear and undies, and a cute top and drawstring pants to change into. Then a leisurely stroll around the nearest Target for overnight items she would need: toothbrush, toothpaste, energy bars. Her emergency makeup and a hairbrush were in a cosmetic case in the car.

Official check-in time at the hotel was four-o'clock, but Claudia sweet-talked her way into her room an hour earlier. After a shower and a brief nap, she checked her email, found nothing of interest, and then it was time to get ready for her meeting with Randi Quinn.

As she was about to leave the room and head down to the bar, Kelly phoned. From the slur in her voice, she was looking for something at the bottom of a bottle.

"I'm on my way out to meet someone, Kel. What's up?"

"Well, shit. I needed to tell you something. But if you're leaving—"

"If it's urgent, I'll stay. Or is it something that can keep for an hour?" No, that would be stupid. Kelly might be passed out by then, and instinct whispered that she had better listen. "Never mind. Tell me."

"Yeah, if I wait, I'll lose my nerve." The sound of her swallowing punctuated her words. "It's just, I didn't tell you the whole story. Between the first time Dickson came on to me and the time when I stabbed him—there was another time."

That sounded ominous.

"What happened?"

Kelly sniffed. "It's embarrassing. Rachel invited me to go with her and Dickson, just the three of us. I said I would. He left the driver's ed car unlocked. She and I got in the backseat and there was the blanket on the floor for us to hide under. We felt really special. We thought it was so much fun hiding there. He got in the car, and told us to stay down and stay quiet until we got where we were going." She started sobbing. "Wait—wait..."

Claudia checked the time. Her rendezvous with Randi Quinn was in fifteen minutes. She had just texted the bartender that she might be a few minutes late when Kelly blew her nose and said, "We drove for maybe ten or fifteen minutes. It got damn hot under that blanket, I can tell you. Rachel said don't complain, it was gonna be worth it. When the car stopped and we got out, we were in the woods behind the school, in that upper parking lot where nobody ever goes. We walked into the woods, Dickson making dumb jokes, and after a couple of minutes, we left the main path. There was this place they went all the time, like in the underbrush. There was an opening and once we went through it, nobody could see us, even if anyone came. And they didn't."

The time was ticking by. This was not the sort of story you could interrupt and say you had to go. Claudia hoped Randi would wait for her.

"The dumb jokes kept coming while we spread out the blanket, and Dickson gave us some weed to smoke. I thought that was cool. But after we got a little high, he gave us some pills, too. Ecstasy, I think. Then he started making out with Rachel. He wanted me to join in with them, but I wasn't into threesomes back then."

"Wait. You mean, he and Rachel were—"

"No, they didn't actually do the deed, but she blew him." Kelly made a sound of disgust. "I didn't want to see that, and I sure as hell didn't want to participate. The minute they were done, I told him I wanted to leave. He grabbed me and kissed me, with tongue—that fool expected me to like it. Ugh! Then he said that next time, it would be just him and me."

She sucked in a shuddering breath. "And that's why, the next time he came onto me I sharpened my pencil and had it ready."

Randi Quinn was a good twenty pounds heavier than her photo, but the ginger hair—two shades brighter than Claudia's own auburn—with its long, Z-shaped coils made her easy to spot. Already seated at a hi-top table in an emerald green tunic, she earned her Irish name—a fairytale version of a beautiful witch.

As Claudia perched on the other barstool and they greeted each other up-close, she saw that the dim lighting in the bar was kind to the bartender, who was older than she appeared at first glance.

"Pioneers rule," Randi said, raising a glass in greeting. "Class of '92."

Claudia was still processing what she had learned from Kelly. "Pioneers rule," she responded automatically. "When Cathi said you were an alum, she didn't mention—"

"That Josh and I graduated the same year? Yeah, we were old friends. He got me the gig."

"And that's why you agreed to meet with me?"

Randi nodded. A waiter came over to refresh her gin and tonic and take Claudia's order for a Stella Artois. "Does Detective Booker know?"

"That Josh and I were friends? No. He never asked if I knew him. I felt like he just questioned me because I was there. Not because the lowly bartenders would notice anything important."

"You didn't think it was important to mention that you saw something?"

"Don't ask, don't tell, right?"

"Is there anything *I* should be asking?"

"You don't have to. You're a fellow EHS alum, so I'll just tell you. Like I said, there's not much to tell. Josh had a lot to drink that night—hard stuff. After five or six rounds at my station, I told him I wasn't going to serve him anymore. Pissed him off. He stormed away." She snickered. "If you can 'storm' when you're hammered. More like he staggered away. I kept half an eye on him, saw him go across the gym to the other bar. Like I said, he wasn't too steady on his feet, and my buddy over there must have told him the same as me, 'cause Joshie flipped him the bird and left."

"Is that when you saw him go outside?" Claudia asked.

"No. What I saw was him stopping to talk to some guy—no one I knew. A couple minutes later, he was going towards the exit door in the back of the gym. After that, I got busy and wasn't paying attention. But I happened to glance in that direction a few minutes later, and I saw someone following him. Well, I say following. It may have been that they were just trying to catch up with him."

"You said a non-specific 'someone.' Does that mean you couldn't tell whether it was a man or a woman?"

"Honestly, I couldn't tell for sure. They'd just lowered the lights for the romantic dancing, but I got the sense that it was a woman. She—if it *was* a she—was wearing a dark jacket and pants, and had dark hair. It was hard to tell from behind and in that lighting. And there was no reason for me to notice anything. I had no idea he was going out there to die. Crap." Randi scrabbled in her pocket. Claudia grabbed a tissue from her purse and handed it to her.

"What was Josh like when you knew him in high school?"

Randi wiped her nose and stuffed the tissue in her pocket. Her face softened. "He was so sweet. I had a major crush on him in our senior year. I had this fantasy that we'd get married and have kids when we grew up."

"What happened?"

Her mouth twisted in a rueful smile. "My dad was in the military and we moved around. He got reassigned when I was going to school at Edentown, and my family lived in San Diego for a while. I didn't get to graduate from EHS. Several years later I moved back to Orange County. I heard Josh was engaged, and by then, I was over him."

Claudia took a long swallow of beer. It wasn't hard to imagine a teenage Josh and Randi. "We all loved him when he was my teacher. He wasn't much older than us, and we thought he was fun."

"Sounds like the Josh I knew. He liked to joke around, never wanted to talk about anything serious. Kind of a class clown."

"What about drugs?"

"Drugs?" Randi looked startled. "No. I know he sneaked cigarettes sometimes, but I never saw him smoke a joint or do anything harder."

Claudia decided not to tell her what she had learned from Sue Goldman. "When did you move to San Diego?"

Randi thought about it. "Would have been around the end of the first semester."

"If he did get into any 'chemicals,' you wouldn't have been around to see it, right?"

"That's true."

"Would it surprise you to know that he preyed on his female students for sex?"

"Jeeez, Claudia, are you serious?"

"Sadly, I am. And apparently, he didn't get caught."

The bartender hesitated, and Claudia saw something reflective pass across her eyes. Randi tossed back the rest of her G&T and stood up. "I think you should talk to Coach Wilson. Josh was on the football team and they were pretty close. He used to spend time with Coach after school."

Like Lucy and Ms. Goldman. Interesting

Claudia started gathering her things, too. "Ernie Wilson is a legend. When I was at EHS, he was the guy who led our team to winning in the league every year. There are photos of him in the trophy case in the main building. He must have retired long ago."

"For sure," Randi agreed. "I bet he must be in his late eighties, if not older. You should Google him. If he's alive, you might be able to find him."

"I will."

And if that didn't work, as managing editor of the *Gazette,* Lupe knew everyone in town who had ever been important. And on the slight chance Lupe didn't know, Cathi would.

As it happened, Coach Wilson was alive and well, and living at a retirement home in Greengrove, right next to Edentown. When Claudia called, Lupe offered to pave the way for a meeting by making a call to ask if he would see her the following morning.

He would.

"I could meet you at his place and introduce you," Lupe proposed when she phoned back with the news. "He comes to the monthly Alumni breakfasts, so he knows me."

All I need is Lupe interfering. "That's not necessary, but thanks."

"But why Coach Wilson?" Lupe pressed. "Lucy wasn't into sports. He wouldn't have known her."

Lupe had helped her, but that didn't mean she should know what the topic of the meeting would be, not Lucy Valentine, but Joshua Dickson.

"Coach was the big enchilada," Claudia said. "He can provide some background about the school for the documentary."

Lupe wasn't buying it. "Something stinks, Bennett. What are you up to?"

"Keep up, Garcia, I haven't been Bennett in more than two decades. Gotta go, but thank you, I owe you for setting it up."

"You'd better let me know if you find out anything I should know," Lupe sounded suspicious, but short of directly accusing Claudia of lying, there was not much else she could say.

"If there's anything you should know, I promise I will call you," Claudia lied.

Chapter twenty-eight

Tuesday, October 17

Coach Ernie Wilson was a resident of the Elmhurst Senior Living Village "for active elderly adults." A modern, well-kept facility made up of two two-story buildings surrounded by a tidy garden, it abutted a private golf course and tennis courts. On her way to the front entrance from the parking area, Claudia passed several residents, some waved at her from golf carts, one was pushing a walker, accompanied by a little pug dog who was trying to keep up.

Coach Wilson met her in the lobby. A tall, fit, African American man, dapper in a chestnut-colored sweater over a tan golf shirt and slacks, he could have been ten years younger than his presumptive age. They shook hands, and he explained that he had promised to take his wife out to lunch and to the mall. "I detest shopping," he confessed. "And I'm happy to spare a half-hour for a chat with an EHS graduate."

The rain had fled and left a sunny day with the occasional puffy cloud in a brilliant blue sky. The coach ushered Claudia back outside to a park bench. They spent the first few minutes sharing memories of past Edentown High football victories.

With the introductory small talk behind them, before Claudia could give him the reason for her visit, Coach Wilson asked, "What's this about you wanting to talk to me about that girl who went missing? Naturally, I remember when it all happened, but..."

Claudia felt herself blush over the small deception. "The truth is, Coach, I want to talk to you about Josh Dickson."

"My God, what an atrocious business, him dying that way—" He paused, frown lines forming wrinkles on his forehead. "But I don't understand. Lupe Garcia said..."

"What Lupe said is true. I *am* helping Matt Macedo with a documentary he's making about Lucy Valentine. Matt is also an alum. But after what happened to Mr. Dickson, things have taken a turn, and—"

"Macedo, eh?" he nodded approvingly. "I remember him. Good kid. Wasn't he on the swim team?"

"Yes, he was."

"I'm a little confused. What does any of this have to do with Josh, Claudia?"

"Do you remember Josh well?"

"Why, sure. We kept in touch some. He always sent Christmas cards and would call once in a while on the phone for a chat. Some of the boys on the team do that, you know, long after they graduate." Coach Wilson smiled. "Team spirit doesn't just go away because you're not in school any longer. In fact, Josh came by to see me a couple of days before the reunion. He'd told me he was going to be in town for a few days, so we had lunch."

"It sounds like you were close." She had considered how best to approach him, but it was undeniable that the elderly coach cared about Dickson, and that changed things somewhat.

He picked up on her hesitation. "What is it, Claudia? I can see you want to say something. Go on ahead."

There was no point in delaying it any further. Claudia plunged ahead. "I don't know whether Lupe told you, Coach, but I was the one who found him, Josh Dickson."

"Oh, honey, it's a terrible thing to have happened. I'm so sorry you had to see that." Coach reached over and took her hands in his gnarled ones. "I heard he drowned."

"Yes, he did drown." Again, she wavered. The day was so peaceful, it was a shame to ruin it. And then she did.

"I'm sorry to tell you, Coach, but it wasn't an accident. The police have just announced that he was murdered."

The coach darted a troubled glance at her. "Dear God, I am so very sorry to hear that."

Claudia shifted on the bench and twisted her head to peer into his face. "If you don't mind me saying so, you don't seem all that surprised."

"It's a shock, of course." Coach Wilson's lips formed a tense pucker. "But there was a kind of darkness in him."

"Darkness?" Claudia prompted when he fell silent.

"Oh, he covered it up with jokes and laughter—except on the field—he was damn serious about football—captain of the team, and a good one. All those boys looked up to him—wanted to be him. The girls all had crushes on him. After he graduated college I was real glad he came back to Edentown to teach. Hiring him as *assistant* coach was a complete waste of his talents," he said with a disapproving shake of his head. "I suppose that's all that was open at the time. I never understood it when he switched over to driver's ed."

Claudia kept her thought to herself—that teaching driver education gave Dickson access to young girls that football didn't, as well as the use of a car. All he had to supply was the blanket for them to hide under when he 'took them for rides.' "You mentioned that there was a 'darkness' in him," she said. "Can you tell me what meant by that?"

Coach looked as though he was about to refuse. Then he said, "I don't suppose there's any harm in talking about it. He's not around to be hurt by it." He sighed heavily. "Things weren't good for him at home. His mama died when he was a little tyke, and he was raised by his old man and his uncle. I didn't know him until he got to high school, of course." The coach reflected for a moment or two, and shook his head regretfully. "By that time the damage had been done. I could see that something was wrong, but for a long time, he kept it inside. I used to encourage him to stay after school and talk. We did a *lot* of talking. I hoped I could be a good role model for the boy."

"Did he ever say what was going on at home?"

"Eventually." Coach Wilson stared down at his sneakers. "There was abuse—"

"He was being beaten?"

"According to Josh, his father did beat him. But worse than that, his uncle took a shine to him. A shine of the wrong kind, I mean. The uncle was quite a bit younger than Josh's dad—a young teen. Even when he got old enough to fight back, Josh didn't stand a chance against those two. He told his daddy what his uncle had been doing to him, but..."

"Let me guess," Claudia said. "He chose to believe his sicko brother over his own son."

"Beat the living daylights out of him for making those claims. Josh told me he had to stay home from school for a week to let the bruises heal, so nobody would see them. As he got older, he did anything and everything he could to stay out of their way. There were many nights I let him stay in the locker room so he wouldn't have to go home."

All at once, the day felt colder. Claudia huddled in her jacket, but the chill was inside her. "If you knew that kind of abuse was going on, you were obligated to tell the authorities. What happened?"

"His father and his uncle *were* the authorities," Coach Wilson said with something akin to pity. "They were both cops on the local force. Josh's father was a chief in the department and he ruled with an iron fist—no velvet glove for him. He wasn't popular, but in those days nobody would have dared try to prosecute either of them. The uncle became a patrol cop. Josh begged me not to tell. It would have made it worse on him." Wilson hung his head. "To my eternal shame, I let him persuade me to keep it between us. It was easier that way ... easier for me."

It was all making a horrible kind of sense. There was nothing that could excuse Josh Dickson's behavior as an adult, but Coach Wilson's story explained why seducing high school girls might have made her teacher feel like more of a man. A little boy having been abused in such a horrifying way could easily grow up questioning his manhood. Claudia wanted to weep.

She knew it would punish the old man, but he needed to know. "Were you aware that he was sexually abusing some of his female students?"

His eyes went wide. "What? No. No way. He wouldn't—"

"Unfortunately, he did. And now, someone has murdered him. Do you have any idea what happened to his father and his uncle?"

"I-I think I heard that his old man retired and moved to Texas. I don't know about the uncle."

"What if coming back here brought it all back and Josh threatened to tell? It would give his uncle a powerful motive to kill him—to shut him up."

"Is that what you think happened?" Coach looked sick, and Claudia began to feel bad that she had dropped it on him without warning.

"I don't know. First, I wondered if it might be one of the girls he abused, but what you've just told me opens a whole new area of inquiry." She caught his eyes and wouldn't let go. "I'm going to have to tell the detective in charge of investigating Josh's murder about this. I'm sure he'll want to talk to you."

"I'll make myself available." Ernie Wilson's face had gone ashen. "Dear God, I should have turned in those bastards decades ago."

"Yes, you should have." She could not keep the coolness out of her tone. "Better late than never, I guess."

Coach pulled himself to his feet. "I need to go. This is too much. I—"

"Thanks for talking with me," Claudia said. "I'm sorry to have upset you."

He held out his hand to her. "I'm the one who is sorry."

As they shook hands, she could feel his trembling. He walked away with drooping shoulders. His age seemed to have caught up to him.

Claudia was on the way back to her car when her phone rang. She recognized the number. "Hi, Detective Booker, what can I do for you?"

"Ms. Rose, I'm glad I caught you. I have some photos I'd like you to take a look at."

"What photos?"

"You may have noticed that Ms. Soden, the reunion chair, had someone taking candid shots. At my request, she's sent them to me and I've been going over them. I'd like to know whether you recognize some of the people in a couple of the shots."

"Sure, but I doubt I could see them properly on my phone, and I'm not in my office," she said. "Hey, I'm in Edentown and I have something new on the Dickson case for you, too. If you like, I can be at the police department in about thirty minutes and you can show me the pictures."

"That would be just fine," he said. "I'll see you then."

He sounded more pleased than she believed he ought to.

Chapter twenty-nine

The Edentown Police Department was beginning to feel to Claudia like a familiar haunt. Detective Sam Booker showed up within a few minutes of her presenting herself at the front desk. When he escorted her through the same corridor, she had to lodge a protest. "Don't tell me we're going back to the cubbyhole?"

The detective chuckled. "You don't like our luxurious accommodations?"

She rolled her eyes. "I can't wait to enjoy all the amenities. It's about the size of my bathroom."

"It's less distracting than my desk with all the activity going on around it," he said, opening the door for her to precede him. "I prefer to use it for the kind of thing we're doing." He gestured her to a chair at the table.

Claudia seated herself and the detective took the chair opposite. "You said you have some new information for me?"

"And you said you have some photos to show me."

"Let's start with yours."

"It doesn't have to be ladies first..." Claudia said, impatient for what he was so keen for her to see. But he waited her out, observing her with an implacable manner that told her she might as well surrender. "Okay, here it is. I've just learned from his old coach that Josh Dickson was sexually abused for years by his uncle, who was a beat cop *in this very department.*

It was never reported." She paused, and caught his gaze. "What if Josh threatened to spill the beans?"

"Oh. I see," Booker said. "You've got it all worked out that this uncle killed him?"

"I don't know whether he did or not, but it's plausible, don't you think? Something worth investigating?"

"Was the uncle at the reunion?"

"Not that I know of. He wasn't in our class and he wasn't a teacher. But if he knew Dickson was going to be there, he could have showed up and followed him out to the pool? Dickson was a student at EHS, so his uncle probably was too, and would know the layout. Or, he could have lured him out there and laid in wait."

The detective's casual body language—the way he sat, apparently relaxed, in his chair, head tilted forward, the way someone paying close attention would—none of it fooled Claudia. She could read his doubts in the slight frown that formed—likely without him realizing it—even before he gave himself away with his words.

"Do you think maybe you missed your calling, Ms. Rose?" he said, casually slipping the blade between her ribs, hidden as a conversational bon mot. "Maybe you always wanted to be a detective?"

She considered him through half-lowered lids. "No need to patronize me, detective. If you'd pretend to be impartial for a half-second and think about it, you have to agree that it's reasonable to consider as a possibility." Then, she brought out her own knife. "Or, are you one of those cops who's inclined to look the other way when it's a brother in blue?"

The coffee-colored eyes turned to ice. Leaving her taunt lying on the table between them, he said nothing for several seconds. Then, as if she had not insulted him: "Do you have a name for this uncle?"

"No, but it can't be hard to find. Josh Dickson's father was Chief of Police here in the 80s. I assume they had the same last name. He was a patrol cop."

For the space of a blink, Sam Booker was as stricken as if she had announced that a meteor was about to hit the earth. When he spoke, his face was wiped clean of expression. "I'll look into it," he said. "Right now, I'd like to show you these photos and have you tell me whether you recognize anyone in them."

There was a file folder in his hands. Laying it on the table, he slid it towards her. "Please take your time, Ms. Rose."

Claudia removed several enlargements from photos of the reunion cocktail party. Couples were dancing in some. Others showed classmates milling around the two bars at either end of the gymnasium. Recalling the professional camera Matt had around his neck early in the evening, she was confident that this was not his work.

"They're so dark and grainy—"

"Best we've got, unfortunately. I'm told the lights in the gym were low, which impacted the quality, even with flash."

"Let me get closer look," Claudia said. She reached into her bag for her phone, and opened the camera app, then positioned it over the faces, one at a time, stretching the screen to enlarge them, and moving the lens around to see if she could identify any of the subjects.

"These are some of the reunion committee members." She pointed to three women wo appeared to be in conversation near one of the bars.

"These ladies at the bar are Sharon Bernstein and Espie Rodriguez, and that's Becky Condren. And the female bartender is Randi Quinn."

Booker cast a quizzical look at her. "You're friends with the bartender?"

"Not friends," she said noncommittally. "She's an EHS alum."

One of the photos was relatively clear, and showed Randi gazing off into the distance while pouring a drink. Claudia followed the direction of her gaze. There, at the edge of the picture, just about clear enough to recognize, she spotted Josh Dickson. He was talking to someone who was faced away from the camera. The other person wore dark hair and clothing, and blended into the background. It was impossible to see his or her face. Dickson was leaning forward and appeared to be talking animatedly.

In the next shot, either the photographer had moved, or the person he was talking to had turned to the side enough to identify them.

"If I'm not mistaken, that's Rachel Thomas," Claudia said. Booker was busy making a note when she dropped the latest revelation on him. "Rachel had a sexual relationship with Josh Dickson during senior year when he was our teacher."

The detective's eyes popped up from his notebook. "You're just now telling me this?"

"I didn't know about it until last night. A friend of mine told me about an 'encounter' she had in high school with Rachel and Dickson. She personally witnessed them engaging in sexual activities—not intercourse, but as close as you could—uh, never mind. As Ms. Goldman says she told you—and thanks, by the way, for telling her I snitched her out—Dickson supplied several girls with drugs. She didn't know about the sex. She does now."

"This guy was a real prince," Booker said, ignoring the barb she had inserted. "What about your friend—the eye witness? I'll need to talk to her."

"I know, but you need to be aware that she's kind of fragile right now."

"What does that mean?"

Claudia gestured tipping a glass into her mouth. "This has brought back some unpleasant memories. You might not get the kind of coherent information you need."

"Give me her contact information. I can give her a day or two while I work on other angles."

During the time Joel had worked sex crimes, he had never become jaded about the victims. Claudia could tell that Detective Booker was the same, and it made her feel kinder toward him. She gave him Kelly's name and phone number and said, "She didn't kill Dickson."

"I see. You're certain of that, are you?"

"Yes, I'm quite certain. You can find Rachel Thomas at the Eternal Peace Funeral Home. She's a mortician."

Booker scratched his bald head. "This just gets better and better. Anyone else you recognize in those photos?"

Claudia passed the camera lens over them again, and pointed. "That's Natalie Parker and her husband, Tom. And Nat's cousin Andrea is there. Those two were inseparable. I guess they still are. This one is Ginny Vernon. She was friends with Andie—Andrea."

Ginny was gone from the next shot, leaving Tom Parker, Nat, and Andie huddled together. And then, Tom was gone, leaving the two cousins alone together.

"Are you talking about Natalie Parker, who's on the city council?" Booker asked her, although he must know they were one and the same.

"That's her. She's gearing up to run for mayor of E'town."

"I saw her name on the list of attendees," the detective allowed. "She's been very vocal on environmental issues—gets a lot done. I've also run into her husband in court a time or two."

"Oh, that's right. I forgot he's a defense attorney. The kind of guy you and my husband like to refer to as being 'on the dark side.'"

Detective Booker made another note and glanced over at her. "I spoke to your husband on the phone. Sounds like a stand-up guy."

"Yeah, he is. Maybe you two can get together for a beer sometime. Now, detective, I am going to head for—uh—" Claudia fell silent. All at once, her mind was twirling out of control like the ballerina in the *Black Swan*.

Booker eyed her intently, as if he was looking inside her head. She slipped her phone into her purse and forced a smile. "Detective, it's been—well, I'm sorry I can't say a pleasure."

"What were you about to say just now, Ms. Rose?" He was holding on too long to the hand she offered.

"Huh? Oh, nothing."

Booker cocked his head, not believing her. "I got the impression it was going to be something significant."

"Oh, no, no, not at all. My mind took a left turn and I completely lost whatever it was. You know how that happens sometimes." She was talking too much and too fast, but it had become important to get away and follow the connection her brain had made—a connection she had not been aware it was searching for. She stood and moved toward the door. "Good luck with your case. I'll give you a heads-up if I hear anything else that might help."

"I'd appreciate that," Booker said with a wry raise of a brow. "You've been quite the fountain of 'interesting' information."

Chapter thirty

In the car, Claudia tapped out Andrea Adams' number. She would have to send a thank you bottle of good wine to Cathi Soden for all the helpful phone numbers she had provided.

The number rang five times. She was mentally preparing a voicemail when Andie answered sounding out of breath. "Hi Andie, it's Claudia Rose—er, Claudia Bennett, from high school. Did I wake you? I'm sorry if I'm calling at a bad time."

"Oh, wow, Claudia. How are you? It was so great to see you at the reunion."

"It was great seeing you, too, after so long."

"I know. What a blast, getting together with all those people we used to know. I hope you had a good time."

"I did, thanks. Living in L.A., I rarely see anyone from high school."

"A lot of them still live in the area, so we see them at the alumni events. But the others—it was interesting to see how many of them you could recognize, don't you think?"

That was a happy way of viewing it. "Yes, the reunion was great," Claudia said, thinking, *If you didn't find a dead body.*

Andie's eager greeting didn't match the tired droop in her voice. Claudia picked up on the droop, but after the thunderbolt that had landed on her at the police station, she did not want to delay the hard questions that needed to be asked—questions that involved Natalie Parker. Instinctively, she knew that the way to Natalie was through her cousin. And she did not want to return to Edentown again for as long as she could help it. So, she leaned harder on her old classmate than she normally would have.

"Hey, Andie, I'm in town just for this afternoon, and there's something I want to ask you about. Do you have time for a short visit? It's important, or I wouldn't ask."

At first, Andie was quiet. It must have taken an effort to brighten her tone the way she did, but she was the same good girl who wanted to please as she had been long ago. "Um, sure," she said. "I'd love to see you."

"I appreciate it. I promise not to take a lot of your time. Where can we meet?"

"I'm working remotely today," Andie said. "So you'll need to come to my house. I live in the Hills. I'll text you my address when we get off the phone." Then, belatedly, "What's this about?"

"Can I tell you when I get there?"

"That sounds mysterious."

"No, it's just, I'd rather talk about it in person."

"All righty, then." Andrea sounded uncertain, but to argue was not in her nature. "You've got me curious now."

Claudia checked the dashboard clock and made a quick calculation. "I can be there in forty minutes, if that works for you."

"Wonderful. I'll start the coffee."

"Thanks again, Andie, see you then."

She clicked off and almost right away, the phone pinged with her text. Claudia tapped the address into Google Maps. She had a clear recollection of when the hillside land was developed and tracts of large homes built there for the upwardly mobile. It had not taken long for Edentown Hills to become the ritzy end of town. Expansion and growth had continued with the building of successful commercial centers, its neighborhoods no longer strictly residential as they had begun.

It was widely known that a chunk of the residents' homeowner association dues went to the management of the parklands and horse trails that surrounded the highly desirable neighborhood, where doctors and lawyers and financial advisors comprised a good percentage of the residents.

The GPS took her to an attractive two-story home with a three-car garage in one of the recent developments. Andie must have done well for herself to be able to afford the neighborhood. If her cousin was as demanding and imperious as she had been in high school, working for her would not be an easy job. Judging from Nat's behavior at the reunion, it appeared that she had not changed much. Andie deserved to be well-paid for putting up with her attitude.

Claudia parked on the street and took the path around to a tall wooden gate at the side of the house. She reached over to unlatch the gate, and followed a flagstone pathway made pretty by golden chrysanthemums, sweet peas, and nasturtium that edged the house. At the end of the path was the front door. She could hear the doorbell chime inside, but it was a minute or so before the door opened.

Claudia had to stifle the exclamation that jumped into her throat. At the reunion Andie had been thin. A mere two weeks later, she was gaunt. The flesh of her face stretched taut, parchmentlike, against her cheekbones. The warm brown eyes had dulled and become sunken. The pageboy hairstyle looked natural, yet it clanged dissonantly against the rest of the picture and was, no doubt, a wig.

Dressed in a long, heavy sweater and fleece sweatpants, Andie opened the door wide with a tremulous smile. "C'mon on in."

"You could have told me if you're not well," Claudia said with a pang of remorse as she stepped into the entry and closed the door behind her. "I'm feeling bad for bulldozing you into letting me come. I seem to have developed a habit of barging in lately."

Andrea's welcoming smile faded. "I heard. Rachel called right after you did. She told me about your visit to her. I have a feeling you're here for the same reason, though I don't know what's so urgent about a case that old."

"Just me being selfish, trying to avoid driving down here again. I'm sorry to—"

"Don't worry about it for a minute," Andie said, motioning her to follow. How about some coffee?"

"I'd love some, thank you."

They passed through an immaculate living room into an open plan kitchen with an impersonal minimalist design—marble worktops and grey slate facings on the cabinets. It might have been a show home that had just undergone the white glove treatment from a cleaning service—well-appointed, everything spotless. Wide picture windows overlooked a small wrought iron gazebo in the middle of a manicured garden.

Wondering what Andie was doing, living alone in a house made for a family, Claudia said "This is really lovely." Did she like rattling around in what had to be close to 5000 square feet? It would be like living in a boutique hotel.

Andie shrugged. "It's a place to sleep and eat." Her hand shook as she poured coffee into china cups. "How do you take yours?"

"Black for me, thanks."

The cup rattled in its saucer as she handed it over. "Let's go to the den. It's kind of a mess, but it's more comfortable than out here. I hope you won't mind."

"Dropping in practically unannounced takes away the right to mind. But I'm sure it can't be that bad."

"You'll see."

It was true, the den was the lived-in room—an overheated room—where all the untidiness in the house must have gathered. A basket of unfolded laundry sat on a recliner that faced a big screen TV that was currently turned off. A half-dozen stacks of paper littered the floorspace and coffee table.

Andie plucked a plaid blanket off the sofa and dumped it in a heap on top of a bed pillow. "I rest in here quite a bit. Sometimes I don't have the energy to drag myself upstairs."

Claudia removed her jacket and sat at the other end of the sofa from the pillow. "I didn't know you weren't well."

With a faint smile, her hostess moved the laundry basket to the floor and settled into the recliner like a mouse burrowing into its nest. "I bet at the reunion you expected me to be the chubby girl I was in school."

"Uh, that's not quite how I would have described my expectation," Claudia said with a sheepish grin, remembering she had thought exactly that. "But to be honest, you do look different from how I remember you."

Andie nodded. "Until about eighteen months ago, you would have easily recognized me. Things changed when I was diagnosed with stage four ovarian cancer."

Any response to an announcement of that magnitude would be threadbare and meaningless. But something had to be said. Settling for the simple truth, Claudia said "I'm so very sorry you've had to deal with that, Andie."

"Half the women diagnosed are alive after five years. I'm not going to be one of them. I've had all the treatment that's available, and it didn't work for me." Her shrug was philosophical. "I've made my peace with it;

I'm ready to go. Well, I will be soon at any rate. I'm not quite ready for hospice yet. Some things need to be wrapped up."

She indicated the piles of paper. "It turns out that closing down a life is more complicated and untidier than you would expect. I've been sorting and tossing. Didn't want to leave it for Nat to have to deal with my stuff." There was something ironic in Andie's chuckle. "What's gotten into me? She'd hire someone to do it for her. This way, I'll know that the things that are important to me will be handled like I want them to be. This house belongs to Nat and Tom, so that's one less thing to worry about. They can easily get a renter."

Which explained how Andie could afford to live in Edentown Hills.

"I'm sure they can." Claudia took a sip of coffee, which had already cooled in the shallow cup, and got to the reason for her visit. "I promised not to keep you too long, so ... you were right that I wanted to talk to you about Lucy Valentine. Since you've talked to Rachel, I guess it's safe to assume that she told you about the documentary Matt Macedo is making about Lucy's disappearance?"

"She did mention it, yes."

"I'm helping Matt with some of the interviews. We're widening the scope, talking to people who knew her, even if they weren't close, hoping to get some additional points of view." It sounded plausible to Claudia. She hoped it did to Andie too.

"That was such a scary time." Her classmate looked down at her hands, which were clenching and unclenching in her lap. "It's something I don't like to think about."

"We were all traumatized by it, weren't we? I'm sorry to bring up something so upsetting. I have to admit, some of the information that's come up is—well, disturbing." Claudia paused. "You were friendly with everyone. Were you friends with Lucy?"

Andie gave a quick shake of her head. "Not really. Rachel was, though. She must have told you."

"She did. It seems Lucy didn't have many friends."

"I know. I used to feel bad when some of the girls messed with her because of the way she dressed—that emo style. Afterwards—when she was—was—gone—I felt bad that I wasn't nicer to her, but I couldn't—" Andie spoke haltingly, and when she broke off, two spots of color popped up on her cheeks.

"Because Natalie was one of those girls?" Claudia asked.

Andie nodded.

"I visited Sue Goldman yesterday—our English teacher? It felt a little weird to be back in a classroom. The desks don't fit as well." Andie did not return her smile. "She was talking about what a gifted writer Lucy was—she loved to write dark stories in the style of Edgar Allan Poe." Her classmate's silence continued. "Last week, Matt and I had a meeting with the detective who worked on Lucy's case."

That made Andie's eyes fly open wide. "Oh. What did he say?"

"He believes Matt killed her and got away with it. I don't think the police looked any further than him."

Her hand went to her throat. *"Matt?* But why him?" If she had been pale before, Andie was ashen now. Her voice dropped to a near-whisper. "Would you mind handing me that blanket?"

"Of course." Claudia took the plaid blanket from the sofa and wrapped it around her stick-thin frame. "Are you all right, Andie? Is there anything I can get you?"

"No. It's just—I'm sorry. Talking about it brings it all back. It was so...so...." She clutched the blanket up high around her neck, her fingertips peeping over the fringed edge. The nails had been painted shell pink, but were chewed ragged.

The seconds passed, strained, uncomfortable. Claudia had not realized that in coming here she would be hurting a terminally ill woman. "Would you like me to leave?" she asked

Andie released a soft sigh. "Frankly, coming to the end of my life, I'd prefer to focus on happier things. But there are some things that need to be said before I go."

"Let me know if you want to end this at any time." Claudia left a space, and when it remained unfilled, continued. "They picked on Matt because Rachel told them that he and Lucy dated for a little while. Lucky for him, there was no evidence that he had done anything wrong. But that's why her disappearance haunted him all these years, and why he's reinvestigating it now."

"I didn't know that about Matt and Lucy."

"We also talked to her brother, Troy. Their mother got cancer several years after Lucy disappeared. Troy said she died of a broken heart."

"Oh my God," Andie said faintly.

Claudia got up and went over to the window. In the garden everything was perfect, not a weed in sight. Just like Lucy's story. She turned back to Andie. "I expect Rachel told you that Lucy was pregnant when she disappeared."

"No," Andie said, and started to cry softly. Claudia took her a box of tissues from a side table, cursing herself for tormenting her old friend when she was so sick. She was tempted to comfort her instead, but this was not the time to be soft. If she was to uncover Lucy's fate, she had to be relentless, not give out hugs. Returning to her seat on the sofa she said, "Andie, I think you know something about what happened to Lucy."

Andie's tears, which had started as a trickle, became a steady stream. Her chest was heaving. The words "Lucy" and "Natalie," and "Omigod, how could—" came out on quick pants. The rest was incoherent.

It felt as though they had reached a turning point. There was no going back from here; Claudia was watching her classmate break apart. She got up again and went to kneel in front of Andie's chair. "Was Natalie one of the girls who used to go with Mr. Dickson in the driver ed car after school? I know Rachel was."

The sudden sound of the front door closing said someone else was in the house.

A voice called out, "Andie?"

Chapter thirty-one

Hurried footfalls on the tiled corridor stopped at the den door. Rachel Thomas stood in the doorway in her pale blue scrubs, glaring like an avenging angel, ready to protect her ailing friend. Andie must have called her for reinforcements after Claudia asked for the meeting.

"Don't you say a word, Andie." Rachel strode across the room and got in Claudia's face. "What the hell is wrong with you? Can't you see she's in no condition to be interrogated?"

Claudia straightened and faced her head on. They were about the same size. "One question is hardly an interrogation, Rachel. And it was a long time ago; it shouldn't be hard to answer."

"Well, it is." Anger flared in her eyes. "In case you've forgotten, I was at the table when you heard that Nat is going to run for mayor. Something like what you're talking about could put an end to those hopes."

"Something like what? Being abused by a teacher when she was in high school more than twenty-five years ago? A teacher who is now dead? Even if it did get out—and there's no reason why it should—it would make her more sympathetic. Which, by the way, she could use."

"Natalie is popular," Andrea piped up from her recliner. Having someone to side with her seemed to have restored some of her strength. She pulled a tissue from the box, wiped her eyes, and blew her nose. "She's worked hard to do good. She's devoted her whole adult life to working for the community and making things better."

"Bully for her," Claudia said with a mental yawn.

"She's been involved in environmental issues—protecting our ecologically valuable natural areas. She got them to stop using pesticides in the neighborhood, and to make use of food waste in composting, and—"

Claudia held up a hand to stop what was beginning to sound like a campaign brochure. "Okay, thanks, I get it. You do a great job as her PR person. That doesn't mean—"

"You don't understand, Claudia. In politics, any tiny little thing can be used against you. Natalie has paid for anything she did in the past, and then some."

"Paid for what?"

Years of giving testimony in court had taught Claudia not to answer more than she was asked. Andrea had not learned that lesson. She started to dither.

Rachel's livid glare spoke volumes. "She's not a cop, Andie. You don't have to talk to her. Leave the past in the past. No stupid documentary is going to bring Lucy back from ... from wherever she disappeared to."

"The police found a note, supposedly left by Lucy after she disappeared," Claudia said, ignoring Rachel's attempt to stop her. "Did you know that? Her mom hung on to the original. Troy Valentine gave it to me to analyze the handwriting.

"It was obviously written with an awkward hand—one the writer wasn't used to writing with. That's a way to disguise who wrote it. The disguise made the handwriting look bizarre, which makes it harder to identify. I had to ask myself, if it *was* written by Lucy to her mom, why would she disguise the writing? And, if it was written by someone other than Lucy, why would they sign her name to it?"

The two women froze as if they had been hit with a 'stupefy' spell. She paused to give them time to catch up. "It occurred to me to compare the writing in the note to some of the handwritings in my eleventh grade yearbook, and to some other older handwriting I had in a box of high school memorabilia—been sitting in my garage for more than two decades. Who knew it would come in handy now?

"There were a couple of idiosyncratic features in the note. That means they were unique formations that are not likely to be found in the handwriting of the general population." She stopped again, to make sure the impact of what she was saying was not lost on them. "Of all the handwritings I examined and compared, only one had formations that were similar to those idiosyncratic ones in the note. And they pointed in a particular direction."

"What direction?" Rachel asked faintly. "Whose handwriting..."

"Natalie Parker's."

The blood drained from Rachel's face. She sank onto the floor next to Andrea, nearly as pale as her friend.

Claudia looked from one to the other, wondering what memories were silently passing between them. "I asked myself why Natalie would write that note," she said.

Andie closed her eyes, the pale lashes close to invisible against her pallid skin. "I didn't know Lucy was pregnant until Rachel told me today. Neither did Nat. *He* told us she was going to rat him out to her mom about the drugs, and we needed to—"

"Andie, stop it! Shut up!" Rachel cried out, but Andie wasn't listening. Two red spots marked her pale cheeks. Her voice rose on a hysterical note.

"I never wanted to go with you guys. I *hated* going. I hated every goddamned second of it."

She glowered at Rachel in a most un-Andie like way. "You two shouldn't have made me go. You *ruined* my life."

Claudia and Rachel both stared at her, each for her own reasons. Claudia recovered first. "What happened, Andie?"

"Andie—no!" Rachel moved as if to prevent her from speaking. But Andie kicked her away and pushed to her feet. *"We didn't mean for her to die."*

With an anguished howl, the dam Andrea Adams had defended for twenty-six agonizing years cracked open. The emotions she had been forced to suppress flooded out of her, and all the fear and guilt and resentment. Her eyes stared wildly at Rachel as she relived her nightmare out loud. "We were only supposed to get her not to tell her mother what was going on. We weren't supposed to *kill* her!"

Chapter thirty-two

"Good God, Andie," Claudia cried in horror. Whatever she had imagined, it was not this.

And Andie wasn't finished.

"You and Nat, you kept pushing her down and she couldn't breathe and Nat kept holding her head under the water. She wouldn't stop and poor Lucy was struggling and gagging and begging you every time she could catch a breath, but you wouldn't stop her. Why didn't you stop her?"

She collapsed back in the recliner and closed her eyes, her whole body visibly trembling. "I've lived with it for all these years. I *can't* die with it on my conscience. Somebody needs to know what happened to her."

Rachel, who had remained frozen through the broadside, looked stunned. "Is one of you going to tell me?" Claudia asked.

"Yes," Andie said softly.

Claudia picked up the plaid blanket and wrapped it around her, asking herself as she did what she was going to do with the information once she knew the whole story. As if there was a choice.

Rachel closed her eyes and bowed her head as if she had resigned herself to whatever came next. Andie began in a dull monotone to tell the sordid tale she had kept secret for so long. "He would tell us when we were supposed to meet him at the driver's ed car after school. The blanket would be waiting on the floor of the backseat. We had to cover ourselves with it—three of us squashed back there and one up front, crouched under the dashboard. Unlike me, the others were thin, and Natalie never let me forget it."

"You weren't all that heavy, Andie," Claudia could not help objecting.

"My reflection in the mirror was." Andie gave her a self-deprecating half-smile. "He would drive us into the woods in back of the high school. There's a place called Wildwood Pond—a little pond hidden behind a copse of trees. When you went through an opening in the trees, you couldn't tell anyone was back there. It would have been a beautiful spot, except for the things that happened there.

"Most days, he brought weed and got us high. I guess it was to make sure we were compliant. The others liked it, but I didn't. It made me feel sick, and I'd get dizzy, but he insisted we all take a couple of hits. He'd say something like, 'if you girls are very, very good, I'll have something extra-special for you.' Which meant a new drug or a new 'activity.'" Andie's face twisted into a grimace of disgust. "He'd get this grin like a little boy with a secret, and everyone said he was so cute and adorable. He said he wanted to introduce us to his 'new friend, Molly.'"

Molly. MDMA...

"He gave you *ecstasy?*"

"He'd put it on our tongues," Rachel broke in, now that the story was laid bare. "He liked to French kiss each of us until it dissolved. And then we had to do things to him—sexual things, obviously—until the drug took effect. I didn't understand back then what a sick bastard he was. He'd tell us what he wanted us to do to each other while he watched, until he was excited, and started to—" she trailed off, looking sick.

Andie picked up the narrative. "God, it was humiliating. I was already embarrassed about my body, and to have to be so exposed like that, defenseless—" She pulled the blanket closer around her like armor until it hid the lower half of her face and muffled her voice. "Lucy was always there, but she was never quite part of the group. I knew she was friends with Rachel, but you would never know it when we were all together."

Hiding her emotions behind the long, black hair that trailed over her shoulders, Rachel hung her head. Claudia took note that Joshua Dickson's name had not been invoked, even once. Hearing about the details of what he had done made it all the more reprehensible. It was easy to understand why they both wanted to distance themselves from him that way. She wanted to rail against him, do to him some kind of violence.

"Rachel wanted Nat's approval," Andie was saying. "Don't deny it, Rache."

"I'm not denying it. I wish it wasn't true."

"I don't know why Nat was so contemptuous of Lucy. Probably because Lucy didn't bow down to her the way we all did. Why Lucy stayed friends with you, Rache, I have no idea. The way you treated her when Nat was around. Maybe because she didn't have many people to hang out with. And then there was me, waiting for Natalie to pat me on the head like a puppy and tell me what a good girl I was. She was so beautiful and full of confidence—everything that was out of my reach."

Andie seemed to be running out of steam. She fell silent for a long moment. When she spoke again, her voice was weaker. "When we were little kids, I would do anything she told me to, no questions asked. So, when she started going on these 'fun adventures with Mr. D,' as she called them, and she wanted me to go with her, of course I did, even though I didn't like it from the get-go."

"Did she know that you didn't want to go?" Claudia asked.

"Oh, I may have protested once, but she made it abundantly clear that if I wanted to stay in her orbit, I'd better put up or shut up."

"Lucy had gone with him alone a couple of times," Rachel said. "She told me they'd had full-on sex, which stopped after we three started going. She was so miserable about that."

Andie glared at her. "And now I find out she was ... Omigod, are you *sure* she was pregnant?"

"That's what you told the police, isn't it, Rachel?" Claudia said, giving her a pointed look.

"That's what she told me."

"But you didn't tell them Josh Dickson was the father."

"Of course not. That was the whole point of what happened to her—stopping her from telling on him."

"Jesus Christ, Rachel, you pointed them at Matt Macedo and screwed up his life too."

"I didn't tell them Matt was the father; just that they'd dated," Rachel said defiantly. "And they did, so it wasn't a lie."

Andie frowned. "Why didn't you ever tell Nat and me that Lucy was pregnant by that monster?"

"She made me promise not to tell a soul, and then after she was—you know, dead—it didn't matter anymore."

Andrea's face cleared, and she nodded. "That must have been what was on her mind that day. You could see this—aura of unhappiness—around her."

Rachel said, "Remember the day he made her stay behind, Andie? She told me later that she'd planned to tell him on that day."

"Of course I remember it. She was utterly miserable."

Claudia was confused. "Are you talking about the day she ... died?"

"No," Andie said. "This was the week before that happened. We were waiting for him at the car. Lucy got there late. She was a wreck—like she'd lost her favorite kitten. Puffy, blotchy face, swollen eyes. He told her she couldn't come with us because he didn't want to be around anyone who looked like that. Nat was giggling. I was mortified on her behalf."

Rachel added, "He pulled Lucy aside, and I don't know what else he said to her, but it was obvious she was begging him to let her come. She grabbed his shirt, trying to hold onto him when he turned away from her. He was shaking his head, and he unhooked her fingers and shooed her away. When he came back to the car, where the three of us were waiting, he said she wasn't up for going that day, maybe next time. We left her there in the parking area, alone and sobbing. The rest of us knew better than to ask questions. We didn't want to get left behind like Lucy."

A bolt of fury shot through Claudia like a red hot poker. "What an evil fuck. I can't believe the way we all hero-worshiped him. I've been told about his horrible childhood—and it truly was appalling. But lots of people have horrible childhoods and don't grow up to be child molesters. He should have been arrested and thrown *under* the jail."

"No kidding," Andie agreed. "For once, that day he didn't have any asinine jokes. He didn't say anything until we got to the pond. And when we got there, he gave us a very stern lecture. He said Lucy was threatening to tell about our 'little parties.' He said we couldn't let that happen, that it was up to us to convince her that she couldn't tell a soul, or else he would go to jail and we would be taken away from our families and end up in juvie."

"We believed him," Rachel put in. "He was an adult and our teacher who we trusted to tell us the truth—ironic as that is."

"None of us wanted him to go to jail. Or be taken away from our family." Slumped in her chair, Andie was spent. She paused for a few labored breaths. "We were scared to death. We talked afterwards about what to do, but I didn't know until much later that Nat and Rachel got together without me and decided how they were going to make Lucy agree not to tell."

Rachel didn't look at her. "Nat said you were the weak link. She was afraid you'd warn her if you knew the plan. We tried to tell *him* what we were going to do, which basically was just to threaten her—we didn't intend to happen what happened—he didn't want to hear it."

She went quiet, and Andie took up the story again. "The next week when we went with him, Lucy was allowed to come. She kept giving him this big fake smile. I've never forgotten it; she was so afraid he would leave her behind again. We got to the pond, and after he gave us the molly, and after the other—well—when he finished—he told us to undress each other."

Rachel made a sound of protest. Andie's face flushed bright red. "Don't worry, I'm not going to say what he made us do, and I'm sure Claudia doesn't want to hear the details."

"You're right, Andie," Claudia said. "I really don't."

"It was a warm day, and after he was done with us, he told us to go splash around in the pond for a while. He walked off into the woods by himself. Looking back, I know it was because he didn't want to see what was going to happen to Lucy. He didn't want to feel responsible if she got upset. He knew Nat could be kinda harsh."

"'Harsh?'" Claudia echoed. "That's a mild word after what you described."

"I don't mean to soft-pedal it. Look, I didn't participate directly, but I was there and I didn't do anything to stop it. That makes me complicit. All I did was yell at Nat to let her go when she started choking. I didn't pull her off like I should have. I could see Nat's face. She was enjoying the power."

Suddenly, Andie's body spasmed. She hunched over, hugging her midsection. "You can never forget something like that," she gasped. "I've seen it over and over in a thousand nightmares. We were just kids who got carried away in a horrible moment. None of us are monsters."

Rachel was crying. Claudia felt lightheaded, her stomach churning as if she had a bout of food poisoning. She wanted to tell Andie to stop talking, that she did not want to hear any more. She could not bring herself to do it. "What happened afterwards?"

Rachel reached for a tissue and wiped her eyes. "When we got home, Nat wrote that stupid note and I snuck it into Lucy's house. I'd been there, and I knew where her bedroom was—she had a private door to the outside. We promised each other never to talk about it again."

"I meant what happened when he came back and saw Lucy—when he saw what you had done?" Claudia said impatiently.

Andie said, "We had pulled her out of the water and—"

"I tried to give her mouth-to-mouth," Rachel said. "I didn't know what I was doing; just did what I'd seen on TV. It was too late. She wasn't coming back. We just stood there. We couldn't believe it. None of us had ever seen someone dead. He totally lost it, started bawling like a baby, asking us what the hell we'd done—like he wasn't part of it. After he pulled himself together, he said we had to make it look like she ran away. He made us stay there with her while he went to the hardware store. He came back with a couple of shovels..."

Claudia stared at them. "You *buried* her out there?"

Andie turned wide, frightened eyes to her. "God forgive us, we did. Under a tree next to the pond. We had to take turns digging. Even him. It's way harder than it seems, digging a grave. My hands got blisters—small penance. We dug a couple of feet down; just deep enough for the dirt to completely cover her and a bit more. She was a small girl. He laid her in the grave curled up like a fetus so we didn't have to make it very big." She was panting a little as she paused.

Once again, Rachel took up the narrative again. "We broke branches off some trees and put them over it. He said we should say a silent prayer, if you can believe that."

"I could have cried with relief when he said the 'parties' would have to stop." Andie said. "Eventually, a long time later, there were times when I could pretend to myself that it never happened. Especially when he moved out of state, the coward." She covered her face with her hands. "We believed we had gotten away with it. The truth is, we hadn't; it's haunted me literally every day of my life. Every night, I pray to Lucy to forgive us."

Claudia could find nothing to say. She was thinking of Stephanie Valentine, who had spent the rest of her life believing her daughter would come home to her someday. She never got the closure of knowing what happened to her. Never got to bury her child in a decent grave. Sixteen-year-old Lucy had been abandoned in the ground for animals to find and gnaw on her flesh and bones.

"After so long, I didn't think I would ever have to see him again. And then, there he was, at the reunion." Andie pointed her gaze at Claudia. "That one wasn't their fault, Rachel and Nat's. This time, you can't blame anyone except me."

"Andie, stop," Rachel begged her, "Please don't."

But Andie was past listening. She was on a roll and she was determined not to be interrupted. Her face was drawn and haggard, a death mask. Her breaths juddered, quivering gasps. "Seeing him unexpectedly like that—it triggered every hideous feeling I'd had since the day we killed her. There he was, exactly the same as always—the charmer, the joker, having fun at the party. I bet he never lost a night's sleep over it. In fact, I'd be surprised if he remembered who Lucy Valentine was."

Ice cold dread spread through Claudia like frostbite. "What did you do, Andie?" Knowing what was coming didn't stop her from holding her breath.

Her laugh sizzled with bitter acid. "I know it's hard to imagine. I made them do it. Can you believe it—dying little Andie, *making* Natalie Parker do something? I have nothing to lose, and they have everything to lose. Nat's political dreams mean more to her than anything or anyone in the world, including Tom or their girls. Rachel has her career.

"I told them they had to do what I said or I would spill my guts about Lucy. Rachel would promise him some fun if he would go outside with her—which is hilarious if you think about it—she's a lesbian, right Rache? Of course, he didn't know that, and he was more than half in the bag, so he jumped at the chance. Same old randy Josh."

Her eyes glittered with fury. "Rachel and I went outside first. We were waiting by the pool when he showed up, closely followed by Nat with a couple of bottles of beer. He didn't expect to see all three of us. He actually had the gall to say how great it was, all of us together again. I had intended to make sure he knew why he was going to die, but hearing him say that was the last straw." She paused to catch her breath. "I grabbed one of those bottles from Nat. He was turned away from me and I slammed it in the back of his head as hard as I could."

"I didn't have the strength to knock him out, but it felt so satisfying, so good—like one of those games at the fair where you hit the hammer and make the bell ring. In the state he was in, it was easy to knock him off balance. Nat hit him with the other bottle and he was down for the count. I gave my bottle to Rachel. It was easy, and there wasn't any blood.

We rolled him into the pool and let nature take its course." A humorless smile stretched her lips. "Does that make us serial killers?"

"We left by the back gate," Rachel said in a low voice. "We had checked for cameras, and knew we were safe."

Andie took the last word. "That night when I got home, I poured a big glass of wine and told Lucy that we had delivered justice for us all."

Her confession complete, she started to retch. Claudia grabbed a wad of tissues from a box on the end table, too late to catch the oily green mess that spewed from her mouth.

From the doorway, a new voice said, "Omigod, that's gross."

Chapter thirty-three

As one, their heads turned. How long had Natalie been standing there, listening?

She held her phone pointing at Andie with one hand, a restaurant bag in the other. "Hey there, cousin, I brought you lunch, but it looks like that isn't going to work." She tapped the phone screen and dropped it into her purse. "I didn't know you had company until I saw Rachel's van in the driveway."

Claudia made a cynical guess that it was to have been a TikTok video intended to show her constituency how kind and generous their city councilwoman was, delivering food to her sick cousin. Maybe she had not been there long enough to hear their confessions.

The aroma of chicken soup wafted across the room and Andie fell back onto her chair, retching again. Her face was waxy and she hugged her belly, shivering. There was nothing left for her to bring up.

Forcing down the bile that rose in her own throat, Claudia kicked aside the soiled blanket and cleaned the dribbled mess away from Andie's mouth and chin.

Natalie wrinkled her nose in distaste and handed the bag to Rachel. "Be a love and put this in the kitchen." Then, "Didn't expect to see you here, Claudia. What's the occasion?"

Claudia fought the urge to turn tail and run. She made her voice as level as she could manage. "Quick visit to an old school friend. I was telling them about a documentary Matt Macedo is making about Lucy Valentine. Remember when she disappeared in our junior year?"

Natalie quickly concealed the sick expression that had crossed her face, and constructed a fake smile that showed off white, even teeth. She was not a politician for nothing. Hiding her true feelings must have become a practiced art.

"Matt Macedo?" she said. "Your old boyfriend? Why would he be interested in that old case after so long?" Her cool blue eyes swept Andie, and then Rachel, who had returned after depositing the offending soup in the kitchen. "Have you two been holding out on me?" she said archly.

"Not deliberately," Rachel said in a shaky voice. "I've been slammed at work and obviously, Andie has been too sick to do much of anything." As her gaze slid away, there was no disguising that she had been caught in the lie.

Natalie stared at her for a long moment, letting her know that she knew. It was a surprise when she let it go. She wrinkled her nose in distaste and said, "It reeks in here." Then, perhaps hearing the coldness in her tone, quickly added, "You poor thing, Andie. Rachel, dump that blanket somewhere, preferably outside in the trash. Let's you and I get her into bed. Then we can have a little visit with Claudia."

Not for a moment did Claudia believe that Natalie cared about Andie. It was not in her narcissistic nature to show genuine empathy for anyone else, even her ailing cousin. If she knew, or guessed what they had been talking about, she would be on to damage control. These women had killed twice to hide their secrets. Rachel appeared remorseful, but was that sufficient to change her behavior after a lifetime of doing Natalie's bidding?

"I'll bring her up some water," Claudia said. She would deliver a bottle of to Andie and make sure she was comfortably put to bed, then she would find an excuse to get the hell out of her house.

At least, that was her plan.

Andie's bedroom had the spartan feeling of a nun's cell, with a single piece of wall décor above her bed—a small body of water surrounded by leafy trees. The pond where Lucy had drowned, or one like it, if Claudia's guess was correct—stark evidence of her daily self-flagellation, which she had suffered on behalf of all three of them.

The covers were folded back on the bed where Andie was lying, a flower-sprigged flannel nightgown in a heap across the foot. When Claudia arrived, Rachel was working the heavy sweater over her head while Natalie stood at the door, watching. "You must be used to dressing people," Natalie said with a monstrous lack of tact.

Rachel shot her a glare full of animosity. "Why don't you shut the hell up for once, Nat?"

The other woman's manicured eyebrows rose in surprise, the very picture of innocence. "What? What did I say wrong? Don't you have to dress people before a—"

Claudia shoved past her, not bothering to be polite. "Are you naturally that callous, Nat? Or do you have to work at it?" She went around to the opposite side of the bed, where Rachel was now struggling to remove Andie's sweatpants. "Let me help."

Working together, the two of them got the nightgown over their friend's head and the sleeves over her limp arms. Other than the flicker of her eyelids, there were no obvious signs of life. The emotional toll of unburdening herself had taken a physical one as well. Andie's face was as white as the pillowcase on which she lay.

Heedful not to let the garment bunch up under her back, and taking care to preserve her modesty, they smoothed it down over shockingly bony hips and legs.

When they were finished, Rachel pulled the bedclothes up over her, and brushed the back of her hand lightly across her friend's cheek. "Are you warm enough, Andie?"

When there was no response, she carefully removed the wig, which had become askew. Without the glossy brown hair that had framed her sunken features, Andie had the look of a newborn baby bird, fallen from the nest before its feathers grew in.

Natalie edged out of the doorway. "Bye, Andie. See you downstairs, Rache."

Rachel hung back. "She might need some help."

"Claudia's got it covered, haven't you? She keeps her meds on the nightstand. Give her a couple of the ones that help her sleep. I'll get someone to come and check on her later."

"I'll be glad to stay with your cousin if you're too busy." The dirty look Claudia threw her was as lost on Natalie as the sarcasm.

"No need. The pills will knock her out for a good few hours. She won't know whether you're here or not. And we do need to chat before you leave. Come on, Rache."

Rachel trailed her out of the room with a troubled glance behind her, leaving Claudia to examine the pill bottles. There were several, including one whose name she recognized as an opioid. "Is Nat right, Andie? Do you want meds?"

Her head moved in a slight nod. "Two," she whispered, mouthing the name of the opioid drug.

"This says one every four to six hours," Claudia said, reading the dosage. If Andie wanted to overdose—and she could not blame her if she did—she was not going to be the one to help her do it. She shook one pill into her palm. "I'm sorry, Andie, I can't give you two."

A single tear leaked out of the closed eyes and slid down her cheek. She said something, but her words were inaudible. Claudia leaned close enough to catch the end, "...sleep forever."

Tears clouded Claudia's eyes, too, but it would be a cruel poke at an open wound to say what she would have liked to: "Dickson was a piece of crap, but killing him wasn't the answer." Instead, she opened the Dasani and sat on the edge of the bed, supporting the sick woman, who was having some difficulty swallowing the pill. "What you told me is unbearable," Claudia said. "I wish I could erase it all for you."

Andrea's eyelids fluttered half-open. "No. I deserve it." It was clear that every word she pushed out took a monumental effort. "I'm fine. Go."

"You don't look fine. I don't think I should leave you alone like this."

"Get away from Nat, she's—"

Her head lolled, and for one awful moment Claudia feared she was gone. What had she been trying to say?

Nat's what? Toxic? A pain in the ass? A narcissist?

The Natalie Parker she knew was all of those. For several minutes she sat there, monitoring the rise and fall of Andie's chest, the shallow, almost undetectable respirations. The voices of the other two women downstairs were audible—not what they said, but the urgent tone of their conversation. Again, it came to Claudia—even if she had not heard the full confession, from her manner, Natalie must have heard plenty. What was Rachel telling her?

Her purse was in the den. She would have to pass them to get it and leave. Luckily, her phone was in her pocket. She started to call Joel. Remembering he was in the field, she typed out a text.

'Natalie, Andie, Rachel killed Lucy and Dickson. Heading home.'

When she tapped Send a red message popped up on the screen: "Not delivered."

Paying a mint to live in the Hills apparently did not guarantee a good signal. She would have to try him again from the road once she got out of the area. With a last glance at Andie, whose face had relaxed into a mercifully peaceful expression, Claudia left the room.

They were waiting for her at the foot of the staircase.

"Poor Andie," Natalie said with a remarkable lack of sincerity. "She's been such an awesome admin for me all the time I've been in office; during the campaign too. Of course, she's my cousin. We've been as thick as thieves all our lives. I'm gonna miss her a lot when she's gone."

"I can only imagine, how devastated you must be," Claudia said, doubting she would get the sarcasm.

Natalie reached out and laid her hand on Claudia's arm. She looked down at the expensive nail art—a delicate line painted on each French tip one-third of the way down—and wanted to wrench it away. She had taken the time and energy for an expensive manicure, but was going to "send someone" to look in on the cousin who had devoted her life to serving her.

"Andie's asleep," Claudia said "I'm going to get—"

"Rachel brought me up to date," Natalie interrupted. "All that silly stuff Andie was spouting about that Valentine girl—"

"I have a feeling you're going to tell me it was the ravings of a fevered mind."

"Of course I am. You can see how unwell she is—just about on her last legs, I'm afraid. The treatments have left their mark, too. Her imagination has gone *completely* off the rails. It's a side effect of some of the medications her doctor prescribed." Natalie lowered her voice to a murmur. "It's so sad, the way she hallucinates. I have no clue where she came up with this nonsense. I mean, seriously, can you imagine the three of us *killing* Lucy Valentine, and then Josh Dickson? At the reunion?" She shook her head again, as if she couldn't quite believe what she was saying, and came up with a sad laugh. "You probably didn't know she's always had a crush on Josh Dickson—unrequited, of course. She became obsessed with him. Seeing him at the reunion badly upset her. It brought back her feelings of being embarrassed because he didn't return her affection. Of course he didn't; he wasn't all that much older than us, but he was married with kids, and he was our *teacher*. He certainly wasn't interested in Andie—remember how roly-poly she was back then?"

"We don't blame her," Rachel was quick to add as if she had not been part of the admissions of guilt. "She can't help it. But you can't trust what she says."

Whatever remorse Rachel had felt had either been squelched by the more powerful Natalie, or she was playing along with her for some private reason. Claudia looked from one to the other and forced herself to nod sympathetically. "Poor Andie. That explains it all. It did sound sad, and preposterous when she said it. Don't worry, I won't take it seriously. Consider it forgotten." She could barely keep from rolling her eyes at her own falsity. Was she overdoing it?

Natalie smiled like a shark. "Oh, good. Hey, why don't we get together sometime. Later, I mean, after Andie is—well, let's just say under happier circumstances. I'll spring for lunch."

"Yeah, let's do that," Claudia said with the same degree of insincerity. Rage burned in her gut at what they had done. But there was fear in her too. Did they believe she accepted their excuses about Andie's mental condition? The desire to rush out to her car was an itch that badly needed scratching. She could hardly wait to shake off the dreadful taint of what she had learned; to get the hell away from Edenwood and never come back. Producing a weak smile, she said, "I need to get my purse from the den and get going. My husband is expecting me home before it gets dark."

"Oh, those pesky husbands," Natalie said archly. Rachel remained silent, her eyes darting back and forth between the two of them like a rodent assessing the danger between the cheese and a trap.

Half-expecting them to prevent her from leaving, Claudia held her breath. They didn't try anything, and she retrieved her purse. The three of them walked to the front door together, making goodbye small talk—great to see you, have a wonderful weekend, yada yada. Her car keys were in her hand and she was reaching for the doorknob...

From the corner of her eye, her attention was drawn by a movement from behind. She started to pivot at the same time Rachel yelled, "No, Nat, don't!"

Natalie's raised arm came down.

Something hard slammed into the side of Claudia's head. "I should have listened to Andie," she thought as she dropped to the floor.

Chapter thirty-four

At first she thought the rhythmic, throbbing roar was ocean waves battering a cliff face. Squinching her eyes open in almost-darkness, the sound resolved into a throbbing inside her head. Her brain was refusing to cooperate. Answers floated, tantalizing, just out of reach. She could not remember why her head hurt, nor how she came to be here—wherever *here* was—flat on her back, arms and legs restrained, with little room to move.

Wet beads of condensation formed and trickled down her face in air that was overly warm and humid, oppressive. And yet, an unpleasant cool slickness lay damply against her face. It took a second or two to identify the overbearing smell. Plastic. More seconds passed. Gradually, as awareness grew, it came to her in a fit of panic: her entire body was cocooned in the same material.

Frantic, Claudia thrashed her body. Unsuccessful in freeing herself from the prison that swathed her, and well on her way to hyperventilating, she badly wanted to scream—*needed* to scream, A thick strip of sticky tape across her mouth made it impossible.

She was already shaking and starting to feel dizzy. Teetering on the razor's edge of hysteria. A voice in the back of her mind clamored to warn her. Something told her to listen. Breathing her own air in the enclosed space was causing the oxygen levels in her blood to drop and the carbon dioxide to increase. Her blood pressure was climbing. Soon it would be harder to breathe. She would pass out and ...

Stop it!

Whatever primal instinct slammed the brakes on the runaway fear demanded that she find a way to curb the terror and hang on to whatever control she could find.

The usual breathing techniques were not going to work when her breaths were coming in little puffs above the tape over her mouth. It took some digging to find an optimistic thought to glom onto, but she found one: right now, in this moment, she was alive. The only chance she had to stay that way was to get calm. She forced herself to concentrate on her concrete senses, naming each one and counting to five each time.

Gradually, she was able to stop the frenzied twisting and turning. Little by little, the swirling thoughts slowed and settled. And when she was still, like a dirt-crusted window scrubbed clean, Claudia had a moment of blinding clarity: Natalie had knocked her out. Then another: Rachel was a mortician.

The appalling truth smacked her in the face. She was trapped in a mortuary body bag. What were they planning? To kill her and bury her where Lucy's remains were? Bury her alive in the bag? Hysteria started to rise again like a helium-filled balloon.

Again, she pushed it back down and took stock of her situation. The restraints that crossed her chest and thighs were, she realized, just straps whose purpose was to keep the limbs of a corpse from flopping around. If Rachel had fastened them as she habitually did on her job, they might not be tight enough to secure a prisoner.

Claudia began to experiment. She tested her ability to move, to see how much she could shift her right shoulder and arm. There was some restriction, but, holding her arm against her body, she could bend her elbow and wriggle her arm and hand up across her stomach and her chest. She was maneuvering her hand under the strap and pushing it toward the gag—

Her heart leapt in hope at the sound of muffled voices, and the rattle of wheels on tile. They must have reconsidered, and were coming to let her out. Claudia moaned through the tape on her mouth, squirming as much as she could to get their attention.

"Crap, she's awake." Rachel's tense voice poured ice cold water on the fragile fantasy that they were here to release her.

"You backed the van into the garage, right?" Natalie said.

"I told you I did. If any of the neighbors see it, they'll think it's for Andie."

"Let's get it done, then. You take her shoulders; I'll get her feet."

Feeling their hands take hold of the bag and start to lift it, Claudia thrashed until they dropped her back to the floor. "Damn, she's heavier than she looks," Natalie complained. "How the hell are we supposed to pick her up if she won't be still?"

"You expect her to just stay still? Seriously?"

"Maybe I should knock her out again."

"No, Nat, don't!"

The oxygen in the bag was diminishing. The higher CO_2 levels close to her face were making Claudia lightheaded. Even in her half-dazed state, the futility of fighting them hit her. Her body went as limp as a ragdoll.

"I think she's passed out on her own," Rachel said. "Hey, don't open it. We just have to get her onto the gurney, then I'll raise it and we're good to go. On three. One. Two. Three. *Now.*"

Claudia felt herself lifted just a little, and moved a short distance. They deposited her on a softer surface—the gurney.

"Be careful she doesn't slide off," Rachel cautioned as they started to move.

"Aren't the straps tight?"

"What the hell? Do you think this is the first time I've done this?"

"Truthfully, Rache, I hope it is." Natalie's giggle bore a hint of mania. "Did you notice, in that bag, she looks like a giant caterpillar."

"Omigod, Nat, do you ever think before you speak?"

"I can't help it; I'm nervous. Aren't you?"

"Nervous doesn't begin to cover it. This is completely crazy, Nat. We can't—"

"It's too late to back out now."

The gurney started moving, and there was the sound of wheels on the tile floor again.

"It's *not* too late until we do something irreversible. We could drop her off in some shitty neighborhood and deny—"

Natalie's voice turned frosty. "Rachel, listen to me. Do you want to go to prison for the rest of your life?"

"No, but—"

"Thanks to Andie, we just killed a man in cold blood. It doesn't matter what he did to us in 1998, we killed him *now,* and we can't exactly cry self-defense when it was three on one. Remember why we went along with it—to protect ourselves."

"I know, but Claudia ..."

"She wasn't buying that story about Andie hallucinating. She pretended to, but she's too smart for that. I could see it in her face."

"We'll never get away with it."

"Rachel. Would you get a grip. I'll find a way like I always do. I have no intention of giving up everything I've worked for so long and hard."

The stretcher bumped over something—the interior garage door sill? Claudia could tell when they made a turn. A few seconds later came to a stop.

"Hurry it up would you," Natalie urged. "Let's get this over with."

"Goddamn it, Nat, I'm not Andie. Quit ordering me around. I've done this a thousand times."

"Maybe so, but your clients generally aren't alive and moving around like this one."

The gurney slid horizontally and the wheels folded, then a sharp jounce. The brain fog was starting to descend again, leaving her feeling sluggish. It would be so much easier to close her eyes and just go to sleep and stop struggling.

"Hold on a sec, I have to set the lock so it doesn't roll around." Rachel's words were followed by a loud click and the slam of two doors. The slam jolted Claudia back to awareness, and renewed anger. That Natalie and Rachel would do this to her boiled hotly and erupted into fury. She would not go unresisting like a helpless victim.

Two more door slams were followed by the dull roar of a vehicle engine—the mortuary van. As the van backed out of the garage, her brain started ticking again, not at its normal pace, but well enough that she knew she had to do something to help herself. And she knew that meant stomping her fear to death.

The worst moment, the utter horror of realizing that she was trapped in a cadaver pouch had passed minutes ago. Now she was numb. What she needed was to think rationally about where they might be taking her and how much time she had before the van stopped. It was two against one, and one had a concussion, her oxygen supply depleting fast.

She reached her hand up under the restraints again until her fingertips touched the tape across her mouth. Resisting the temptation to rip it away in one movement, she started working the borders, peeling it back, inch by inch so the skin wouldn't tear. And then her mouth was free and she was gasping the sweetest gulp of air she could have wished for.

The sudden jolt of a vibration against her hip, and Claudia almost leapt out of her skin. She swallowed a crazy laugh. They had taken her purse, but had neglected to frisk her for her phone. Counting her blessings that Natalie and Rachel were not career criminals, and thankful that she had set the ring to vibrate while Andie was unburdening herself, she steered her hand back down and reached into her pocket.

By the time she got the phone close enough to see the screen, the phone had stopped vibrating. Her thoughts were getting scrambled again. She searched through the fuzziness. What was she supposed to do? If she called Joel, she would run risk of the women up front hearing her.

Text message. Send him a text.

> help me. mort van

No! no! no!

The same red error as before appeared on the screen: 'Not delivered.'
She tried Kelly. 'Not delivered.'
Detective Booker. 'Not delivered.'

Hopelessness settled over her like a thick, black cloud. Being trapped alive in a body bag was more claustrophobic than an Egyptian tomb—she knew that from experience. She had no idea whether or when her texts would eventually send. How stupid she had been, staying in Andie's house for even a single minute after Natalie arrived. She had done so many foolhardy things over the past few years. No wonder Joel despaired of her ever learning a lesson...

All at once it occurred to her that something important was happening. With her mouth free of the tape, she was taking in more air that her oxygen-starved blood needed. As the molecules entered the cells throughout her body and woke them up, a tiny ray of optimism stole into her mind and began to grow. They had put her into this shroud, so there had to be an opening.

Body bags had zippers.

Using the phone's flashlight, she laid it on her chest and reached up to grope the plastic surface with her fingertips until she found the zipper. Quickly familiarizing herself with her intimate prison, her efforts were rewarded. She located a pinpoint of exterior light above and just behind her head—a slight opening at the end of the zipper.

Lying on her back, she reached up. She worked her fingernails between the heavy-duty zipper teeth with shaking hands, pushing against them to separate the two sides. Her arms soon tired in the awkward position, but when the teeth began to split apart and a space opened just enough to allow some blessed fresh air in from outside the bag, Claudia could have shouted with excitement. By that time, her nails were chipped and broken, her fingertips sore, but she thanked her lucky stars for shoddy workmanship.

Her plan was to surprise them when they got to wherever they were going. Now that she had made a start, the zipper would be ready to open when the time was right.

Unless they planned to dig a hole and dump her into it, bag and all.

Chapter thirty-five

Rachel's voice sounded through the opening in the bag.

"... at the funeral home until we can figure out what to do."

"What about the family? How the hell are you going to keep them from seeing her?"

"They've gone to Mexico for a week. The place is closed up until Monday. I wouldn't have suggested it otherwise."

"Well, isn't that convenient."

"*None* of this is convenient."

Natalie made a disapproving cluck with her tongue. "You're not going to pull an Andie on me are you, and spill your guts to the wrong person? This is no time to go soft, Rachel. Listen to me. After I'm elected mayor I intend to work my way up to the governor's mansion, and I'm not about to let either you or Andie—nor our friend in the cargo bay—slow me down."

The van swerved a little, then accelerated. "Are you *threatening* me, Nat? Frankly, I wouldn't be at all surprised if you were planning to get rid of me too."

"Don't be stupid. That would be too obvious. Anyway, we can't keep her there too long. Only until we figure out what to do with her."

"Her husband's a cop—"

"So what? Nobody knows you or I were at Andie's. If she told anyone she was going there, I can make Andie say she never showed up. Or that she was there and left for home and we don't know what happened after that."

"That's not very bright, Nat. There was an old Jaguar outside Andie's place. I think it must be Claudia's. That was the only car parked out there when I arrived."

"Good point, we need to get rid of it. Okay, let's lock her up in the mortuary, then you can drop me back at Andie's and we'll take the car somewhere and leave it. I'll give Andie enough pills to keep her quiet for now. Maybe if we're lucky, she won't wake up. That would be a good distraction."

"Omigod, don't you have any conscience at all?" Rachel sounded appalled.

Natalie laughed. "A conscience in politics? You must be joking."

"And what about Claudia?"

"I've been thinking about that. How about an overdose of Rohypnol? Or shoot her up with embalming fluid, or—"

That was when Claudia tuned them out.

She guessed they had been driving for about thirty minutes when the van came to a halt. Rachel had said they were going to the funeral home, and the motor of what sounded like a creaky rollup door seemed to confirm it. Earlier in the day, when she had visited Rachel, she had not seen the loading area, which, logically, must be around the back of the main house.

Her exertions mixed with agitation had worsened the throbbing in her head. She touched her fingers to the area above her ear, and bit back a cry of pain. Whatever Natalie had struck her with had left a serious goose egg. Claudia knew what a concussion felt like, and it felt like this.

She heard the front doors of the van open and shut. Lying still and silent, she barely breathed as they came around and opened the rear doors.

Rachel unlocked the gurney and wheeled it out. Neither she nor Natalie mentioned the small opening on the zipper.

"Why isn't she flopping around like before?" Natalie's voice said as they rolled her along rough flooring.

"As hard as you hit her, she probably has a concussion. And there's that little fact about breathing your own carbon dioxide for too long—"

"I didn't think about that." Natalie's tone brightened. "We can just leave her in the bag. Maybe we don't have to do anything else. It'll happen naturally. She'll suffocate."

"In case you've forgotten, *Jack the Ripper,* that still leaves a body to dispose of."

"Don't call me that."

"Why not? You don't seem to mind—"

"Shut up, Rachel. Disposal is a problem any way you look at it." Natalie's voice sagged. "I don't know about you, but I could use a minute. I don't suppose you keep any tequila here?"

"There's a bar up in the residence," Rachel said. Sudden anger shook her voice. "Dammit, Nat, why did you have to make everything worse?"

"Me? It wasn't me, it was Andie and you, with your 'true confessions.' I'm just trying to fix your screwup."

Rachel's voice rose to a near shriek. "Fix it? By killing *again?*"

"Chill out, would you? Do you think this is easy for me? Let's go find an adult beverage and relax for five minutes while I figure out what the hell we're going to do."

"You have to be the coldest damn bitch I ever had the bad luck to meet."

"Nice way to talk to your oldest friend. You need to calm the hell down."

The gurney stopped, and Rachel said, "Open the door. This is my prep room. We can leave her in here for now."

"Aren't you going to put her in the freezer?"

"No, Natalie, I am not."

"Why not?"

"She's not dead."

"Yet. She's such a troublemaker, we ought to 'put her on ice.'" Natalie laughed without humor. "Isn't that what they used to say in old movies?"

"She's fine right here. Doesn't look like she's going anywhere, does it?"

"Mmm, I guess not. Let's go then. Lead me to the tequila."

Claudia felt the gurney turn a corner and move a few feet. A door closed and the sound of their voices started to fade.

Freedom was a matter of millimeters away. Her feverish tugging and pulling on the opening she had started in the zipper paid off. Seconds later, with a crinkling of plastic, the two sides of her horrid shroud came apart.

With the bag open, she could see that the restraints were like vehicle seatbelts. Unclasping the one across her chest, clammy and shaking, she pushed herself up on her elbows. The room spun.

Claudia squeezed her eyes shut and held herself perfectly motionless. She inhaled deeply and exhaled on a long breath before struggling into a sitting position. Conscious of every second that raced by, she gradually opened her eyes.

The prep room was no longer moving. She was still lightheaded, the throbbing was just as strong, but the minutes were passing too fast.

The three stainless steel body trays were empty. If she'd had to face a corpse it would have been the last straw. She scanned the room, looking for a weapon, and noticed the instrument tray, which was covered with protective paper.

Claudia unclasped the lower belt still fastened across her thighs and swung her legs over the side of the gurney. She sat for a few seconds, then slid off it. Her legs were wobbly, but with her feet planted on the floor she could stand without support.

Under the protective covering on the instrument tray, medical implements had been lined up, ready to embalm the next body. Forceps, hemostat, needles. Those were the familiar ones. Others looked like something Vlad the Impaler might use, and Claudia preferred not to know their purpose.

Without warning, the door swung open with a loud squeak, and there was Rachel. They both froze, staring at each other across the gurney. Rachel's eyes flicked to the body bag splayed open. "How did you get free?"

Claudia glared at her. "Where's your partner in crime?"

Rachel, her hands outstretched in an appeasing gesture, took a step into the prep room. She spoke in a low, soothing tone, "Listen to me, I'll help you get out of here."

With a glance at the door, Claudia calculated what it would take to get past her. The odds did not look good. "You *kidnapped* me and put me in a goddamned body bag." She strained to hear any indication that Natalie was close by. "Is your career really worth *killing?*"

"*I* don't want to kill you," Rachel said reasonably. "That's all Nat. And she'll be down here any minute, looking for me. I'm just pretending so—"

"Get out of my way, Rachel."

"I'll help you get away."

"I wouldn't trust you as far as I could spit." Claudia's fear had morphed into fury, driven by the determination to survive. Adrenaline charged through her blood. She grabbed the side of the gurney and rammed it into Rachel with all the force she could muster. The aluminum frame was too light to do any lasting damage, but it caught her just below the ribs.

The air rushed out of her in a big "oof." She staggered off-balance as the gurney clanked against the wall.

Claudia grabbed the closest instrument on the tray—a scalpel. It was smaller than she would have liked, but a scalpel was sharper than a razor, and could be lethal. Besides, beggars could not be choosers; it was better than being emptyhanded.

Her heart pumping hard enough to power a city block, she entered the corridor. Claudia swung her gaze to the right, then the left. Which way to go? She had only seconds to decide before Rachel would recover her balance and come after her, and the throbbing in her head was a vice, tightening with every pulse until she was almost blind with the noise.

Focus. Concentrate.

Not to the right. That way led to the staircase from the first floor. At the end of the corridor the other way was a sharp turn. She remembered the waft of cold air she had felt that morning. Praying that it led to an exit, she staggered in that direction. She was at the L when she heard a distant door bang, then Natalie's voice on the stairs. "What's happening? Rachel, what—"

In Claudia's imagination, the voice expanded and filled the air; this woman whose need to satisfy her overblown ego had destroyed lives. Rachel's voice pulled her back to reality. "She got away. I don't know how—"

"For fuck's sake, Rachel, can't you do anything right? Don't just stand there, stop her!"

The echo of expensive high heels clattered down the steep staircase—too bad she didn't fall and break something important. The sound followed Claudia to a wide door. She flung it open, and there, thank God, was the mortuary van and a ramp leading to the open rollup door.

She emerged into a deserted concrete parking area feeling more defenseless and afraid than she ever had in her life. Risking a quick glance behind her, she saw Natalie, tottering into the loading bay in her ridiculous shoes. Rachel was closing in, her soft soles pounding on the concrete. How had she caught up so fast?

Abruptly, Claudia stopped running and whirled around, the scalpel clenched in her outthrust fist, blade first. "Go on, Rachel. Give me an excuse."

Rachel swerved to a halt, her eyes wild as they landed on the scalpel, then went back to Claudia. She tried to smirk, but her voice was less than certain. "You know you're not gonna use that."

The taunt flashed through Claudia like a bolt of forked lightning. She widened her stance, keeping her eyes on the other woman, and readied herself. She spoke in a low, dangerous tone, "You think I'm bluffing? Try me."

Rachel lunged at her. Claudia stepped to the side and brought the blade in a downward arc, catching her upper arm, splitting the fabric of her long-sleeve T-shirt and the flesh beneath it. Continuing on its arc, the scalpel caught her across the abdomen. A cherry red patch flowered and spread on her baby blue scrubs. Rachel's face went slack with shock.

The shock reverberated through Claudia too, that she had done it. But her legs threatened to give way, and there was no time to concern herself with Rachel's condition.

In a desperate scan of the neighborhood, she saw no lights on in the houses across the street. The gathering dusk meant it must be around four o'clock—too early for the residents to be home from work. And even if they were, who would open to a strange woman banging on the door, yelling for help? Across the funeral home's small parking area was Edenwood Memorial Cemetery. Claudia started running that way.

The graveyard dated back to the 1800s, with rows of headstones in all shapes and sizes. Only one place would hide her long enough to make a 911 call—a family mausoleum several rows of graves over and across from the ten-foot-high obelisk where she now stood.

Without warning, the adrenaline of the chase wore off and vertigo kicked in. The world was suddenly off kilter—trees down, graves up. The ground tilted as though she was falling. Claudia stumbled to her knees. Shaky and faint, she rolled onto her back in the damp grass and reached a hand into her pocket for her phone. Not there.

Over the ringing in her ears, she could hear Natalie and Rachel quietly calling to each other, hunting her down. With a sick sinking in the pit of her stomach she closed her eyes and rapidly walked backward through her mind, struggling to recall the last time the phone was in her hands. She had placed it on her chest while she worked on the body bag zipper. It must have slipped off, and in her urgency to get free, she had failed to notice.

Tears gathered and slid down her cheeks. Between them, Natalie and Rachel would soon find her, and in this weakened state, she would not stand a chance against the two of them. Gingerly, she opened her eyes and saw a sliver of moon peeping out from a bank of clouds in the darkening sky. The branches of the trees were once again above, where they belonged. Claudia risked turning her head a little to the side, relieved that the graves were holding steady on the ground. Miraculously, the scalpel was still gripped in her fist. It was slick with Rachel's blood. There was blood on her hands, too.

She inched along the grass toward the mausoleum. Almost home free. Claudia scrambled to her feet ...

And Natalie stepped out from behind the obelisk. "There she is!"

Rachel appeared from the west, where the road ran alongside the cemetery and the funeral home.

Claudia started running, weaving between the graves. Her pursuers were closing in from both sides. If she could make it across the street from the cemetery, or around the corner from the funeral home, she could hide in one of the backyards. If she turned back and went the other way they could reach her still. The only possible route was to go between them.

Focused on the road, she pushed her unwilling legs to pump faster than they wanted to go, and was ten yards away from the street when she tripped on a tree root. Sprawling headfirst, her chin scraped the rough granite edge of a gravestone as she landed on the grave. The warm dribble of blood slid down her cheek and neck, and a wicked pain in her face jarred her from the top of her head to the soles of her feet.

Natalie was bent over her, giving her no chance to pick herself up. "Get up, Claudia," she hissed, yanking on her shirt. "This is not going to end well for you." And to Rachel, "Get over here!"

Then, out of nowhere, the piercing wail of sirens split the dusk. Natalie turned to look, and hesitated a moment too long. Hanging onto the scalpel as if it were glued to her, Claudia slashed it across her outstretched palm.

With an earsplitting shriek, Natalie stared at her bleeding hand, wiping it across her yellow designer jacket and continuing to shriek. Rachel, behind her, was pale-faced and bleeding too.

Holding onto the scalpel, Claudia pushed to her feet as a string of police cars—a half-dozen or more—lightbars strobing red and blue on their roofs, rounded the corner and pulled up outside the mortuary. The sirens shut down with a couple of "whoop whoops," and high-powered spotlights lit up the spectacle like a stage play. Officers poured out of their vehicles.

"Drop your weapon," the lead officer shouted, "Drop it. Drop it and get down on the ground."

Their guns were pointed at Claudia.

Chapter thirty-six

Claudia hated guns, always had. Couldn't bear to touch Joel's service weapon when he left it on the nightstand. Having ten or twelve of the deadly weapons pointed at her was a whole new level of terror.

"I'm not armed," she cried out. She threw the bloody scalpel away from her and dropped to her knees with her hands up. "They kidnapped me. I was protecting myself."

Someone was barking commands at her. "I need you to stop talking, ma'am, and lie down on the ground."

He couldn't mean her. *Could he?* He could, she discovered when he pushed her facedown on the sidewalk. Another cop strode over. "Put your hands behind your back," he ordered, pulling a pair of nitrile gloves on over hands that looked enormous.

Claudia, not in her right mind, attempted to twist away and sit up. "Wait! I have a concussion. That woman in the yellow suit over there—she hit me on the head." She heard her voice rising frantically and could not seem to stop it.

The cop pushed her down again, harder. "Ma'am, I said to *stop talking and put your hands behind your back.*"

She had no trouble hearing the command. It was the anger, humiliation, and outrage at the injustice that would not let her stop.

"Call Detective Booker—Sam Booker, Edentown PD. Please call him. He'll tell you. Or call my husband at LAPD. He's a detective."

The cop yanked her hands behind her back and slapped on handcuffs. "You can call whoever you want when you get to the station. Now, we're going to stand you up and put you in one of the units."

The ignominy hurt as much as having her arms stretched behind her. Two of them pulled her up off the ground. They walked her past another officer—the one who looked like a high schooler who was on his radio, calling for medical help. "—two females bleeding from knife wounds."

Unable to contain herself, Claudia yelled out, "It's not a knife."

Natalie was with another officer. As Claudia neared her, she broke off moaning about her ruined jacket and injured hand, and in her most officious tone said the magic words: "Do you know who I am? I'm your city councilwoman. That woman over there—Claudia Bennett—she tried to kill me."

"It's not Bennett," Claudia shouted at her. Neglecting the fact that, given she was in handcuffs, her last name was inconsequential, she added "It's Claudia Rose, and *you're* the killer!"

The officer who seemed to be in charge, said, "Watch this one," and handed Claudia off to one of his subordinates. Taking Natalie to his unit, he popped the rear hatch and seated her on the bumper—not handcuffed, Claudia noticed resentfully—as he got out a first-aid kit and wrapped Natalie's palm. Rachel was getting similar first-aid at another unit, while she, the victim, was being treated like a criminal.

They stuck her in the backseat of a unit, where she could hear one of the cops on the radio. "...city councilwoman...victim of a single stab wound to the hand. Roll a supervisor."

Of course they would bring out a supervisor for a politician who was married to a well-known defense attorney.

"I did *not* stab her," she said sullenly to the female cop who was none-too-gently wiping blood off her face. "I was defending myself."

The cop ignored her.

An ambulance arrived within a few minutes, and paramedics checked their injuries. Natalie and Rachel were taken to the hospital, and things got quiet. Claudia, having refused to go with them and have her head wound examined, was returned to the backseat of the police car. She didn't know what they were waiting for, but time slowed down and soon it was fully dark. The knot of local residents who had gathered in the street dispersed.

Her eyes were drooping—the concussion, she supposed. At last, an unmarked city car pulled up. Saving her from plunging over the cliff of misery, Detective Samuel Booker climbed out. Smart and well-pressed as usual, in a natty charcoal pinstripe suit, he took in the scene and went to speak to the officer in charge, who pointed in Claudia's direction. Booker walked over to the vehicle where she was sitting in an awkward position with her hands cuffed painfully behind her. He leaned down. "Hello again, Ms. Rose."

Claudia dredged up a weak smile. "I never thought I'd be happy to see you, detective."

"I'm happy to see you too," he said, surprising her. He turned to the nearest officer with an irritated glare. "Unhook this one. Now. She's a *witness,* not a suspect." He might as well have added "dummy."

Sam Booker gave Claudia a ride to the police station. On the way, he explained that he had taken an urgent call from Joel, who had eventually received her text message and was then unable to reach her. Booker, who had been interviewing a suspect in another case, had missed the text.

The moment he got Joel's call, he had put out a call for assistance at the mortuary.

Unfortunately, the message about who the victim was had not been accurately passed on. Responding units, seeing Claudia holding what appeared to be a weapon, and at least two of the three women bleeding, did what they were trained to do—neutralize the apparent threat. That information did little to assuage her sense of umbrage.

Before they left the scene, Booker retrieved her phone from the body bag, allowing her to call her husband and reassure him that she was more or less okay. Joel, whose controlled tone Claudia understood hid more turbulent emotions, told her he was on his way to Edenwood, and was in the middle of rush hour traffic. He would meet her at the police station as soon as he could.

After the day she'd had, the cup of burnt coffee Booker gave her tasted heavenly. By the time he was done taking her statement in the now-familiar interview room, she was half-comatose and finding it hard it to follow what he was saying. When he left her in the room and went to speak with Natalie and Rachel, who had been transported from the hospital to the police station, Claudia laid her head on the table and promptly fell asleep.

The interview room door opened and there was Joel in his leather motorcycle jacket and Levi's, looking every inch the outraged husband/worried lover/calm detective. The sight of him had Claudia ready to cede her independence and let him take over. Temporarily, anyway.

"I'm getting a sense of *deja vu*," Joel said, once he had finished kissing her and telling her how much he loved her.

"I was hoping you wouldn't notice."

"A little hard not to."

She tightened her arms around him, never wanting to let go, and at the same time, feeling sheepish because he was right. "I know I've put us in this position too many times."

He lowered his head until their foreheads were touching. "You are so brave, and so crazy sometimes. I don't know what to do with you anymore. What the hell would I have done if—"

Claudia shuddered. "Don't say it. One thing I know—I *never* want to see the inside of a body bag again. If I die, find another way to get me to the morgue."

"God forbid." He held her tighter, and she could sense the tension still raging through him. "Is there any way to get you to hang up your investigator hat and stick with being handwriting examiner?" he asked.

That made her grin. "If I start getting involved in another investigation, just say 'body bag.' I'll drop it like a hot coal."

"I'm gonna hold you to that."

They both knew it wouldn't last.

Chapter thirty-seven

Booker was absent from the interview room for what felt like a very long time, taking statements from Natalie and Rachel. He returned looking peeved.

After shaking hands with Joel and exchanging some detective chat, he took a seat at the table and got right down to it. "Bottom line, Claudia, without Rachel's testimony, your version of Andrea Adams' confession is hearsay. It can't stand on its own. We don't have a case for murder."

Claudia shot upright in her chair. "But Rachel was *part* of the confession, plus she was an accessory in two murders. How is that hearsay? And let's not forget she and Nat kidnapped me."

"She's saying that she doesn't know anything about any murders; that she didn't hear Ms. Adams confess to anything."

"Well, shit," Claudia said inelegantly. "I should have recorded it."

"That would have been helpful," Joel agreed, and asked Booker, "Has she asked for an attorney?"

Booker shook his head. "Not yet. But I'm sure you won't be surprised to know that *Ms. Parker* has lawyered up, so that's shut down for now. Rachel's not admitting to anything right now. I'll keep working on her about a deal. If we can make her a cooperating witness—if she can give us something concrete, *and* she testifies against Ms. Parker—I can ask the D.A. for a lesser sentence on the two murders. Otherwise, Claudia, it's your word against hers, and that doesn't cut it."

"What would it take for her to be a cooperating witness?" Claudia asked.

"She would have to enter a guilty plea, testify against Ms. Parker, *and* show us where the body is buried. That's the only way the district attorney can offer a voluntary manslaughter deal."

Joel pursed his lips, looking contemplative. "Without her testimony to make a case for murder they can only be charged with kidnapping Claudia. And I'm not so sure we—I mean you, Sam—can make even that stick."

"You and I know that," Booker said. "She doesn't. And she doesn't know what Ms. Parker has or hasn't said about her involvement."

"What kind of reduction are you looking at?"

"If we can get to two first degree murder charges—Lucy Valentine and Joshua Dickson—she'd be getting a very sweet deal if she got eleven years instead of twenty-five to life. And without her asking for an attorney, I think we can do it."

"I think she's not asking for an attorney because of her guilt," Claudia said. "I hope she agrees to show you where they buried Lucy."

"That would certainly tie her to the crime."

"From what they told me, you could dig around the pond and find the remains."

"Yes, but it would save a lot of time if Rachel pointed us to the exact spot."

"What's Natalie saying?" Claudia asked.

"She doesn't know anything about anything."

"How does she explain me being at the mortuary with them?"

Booker took out his frustration on a paper cup from the desk, crumpling it viciously. "I can't ask her that, or anything else since she lawyered up."

"How long is the deal on the table?" Joel wanted to know.

The detective looked at his watch and smiled, not pleasantly. "Until I walk back to the interview room where I've got her stashed, and ask for her decision. I'll tell her that Natalie rolled over on her. If she believes me and it's a go, I think she'll be smart enough to take it. Then I'll get on the horn and see if I can find a forensic anthropologist to get digging early tomorrow morning."

"Can I be there?" Claudia asked.

"I don't see why not. But right now, lady, you're looking pretty ragged. I suggest you two find a nice hotel to rest up and call for room service. I'll let you know what Ms. Thomas says."

They took Booker's advice, but before heading to the hotel, went to Andie's house to get Claudia's overnight bag from the Jaguar, which was parked on the street. An ambulance and a police vehicle were there, too.

Joel, who was not ready to let Claudia out of his sight, insisted on having the Jag towed back to Playa de la Reina. While he was making arrangements, the EMTs came out with Andie's still form on a stretcher. Her eyes were closed, her face paperwhite. Claudia watched them place her into the ambulance. Andie would get the care she needed, but to what end—a jail ward for her last days? She could not help doubting that her friend would live to see the trial, if there ever was one.

Joel got them a room with a jacuzzi tub. He climbed in first and Claudia climbed in after him, settling back in his arms. The moment she laid her head against the curly thatch of his chest, she started to cry. At first, it was a single tear rolling from each eye. Then her body was shaking with uncontrollable sobs as all the pent-up emotion of the day poured out in a torrent. Joel held her until she was wrung out and had nothing left but gratitude—for her life, and for their love.

Chapter thirty-eight

Rachel Thomas took the deal. Believing the lie Detective Booker told her—that Natalie had blamed everything on her—she had described in detail how to find Wildwood Pond. The next day, she would be transported to the crime scene in a patrol car to show the exact spot where they had buried Lucy.

An arrest warrant had been issued for Natalie Parker.

At six-thirty the next morning, Claudia and Joel dragged themselves out of bed to join Detective Booker and the forensics team he had gathered for the expected exhumation of Lucy Valentine's skeletal remains. Troy had been informed, and had declined the opportunity to attend, saying he was fine with just hearing about the results.

Matt was allowed to be an observer, which would make the perfect ending to his documentary, but he did not have clearance to film the proceedings.

Joel parked his Jeep beside Booker's ride in the woods behind Edenwood High School. "I guess you got me to a reunion, one way or another," he said with a lift of his left brow—the one that expressed so much.

Claudia rolled her eyes. "Not the way I wanted you to meet my classmates."

They identified themselves to the police officer guarding the site, and Joel showed his badge. Apart from an opening in the trees, the outer perimeter was cordoned off with yellow tape. The officer pointed them to the opening.

Making their way through, Claudia pictured the four teenage girls who had followed their teacher, excited and anticipatory—all except Andie, who had never wanted to be there. Andie, whose mental and physical suffering far eclipsed anything her cousin or Rachel had experienced. And Lucy, pregnant and scared, putting on a pretend happy face so that she would be allowed to go, never expecting the betrayal that awaited her.

Walking into the small glade that October morning, Claudia knew she had rightly guessed that the black and white photo in Andie's room had been taken here. There was the small, natural pond where Lucy Valentine had taken her last breaths. The idyllic ambience gave no clue to what it was: custodian of her remains for the past twenty-six years.

What must it have cost Andie to return to this place and the ghastly memories it held? Had she come here more than once after taking that photograph, doing penance for all of them? Claudia was quite certain that Natalie had never experienced a moment of remorse, or perhaps even given it a second thought beyond how what they had done might affect her personally. As for Rachel, she seemed to waffle somewhere between shame and regret. Luckily, she had decided against allowing Natalie to influence her future any further.

Booker told them that Natalie Parker would be arraigned later that day. "When Rachel gets here, I'll remind her that our deal won't be a deal until we actually confirm there's a body," he said.

"Rachel still hasn't lawyered up?" Joel asked.

"No, but we have her signed confession now, which confirms Claudia's statement and implicates Natalie. We'll re-Mirandize Rachel when she gets here, just to make sure all the t's are crossed."

Then Booker introduced them to a man suited up in disposable white coveralls and booties that would protect the crime scene—and him—from cross-contamination. Dr. Serge Vallen, the forensic anthropologist in charge of the dig, carried a face mask, goggles, and gloves. Once Rachel pointed them to the area where she and the others had dug a grave, they would get started.

"I understand you knew the victim?" Dr. Vallen said to Claudia.

"Yes, though not close enough to be friends."

"What can you tell me about her?"

"I remember her as a smallish girl, maybe five feet tall, not much more. She had medium-length black hair." A glint of memory brought something else back to her. "She always wore the same necklace—silver, with a pendant."

Dr. Vallen looked interested. "Do you happen to remember what the pendant looked like?"

Claudia smiled, wistful in the memory. "I do, because I thought it was so cool that wished I had one. It was a screaming gargoyle. Just the face and wings."

"Now I know what to get you for Christmas," Joel whispered in her ear. She elbowed him in the ribs.

"What do you expect to find, Doctor Vallen?" she asked the anthropologist.

Dr. Vallen's lips pursed as he thought about it. "After twenty-six years of being buried in the ground next to a water source? Assuming she was buried deep enough to preclude animal activity, insects will have consumed the flesh, plus there's natural rot and decomposition. I expect to find bones, hair, clothing, jewelry. She certainly won't be recognizable as the girl you knew."

"Thank you." Claudia's stomach twisted. She wanted nothing more than to grab Joel's arm and pull him away; to go home and forget about the events that had taken place here. But as someone who had known Lucy, she owed it to her to stay and see it through.

Rachel arrived. Booker went to the patrol car to fetch her. She walked beside him into the site, eyes downcast, hands cuffed in front. Her black hair was pulled into a high ponytail. A bandage covered her left bicep. The baggy orange jail jumpsuit hid the wound on her abdomen.

As they entered the glade, her legs buckled and Booker caught her as she started to fall. When he asked if she needed to sit down, she shook her head and straightened her spine, and they walked on.

As they neared Claudia, Rachel faltered. The glance she flicked showed dark, shell-shocked eyes in a face almost as pale as Andie's. Claudia, doing her best to control the hot rage that simmered recklessly in her veins, ignored Rachel's murmured, "I'm sorry." Joel tucked his arm through hers, saving her from doing something insane, like hurling herself at Rachel and beating the shit out of her. Her classmate might be in handcuffs on her way to prison, but right now, it wasn't nearly enough to make up for what she had done.

Then Booker was taking Rachel to speak to Dr. Vallen and she was pointing to an ancient willow at the edge of the pond. Its graceful branches reached down, the tips trailing in the pond like lacy green fingers. As they stood there in the chill of the autumn morning Claudia couldn't help reflecting on the irony. The willow tree was symbolic of fertility and new life, the ability to survive. Lucy's spirit had survived and had reached out at last to get justice for her sixteen-year-old self who had needed so much to be loved.

Having identified the location of the grave, Rachel was returned to the police vehicle, where she would wait while the forensic team staked out the search area and prepared to conduct what was essentially an archaeological dig. Claudia and Joel stayed, watching the crime scene techs form a grid, where they would painstakingly sift through the soil, one section at a time, and layer by layer uncover the burial.

It was more than two hours later, and the sun was high in the sky when Dr. Vallen beckoned Detective Booker over. The team had uncovered what was left of Lucy Valentine: a weathered skull with a few strands of black hair still attached. Disarticulated bones. Remnants of cloth too filthy and deteriorated to identify as clothing. A silver necklace with a gargoyle pendant.

Chapter thirty-nine

Claudia and Kelly walked into the auditorium in the main building at Edentown High School. Most of the theater seats were already occupied by their classmates, but they didn't have to worry; theirs were reserved in the front row.

Matt Macedo, handsome in a grey jacket and dress slacks, was holding court amidst a cluster of classmates. Glancing up, he saw the two women advancing down the aisle towards him, and excused himself to meet them. "Thank goodness you're here," he said, leaning in to kiss each cheek. "Now we can get this party started."

Kelly reached up for a hug. "Are you excited?"

"Excited, nervous, tense, a little scared. Take your pick."

She gave him a suggestive leer. "You do know I'm attracted to mildly neurotic men, right?"

"Mildly?" Claudia echoed with a knowing grin. "Are you brave enough to go there, Matt?"

He looked from one to the other. "Why do I get the feeling I'm being set up?"

They all shared a laugh, then Matt showed them to their seats. As the audience members began to settle, he sprinted up the stairs to the stage and stood behind the podium. With a slight hand gesture from him, the lights dimmed and as silence fell over the auditorium, the air was charged with anticipation.

Matt began to speak with poignancy and passion about the journey that had brought him to this moment. Music filled the auditorium, and on the giant movie screen behind him, Lucy Valentine's junior class picture appeared, and the title — *Looking for Lucy*.

The Edentown High School Class of '99 settled into hushed attention.

THE END

You won't want to miss Sheila Lowe's new memoir, *Growing From the Ashes*, A forensic handwriting expert learns about the Afterlife from the murder of her daughter. Read the first chapter now:

February 19, 2000, 11:30 a.m.

When you pick up the ringing phone, you don't expect that a careless verbal match is about to be lit and set your world ablaze.

It's Saturday morning and I'm dashing around the house, a whirlwind of activity, preparing for a forensics conference in Reno. I have to figure out what I need to pack for the three-day trip, make arrangements for a ride from the airport to the hotel. Talk to the friend I'll be rooming with. Make sure my husband and adult son have enough food while I'm away—not because they are helpless, but because we take care of each other that way. Oh, and the cats. Must remember the cat food for Fritz and Sugar.

In the midst of all the crazy, my cell phone rings; a number I don't recognize. This is 2000, and only close friends and family have that number. Thinking that it's probably a misdial, I follow the ring tone and dig the phone out from under a stack of papers on my desk. I answer, hiding my impatience. "Hello?"

The voice I hear is male, unfamiliar, and expressionless. "—is Kenneth Lowe there?"

In my surprise at his request, I miss who he says he is. "Why are you calling my ex-husband on my cell phone?" I ask, confused. "We've been divorced twenty years."

Instead of answering, he moves right to his next question. "Do you know Jennifer Lowe?"

My stomach tightens. Two months ago, my daughter was placed in a mental health facility on a 5150 hold. That's the legal term for the involuntary commitment of an adult who is in a mental health crisis. Jen had freaked over some boudoir photos she'd had taken by a friend of a friend. Afraid that he would post them online when he refused to give her the negatives, she'd had a meltdown. Things went from bad to worse and her boyfriend, Tom Schnaible, called 911.

Tom carried the credibility and weight of working as a special agent for the federal government, so the doctors listened when he said Jen was suicidal and should be locked up.

She phoned from the hospital. "It's not true," she swore. "Tom is the crazy one, not me. Get me out of here. Please!"

Jen was twenty-seven, which left me powerless to do more than listen to her anguish and fury at being locked up, and to tell her that I loved her.

After the initial 72-hour evaluation period, the doctors refused to release her unless she would 'admit' that she wanted to kill herself. After a week-long standoff, they gave up and let her go.

Now, a stranger is calling me about her. What has she got herself into this time?

With an inward sigh, I mentally check off a few possibilities: jailed for shoplifting? It's been ten years since the last time. Picked a fight at a party in Mexico? A car accident with her friend, the Hell's Angel?

Has she harmed herself after all? *Please, God, not that.*

The questions tumble around in my head and my heart is racing as I say, with the dread of past experience, "She's my daughter. What about her?"

Holding my breath, I brace for bad news. But whatever I am expecting to hear, there is nothing that can prepare me for what this stranger has to say. He says it baldly, and without preamble or warning. The caller is Investigator Joe Homs of the Orange County California Sheriff's Department. He is the one who ignites the match and drops the bomb that changes my life forever: "I'm sorry to tell you, your daughter has been murdered."

Growing From the Ashes is available in ebook, print, and audiobook

A request

Dear Reader,

Did you enjoy Maximum Pressure? If you did, please consider leaving a brief review on your favorite review site. Amazon, Goodreads, and BookBub, are always appreciated, or any other. It really helps when you tell others how you feel.

Get the latest on all my books by signing up for updates at sheilalowebooks.com. I promise never to share your information.

You can find Sheila here:

amazon.com/dp/B08WPQHYG7

bookbub.com/authors/sheila-lowe

facebook.com/SheilaLoweBooks

instagram.com/sheilalowebooks/

youtube.com/@SheilaLowe

goodreads.com/SheilaLowe

Acknowledgments

Thanks to my Anaheim High School Class of '67 classmates for urging me to write a book about a murder at a high school reunion, including those whose names appear in the book. Thanks, too, to my filmmaker friend Matt Macedo for the use of his name and profession, to Derek Pacifico for consulting on police procedure, to Dr. Doug Lyle for answering questions about drowning, to Sara Ostrander for the information on willow trees, and to Jeff Elkins, the Dialogue Doctor, who had some great ideas about high school 'types' twenty-five years later (they never change!). One more thanks due to Tracy and Trish of the Are You Dying to Know podcast, whose episodes helped with the scenes in the mortuary prep room.

And let us not forget the oh-so-important beta readers and amazing writer Kim Taylor Blakemore.

About the Author

Sheila Lowe is the author of the award-winning Forensic Handwriting series and the Beyond the Veil paranormal suspense series. She is also a real-life forensic handwriting expert who testifies in court cases. In addition to writing stories of psychological suspense, she writes nonfiction books about handwriting and personality. Her memoir, *Growing From the Ashes*, details her journey from a strict religious cult to spiritual freedom following the murder of her daughter. She lives in Southern California.

To sign up for the newsletter: www.sheilalowebooks.com
https://www.sheilalowe.com

Made in the USA
Las Vegas, NV
24 August 2025